THE BOOTHEEL

THE BOOTHEEL

KEVIN WOLF

THORNDIKE PRESS
A part of Gale, a Cengage Company

GALE
A Cengage Company

GALE
A Cengage Company

Copyright © 2023 by Kevin Wolf
Thorndike Press, a part of Gale, a Cengage Company.
All scripture quotations, unless otherwise noted, are taken from the King James Bible.

Thorndike Press® Large Print Hardcover Western.
The text of this Large Print edition is unabridged.
Set in 16 pt. Plantin.

LIBRARY OF CONGRESS CIP DATA ON FILE.
CATALOGUING IN PUBLICATION FOR THIS BOOK
IS AVAILABLE FROM THE LIBRARY OF CONGRESS.

ISBN-13: 979-8-88578-840-3 (hardcover alk. paper)

Published in 2023 by arrangement with Talcott Notch Literary Services, LLC.

Printed in Mexico
Printed Number: 1   Print Year: 2023

To Roy Rogers,
Matt Dillion, and John Wayne.
Thanks, pardners.

CHAPTER ONE

1908, New Mexico Territory

Steam rose from the coils of intestines the coyotes had torn from the horse's soft belly. Tyler had done the right thing. Still, his insides boiled and threatened to rage up his throat. He never wanted to kill another horse again. Maybe he could save the other horse.

"Here, fella," he whispered and caught hold of the gelding's halter. "I'll take care of you. Mister Hutt'll know what to do."

The boy snatched up the old Winchester he shot the mare with and led the gelding away from the bloody ground. "We'll get you to the ranch. Mister Hutt and the Bootheel, that's all you need. You'll see."

It was more than a mile. Tyler led the horse, four steps at a time until he urged the limping horse to the ranch. Winter sun burned the day and sweat marked the gelding's hide and stained Tyler's shirt.

"Mister Hutt," Tyler called out. He leaned the old Winchester on the fence and swung the gate open.

The white-haired man came from the barn. "Heard the shot. Thought maybe you got us a deer." He touched the horse's back, bent down, and lifted the gelding's front hoof.

"Coyote's yippin' woke me before first light." Tyler pulled the horse's lead rope tight and stroked the animal's mane. "Found that gray mare all tangled in the wire fence on the south side of that pasture ground. Coyotes got to her. She's all tore up. Had to —" He tilted his head toward the rifle by the fence. "This one lame for good?" Tyler let his forehead touch the gelding's face. "We won't have to . . ."

"Hoof's split to the quick. We'll pull the old shoe and put a new one on." Mister Hutt stood up and eyed the hill above his ranch. "Take some doctorin' but I think we can save him. Get my tools, boy."

Tyler watched Hutt pound the last nails through the horseshoe and into the animal's hoof. In an easy practiced motion, the old rancher spun the hammer in his gloved hand and trimmed away the protruding nails. He set the horse's foot on the ground and stepped away. "We did all we can. Keep a close eye on him the next few days."

On the hill, where the rimrock met the mesquite, a hot flash of the sun reflected from a place in the thick brush. Tyler stepped to the fence and picked up the rifle.

"Put the gun down, boy." Hutt found the small of his back with both hands and arched. "He's been up there most of the mornin'." Hutt opened the gate and led the gelding into the corral next to the barn. "Figure he left his horse on the back side of that hill. Been taught well, that one. Picked that spot 'cause it's downwind. Our stock can't scent his horse and put up a ruckus. Been settin' up there and studyin' on us since you got back with the horse. Learn from what he did, Tyler."

"Do you think it's him?" Tyler still held the rifle.

Hutt stripped off his gloves and wiped the sweat from his forehead. He hooked one boot over the bottom fence rail and smacked his gloves on his pant leg. Fine dust lifted into the chill air. "Put the rifle away." The old man took a deep breath. "Knew he'd come — knew he wouldn't send word — he'd just ride in here one day."

Tyler lifted his hand to shade his eyes. The shiny speck flashed again. "He wants us to know he's watchin'."

"I'm sure of it." Hutt walked away from the corral. "Tyler, run on in and tell Pilar to cook up some frijole beans and our best beefsteaks. Tell her to set three plates at the table. You'll be eatin' in the house with us."

"Sir?" Tyler looked to the hill and then back to Hutt's adobe house.

"You need to hear the story."

The old man kicked his way through a dozen scrawny red chickens. The birds cackled, flapped, and scurried out of his way. Mister Hutt plucked a leather pouch from his shirt pocket, rolled a cigarette, and let the man on the hill come to him.

Case Spencer let his big dun horse pick its way down the slope. The horse stayed away from the rutted wagon road and crisscrossed the rough ground. When they reached the flat near the ranch yard, Spencer touched his spurs to the horse and guided the animal with his knees.

Spencer pulled at the ranch gate and rested one elbow on the saddle horn. "You Virgil Hutt?"

Smoke curled from the old man's nostrils and he nodded.

"I'm —"

Hutt cut him short. "I know who you are.

10

Could tell by the way you set that saddle." Hutt raised a hand and pointed to the barn. "Water your horse and put 'im in the corral. When you're finished, come on to the house. We'll feed you first and then we'll talk."

Virgil Hutt mashed his cigarette into the dirt with the toe of his boot.

It had been Christmas since Tyler and the other hands ate with Mister Hutt in the ranch house. And he'd never eaten the best beefsteaks before. Mister Hutt saved those for the sheriff, other ranch owners, and sometimes the preacher.

Tyler wanted to make his steak last. He cut it into small pieces and savored each bite. Spencer wolfed the meat down and wiped the plate clean with Pilar's biscuits. Try as he might, Tyler could not keep his eyes off Spencer. When Mister Hutt told him that he'd sent for the gunman, Tyler expected a mountain of a man wearing a pair of silver six-guns would ride in on a palomino stallion. That's what a gunfighter looked like on the cover of the dime novels he bought in town.

Spencer wasn't a giant either. Just a couple of inches taller than Tyler. And there wasn't a pair of holstered guns around his

11

waist. Just a saddle gun, and Spencer leaned it on the wall an arm's length from where he sat. But his eyes had the look of the pistoleros on the cover of those storybooks. Cold and studying everything around him.

There hadn't been a word spoken. Forks clanked on tin plates. Steaks and beans disappeared. Tyler figured that Mister Hutt would be the first to say something, but it was Spencer. He tore the last biscuit in two and while he stuffed one half in his mouth, he dug into his vest pocket with the other hand.

"Tell me about that," Spencer said. He tossed a piece of brown wood on the table.

The grip panel from a Colt revolver slid next to Mister Hutt's plate. "I knew that would bring you here," Hutt's calloused thumb rubbed the smooth wood. "Tyler, the bundle the Mexican had with 'im is in the top drawer of my desk. Fetch it for me."

Tyler lifted himself from the table and walked to Mister Hutt's desk. He strained hard to hear every word the two men spoke.

"Somebody burned your brand on that pistol grip," Spencer said. "And my name's burned onto the back."

Hutt's plate scraped across the table. "Ain't your name. It's your pa's."

Tyler turned.

12

The muscles in Spencer's jaws bunched. "My father was one of Roosevelt's Rough Riders. He never came home from Cuba."

"You're wrong." Hutt looked down at the table.

Tyler snapped his head around and looked at the picture over the mantel. The faded photograph showed an assembly of men in uniform. He'd asked Mister Hutt about that picture one day when he'd brought feed receipts to the house. Hutt had tapped the picture and said, "That man there. Short one with the eyeglasses. He's the president of this here country."

"That's Roosevelt?"

"Theodore Roosevelt, hisself. My commanding officer in Cuba."

That night in the bunkhouse, the other hands told Tyler that Hutt had been an officer. And that he'd charged up San Juan Hill right behind Teddy Roosevelt.

Tyler gathered the cloth-wrapped bundle from the desk and took it back to Mister Hutt. He set it on the table in front of his boss.

Mister Hutt twisted the cloth from the package. Inside was a smaller packet made of pinto horsehide cured with hair still on. On the old leather rested a Colt Peacemaker. One of the grips was missing.

13

The old man fitted the wood panel in his hand to the gun.

"You gonna tell me that was my father's?" Spencer's fingers moved to the Colt but stopped short of picking it up.

Hutt nodded. He reached up and pinched the wrinkled skin between his eyes.

"I was with your father the day he got the news your mother had passed. Your grandpa's letter said he should never come back. That your mama's death was his doin' and you'd be better off without him. The war had been extra hard on him and your grandfather's letter took what spirit was left out of the man."

Hutt looked out of the windows at the horses in the corral. "When we mustered out, I brought him back to my ranch here. Told 'im I'd need his help to get started up again. With all the killin' we'd done, thought it would be good for both of us. Just knew that after some while he'd get hisself together and go find you. Months became a year. Then five years. We built this place up side by side. He was more my brother than a workin' hand."

Hutt pushed the Colt across the table to Spencer.

"Some nights he'd say 'Wonder what my boy's doin' now?' "

14

Hutt's tongue licked his lips. "I never said a word. Part my fault he never went to find you."

Spencer lifted the gun off the table. He traced the Bootheel brand with his thumbnail. "What happened to my fath—" The word wouldn't come. "— to him? You didn't have me ride all this way just to give me a rusty old gun."

Hutt smoothed the horsehide with the palm of his hand. "Last fall, an old Mexican vaquero stumbled in here. Showed me that bundle. I gave him a horse and food. He gave me that gun and this map." Hutt pressed a gnarled finger on the leather. "Might be the only way you'll ever learn what kind of man your father was. Felt I owed you that much."

"Go on." Spencer's fingers tightened around the pistol so tight that Tyler feared that bones would tear through the skin on his knuckles.

"Your pa took three men and thirty of our best horses. Mexican Cavalry was payin' top dollar for mounts. Crossed the Rio Grande like he had more'n two dozen times before. This time he had five hundred dollars in double eagles in his saddlebags." Hutt shifted on his straight-back chair. "My money. After he sold the horses, we figured

15

he'd have twelve, maybe fifteen hundred. He was to buy cattle, hire drovers, and head 'em back here. I was going to make him a partner and gonna double the size of this ranch." Hutt cleared his throat. "But I never saw your pa or any of 'em ever again."

"What makes you think he didn't steal your money, old man?"

" 'Cause I knew your father." Hutt pointed to the map. A swirl of lines and angles had been burnt into the hide. "Look close. He carved it with the point of a hot knife just like he marked the brand on the grip of that pistol. Study that corner."

Spencer leaned over the table and peered at the marks on the horsehide. He snatched the Colt and held it close to the leather. The Bootheel brand and the letters *CS* showed black against the gray leather.

"Where is this place?" Spencer touched the map with his fingers.

"Deep in Mexico. They all call it the Valley of Visions. Any smuggler, cutthroat, or rustler can hide there from the whole world. Word has it that the Apaches still run wild. It's like the mountains split open and all hell seeped out."

"You're talkin' crazy, old man."

Hutt's hand shot out and clamped on Spencer's wrist. The wrinkles in the old

16

man's face drew taut. "Go find out what happened to your father."

Spencer shook free of Hutt's grip. He pushed his chair back and stared at the old man. The muscles in his jaws balled tight. "You want your money. That's what this is about and you think that fool map will help find it."

"No son." Hutt's voice grew even and calm. "The money's long gone. If that's all I wanted, I wouldn't have sent for you." The old man's shoulders straightened. "I'll pay for cartridges and what supplies you need. Give you the horses."

"What's in it for you?" Spencer spit the words out.

Hutt looked away from Spencer to where the young ranch hand stood. "I want you to take Tyler with you."

Like he'd been kicked in the belly by a scared calf at nut-cutting time, Tyler's lungs refused to take in the next breath. Mister Hutt wanted him to go to Mexico with Spencer?

Had he heard it wrong?

Spencer's face flamed red. "This old piece of horsehide don't mean nothin'. If you think I'm gonna take your word on this and ride off into Mexico with that kid, you lost whatever sense you had." The gunman's chair tumbled backward as he stood. He tucked the Colt in his belt, snatched up his rifle, and stomped across the wood floor. The front door slammed behind him.

Through the window, Tyler watched Spencer stride across the yard to the corrals. Spencer walked to the front gate and pulled the gun from his belt. He stared out at the rimrock and then looked down at the gun in his hands.

"Is he saddlin' his horse?" Hutt asked from his place at the table.

"No, sir," Tyler answered. "He's just standing there staring at that old gun."

The old man pulled a handkerchief from his vest pocket and coughed into it. The hacking jerked Hutt's shoulders and his face sank into his hands. It seemed to Tyler that more lines wrinkled his face and that his hair was whiter.

"Sir," Tyler asked, "why didn't you ever tell any of that before?"

"I was waitin' 'til the right time. I thought Spencer there would give me a fair hearin'. Guess I was wrong."

"But Mister —"

Pilar hurried into the room. "Señor Hutt, rider, he come fast."

Hutt lifted his face from his hands and pulled himself up from his chair. He shouldered by Tyler.

Rays of the late-day sun angled across the cholla and sage. Dust from the galloping horse's hooves hung like dirty clouds against the far horizon.

Tyler shaded his eyes with his hand and squinted. "It looks like that paint pony Jesus took out this morning. He'll kill that horse if he don't let up on him."

At the top of the bowl that surrounded Hutt's ranch, the horse and rider barreled over the rim. The pinto sat back on its haunches and crow-hopped down the hillside, kicking chunks of the caliche clay into the air. When the two reached the bottom, the rider smacked his quirt on the animal's rump and made for the ranch.

Hutt hurried toward the front gate. "That's Jesus for sure. Something's got him spooked."

As the horse lunged into the ranch yard, Jesus slid out of the saddle and hit the ground running. He stumbled to where Hutt and Tyler waited. Despite the cool of the afternoon, the Mexican cowboy's face shone slick with sweat. He bent over and gasped for breath.

"Trouble, Señor. Much trouble." He wheezed. "Riders come up the small river.

They herd together your cattle, Mister Hutt."

"Rustlers?"

"Sí, Señor."

Hutt balled his fists. "How long ago?"

"Before the sun is straight above."

"How many?"

"Twelve, maybe fifteen." Jesus staggered and fought to keep his feet.

"They see you?" Hutt pointed to the dust still hanging in the air.

"No, Señor. I sneak away and no ride hard for *una hora.*"

Hutt touched his fist to his mouth. "Lord Almighty." He looked at Tyler. "Border raiders. They'll herd together what they can and trail 'em straight to Mexico."

Tyler's stomach turned hot with fear. He tried to breathe in but the air caught in his throat.

Hutt paced away from Tyler and Jesus. He scanned the desert rimrock and measured the sun in the sky. "Tyler, take my horse."

"Sir?"

No one rode Mister Hutt's Thoroughbred but him.

"Hear me. Take my horse. Ride out north. Find Miller and the boys. Tell them what Jesus just told us." The old man turned. "Listen close now. I want you to bring 'em.

20

Meet Jesus and me where the river opens out at the Severed Finger Canyon. I want you to loop around through the breaks."

"That's the long way, sir."

"It'll be dark in three hours. It's my thought that they'll bunch up tonight and wait 'til mornin' to move the herd. I want to be waiting for 'em. Tell Miller to walk the horses in the last mile."

"Mister Hutt," Tyler stammered. "Miller's got three men with him. You, me, and Jesus makes only seven. Jesus said there might be fifteen or more of them."

"I heard him."

Tyler nodded to where Spencer still stood. "What about him? If he's as good as they say we could use his gun."

"This don't concern him at all."

21

CHAPTER TWO

Skies, the color of worn gunmetal, stole back the night shadows an inch at a time. Below the hill, the stolen cattle snorted and began to stir in the dawn.

"Miller," Hutt whispered, "have the men take plenty of cartridges for their rifles. There's extra on the packsaddle. We leave the horses down below." He pointed toward a faint outline in the dawn light. "You and your three slip out on that gully bank. Jesus and me'll sneak down on that other end. They'll be wakin' soon. Most likely build up a cookfire for coffee and such."

Hutt grabbed a kerchief from his coat and muffled a cough into the rag. "When I can make out a target I'll let 'em have it. Soon as you hear my rifle, you let loose. They'll make for their horses and hightail it out here. Snakes like them won't be worryin' 'bout the herd." He wiped his mouth. "I want 'em hurt bad."

"Do you want me to come with you and Jesus?" Tyler spoke softly. He slid his fingers along the old Winchester that Mister kept in the barn.

Hutt turned so that his nose almost touched Tyler's. Dark lines webbed his eyes. He bit back a cough. "No, boy, you stay with the horses. Soon as the shootin's done, we're gonna have cattle scattered from here to kingdom come. Can't afford for our horses to spook."

"But, sir —." He wanted to prove he was as much a man as the rest. He wanted to beg for that chance.

"Do as I say."

Tyler tugged at the rags he'd wrapped around his fingers to ward off the January cold. He glanced at Miller but the foreman looked away.

"Leave Jesus with the horses. I can shoot."

"You heard me, boy." Hutt's teeth clenched.

A shiver ran down Tyler's back. He crawled off the ridge to where the horses were hobbled.

The first rifle shot shattered the morning still. Almost as one four guns boomed from the gully bank just north of where Tyler waited. Horses fought their pickets and stamped the ground. He scooped the Winchester from his saddle's scabbard, looked at the animals, and sprinted for the hilltop.

Shots came from the south. He could pick out the sound of the bolt-action Krag that Mister Hutt brought back from the war. It cracked the air so different than the boom of the hand's saddle guns. Cows bawled. The rustlers' horses milled about in fear. Shouts came from the rustlers in their camp.

Tyler threw himself on his belly and peered over the ridgeline. In the gray light, a man kicked dirt on the campfire. Streaks of orange flashed from gun muzzles as the rustlers fired back at Mister Hutt and the men on the hill above them.

He eased his rifle to his shoulder and peered down the sights trying to pick out a target amid the confusion. The crack of the Krag cut the air again. The man near the fire grabbed his chest and pitched forward onto the smoldering embers.

Another rustler screamed and clutched his leg. Tyler heard bullets smack the dirt and trees around the robbers' camp. A bullet whined over his head. Bile raced into his throat. He turned and emptied his stomach on the sand beside him. The cold stabbed its fingers into the pit of his empty belly.

Tyler lifted his head for another look.

Three mounted men fled the cross fire and galloped up the hill to where he lay. Gunfire snapped all around. Tyler lifted his rifle and pointed it at the lead rider. The sights wobbled. The rustler leaned from his saddle and leveled his pistol at Tyler.

Trembles racked through him. Tyler slammed back on the trigger. The horse screamed and pitched forward. Its rider rolled away from the flailing animal and aimed his gun at Tyler. Tyler jerked at the lever of his rifle. The rustler's bullet sliced the air over his head. The next gunshot came from behind him. The outlaw's head snapped back, blood blossomed around a ragged hole in his shirt, and the pistol fell from his hand.

Another shot boomed from behind. The second rider fell from his saddle. The third rider turned his horse and hurtled off the hill into the riverbed.

Tyler turned.

Case Spencer stepped from behind a clump of cholla, jacking another shell into his big rifle.

Boots crunched the sand and gravel along the hill. Hutt and Jesus scrambled up to the ridge top. The old man looked at the two dead rustlers sprawled on the slope in front

25

of Tyler. "What happened here, boy? You was ordered to stay with the horses."

Spencer walked to the group. "I told the boy to come with me."

Tyler turned toward the gunman. Spencer's tongue traced a circle on the inside of his cheek.

"What are you doin' here?" Hutt snapped.

"Saddled up after you left and just ended up here." Spencer looked back at Tyler. "Might be a good thing I did."

Hutt stared at Spencer and then at Tyler. "Are our horses still in the bottom?"

"I think so, sir," Tyler said just above a whisper.

"If those two," Spencer pointed at the dead men with his chin, "had got over this hill they mighta stampeded 'em. Tyler and me stopped that."

"Señor Hutt," Jesus called from beside the horse that Tyler killed. He waved for them to come. *"Aquí."*

Tyler scrambled down the hill behind Mister Hutt and Spencer.

"Aquí." Jesus pointed at the horse's flank. "Your brand, Señor."

Hutt bent and ran his fingers over the Bootheel mark burnt into the hair and hide on the horse's flank.

"They run off some horses along with

26

your cattle?" Spencer asked.

"No." Hutt handed his rifle to Jesus and knelt next to the dead horse. He pulled open the animal's lips and ran his fingers over its yellowed teeth. "This horse is four, maybe five years old." The old man sat back on his heels. He looked up at Spencer. "The horses your pa took to Mexico were all three-year-olds. No way to prove it, but I'd wager this 'un was part of that herd."

Spencer stepped closer to the horse. He reached down and touched the brand and then looked Hutt in the eye. Neither man spoke.

Hutt stood and dusted the dirt from his pants. Tyler felt the old man's eyes study him. "How many shots you get off, boy?"

Tyler looked down at the dead horse. "Just one, sir."

"And you killed this horse?"

Tyler's stomach knotted. He stared down at the tops of his boots. He didn't want Mister Hutt to say anything more. He didn't want Spencer to hear. Maybe he wasn't to be trusted in a fight. Mister Hutt knew that. That's why he left him to look after the horses.

Then from the robbers' campsite, Miller called up, "Sir, you better see this."

■ ■ ■ ■

Cottonwood trees lined the creek where the rustlers had camped for the night. Burnt gunpowder mixed with the smell of woodsmoke, horses, and cattle. The stench of death hung all around.

Tyler hadn't given a thought to the two that Spencer killed on the hill. But the body of the man he saw fall near the fire made his guts burn. The man's hands were charred black and his blood streaked across the dust around the firepit. The back of his head had burst like a hen's egg and specks of gray brains hung to his hair. Tyler bit hard on his tongue and looked away.

Miller hooked his thumbs in his belt and nodded to where two of the cowhands stood. Both men moved away when Mister Hutt came close.

"There in the brush." Miller tilted his head. "It's a woman, sir."

Hutt leaned forward. He caught a branch in his hand and lifted it. The old man's shoulders slumped.

Tyler stepped between Hutt and Miller so he could see.

Had they killed a woman?

Dark eyes shone back at him. Tyler moved

closer. Hutt reached out his hand.

Her bare heels dug into the dirt and leaves and she pushed back further into the thicket. Scratch marks and blood covered her legs. A colorless gingham dress draped over her bony shoulders. Leaves, twigs, and dirt matted in her dark hair.

"We're not gonna hurt you," Hutt said.

She pressed both hands to one side and inched back. Her wrists were bound together with a leather thong.

"She a Mexican or an Indian?" Miller asked, pushing at the woman with the toe of his boot. "Whatcha think?"

The woman twisted her face. A shiver coursed through her.

"She's cold," Tyler said. Then louder. "She's cold." He pulled his arms out of his coat. He pushed by Miller and Hutt and knelt. The woman's eyes darted from him to the others. He held the coat out and then laid it over her.

"Tyler's right." Hutt stepped back. "Strip the coat off one of those dead men and bring it here. We'll just back off for a few minutes so she'll know we don't mean her no harm. And Miller, have one of the men build up the fire."

Tyler reached out and smoothed his coat over the woman's legs. Her eyes reminded him of the fawn he'd found in the spring. He tried to keep the animal alive but after a few days, it refused to eat and died. "Get her something to eat," he called.

He held the palms of his hands toward her and then slowly moved one hand to his pocket and took out his jackknife. He unfolded the blade.

She cringed.

"I won't hurt you," he whispered to her.

As gently as he could, he folded back the coat and slipped the knife blade into the straps on her wrists. He made a quick sawing motion with the blade and she pulled her hands free. Tears wiped away the dirt on her cheeks. Her lips trembled but no sound came.

She wasn't a woman, Tyler thought. No, just a scared girl. Maybe about his age.

Hutt, Spencer, and the others warmed themselves by the fire and ate the beans Pilar had sent. None of them spoke. They all stared at the girl. Tyler had coaxed her into the dead rustler's coat. His still lay over her bare legs. Spencer pushed himself up and walked over.

"Here." He held out a tin plate. "Let her eat what's left of mine."

"She's mighty hungry." Tyler took the

plate and set it where the girl could reach it. "She ate everything we gave her and licked the plate clean."

The girl's hand darted from under the coat and snatched Spencer's plate. She held it to her chin and scooped the frijoles into her mouth with her dirty fingers.

"Spencer, why do you think she was with those men?"

"Captive, no doubt. I've heard stories 'bout how those border raiders kidnap women and girls. They can sell 'em for big dollars down deep in Mexico."

"You mean for slaves?"

"Or worse."

Tyler looked back at the girl. "You mean —"

"There's a kind of man that will pay a lot of money for a young girl like her. No accountin' for the evil in this world."

Tyler had heard Miller and the others talk about the whores they visited in El Paso. He had seen the stallions take the mares when their season came. Though he'd never heard a tender word come from Mister Hutt's mouth, he knew the Mexican woman, Pilar, shared his bed. But nothing in him could imagine what pleasure a man could take from a frightened girl like this one. He bit down on his lip.

31

"She said anything?" Spencer asked.

"Jesus tried talking to her. She just looked at the ground. Hasn't made any kind of sound at all." Tyler took the plate from the girl. "Spencer." He looked the gunman in the eye. "Thank you."

"What for?"

"For telling Mister Hutt you told me to come up the hill with you when all that shooting started."

"Don't worry 'bout that. Could see he's a hard man."

"You saved my life. That rustler had the drop on me."

"Can't be sure of that. You had your rifle." Spencer plucked a stalk of dry grass and hung it between his teeth. "You sound more scared of Hutt than that outlaw."

"Sometimes I think I am."

Hutt's shadow swept over the dirt near where they sat with the girl. The small hairs on Tyler's neck stood.

"Tyler, best get your coat on." Hutt looked at the sky. "I fear we got weather comin' in. I'm gonna leave Miller and the rest here. Told 'em to gather up the strays and start the herd back in the morning."

"What about her?" Tyler asked.

"We'll take her back to The Bootheel. Let Pilar look her over. Then we'll decide what should be done." Mister Hutt knelt down. He held out another coat taken from a dead man, pulled Tyler's off the girl's bare legs, and replaced it with the one he'd brought. "Fetch my horse. She'll ride double with me. You put your saddle on that roan. If we leave now, we can be at the homeplace 'fore night." He muffled a cough into his coat sleeve.

Spencer said, "I think I'll get my horse and track those raiders out aways. Wouldn't want them to circle back on us."

"I'm thinkin' they're long gone. We killed three of theirs. But it's your choosin'," Hutt said. "You don't draw pay from me."

Both men stood. Spencer's mouth moved like he wanted to say something, but he walked away.

Hutt rubbed his hand over the white stubble on his chin.

"Fetch the horses, Tyler."

By the time Tyler saddled the horses and brought them to the campsite, Spencer was a speck against the gray sky on the horizon.

"Do you think we'll see him again, sir?" Tyler handed Mister Hutt the Thoroughbred's reins.

"Don't rightly know."

"What about the map his father made?"

"Don't know about that either." Hutt lifted the girl and gently placed her behind his saddle. She looked so small. The scratches on her legs had turned bright red in the cold. Hutt bundled her in one coat and tied a piece of rope around her waist to keep it tight around her. He tore the other coat in half and wrapped a piece around each of her skinny legs.

"Jesus." He tipped his head toward the direction Spencer had ridden, never taking his eyes from the girl. "Ride out and follow him. Just in case he finds trouble."

Hutt swung up into his saddle. He reached back, found the girl's hands, and placed them around his waist. He clucked to the Thoroughbred and touched his spurs to its sides.

Tyler and the roan fell in behind. With each hoofbeat, his mind twisted with questions. Would he see Case Spencer again? How could he show Mister Hutt he was man enough to hold his own in a fight? And why had Mister Hutt wanted him to go to Mexico with Spencer? He thought of the map drawn on horsehide and a place called the Valley of Visions. But mostly his mind drew him to the frightened eyes of the girl wrapped in a borrowed coat, stained with a dead man's blood.

34

The snow began to fall when they reached the rimrock above The Bootheel. It swirled around their horses' hooves in the last flat light of the day, like the spirits of all who had walked this land had just begun to stir.

CHAPTER THREE

Lead-gray clouds filled the dawn's sky. Though Tyler knew it couldn't be, even the morning's light felt cold. He made a yellow stain on the new snow behind the bunkhouse instead of walking the extra steps to the privy.

Back inside he stirred the coals in the iron stove and added wood. From the corner of his bunk where he kept it hidden, he took his Bible. Its leather cover was scuffed and the tattered pages stained with dirt from his fingers. Tyler tugged a blanket around his shoulders and ate a dry biscuit while he read.

The fire's first warmth seeped from the stove and began to fill the room when the horses in the corral snorted. Tyler dropped his Bible on the bunk and scraped the frost off the inside of the window with his fingernails. Through the scratch marks, he saw where a single horse had scuffed a path across the yard. The latch on the barn door hung undone and the door hung open not more than a hand's width. Tyler pressed his face on the glass so he could see Mister Hutt's house. Smoke curled from the adobe chimney but no footprints marred the snow near the doorway.

Had one of the rustlers followed them back to the ranch? He scanned the hillside for movement. *Were they after the girl?* Tyler took the Winchester from inside the doorframe and wished that Miller, Jesus, and the other hands were back with the cattle.

He eased out of the bunkhouse and slipped across the yard to the barn. He pressed his back against the rough siding and moved toward the door. From inside the barn, a horse stomped its foot and a leather cinch strap slipped through its rigging. He sucked in a mouthful of cold air and looked at Mister Hutt's house. He could smell Pilar's *tortillas* on the hot stove. Mister Hutt would be at the table with a cup of coffee and a cigarette planning the day's chores.

If Tyler waited too long, Mister Hutt would step onto the porch and call for him. Whoever was in the barn would kill him before the words left the old man's mouth. Pilar would die as she rushed out.

Tyler bit down on his lip and gripped the gunstock. He pressed the rifle's muzzle into the opening of the door. A gloved hand wrapped around the gun barrel. The hand jerked up and forward, pulling Tyler inside. A fist smashed into his side. He tumbled onto the straw and dust on the barn's floor. The rifle wrenched from his grip.

From his back, Tyler raised his hands to protect himself from whatever was about to smash his skull.

"Never poke your gun barrel into a room like that." The gloved hands pressed the rifle butt into his chest. "Surefire way to get it taken away from you. And get you killed." Case Spencer held the gun in both hands. "You ain't hurt, are ya?"

Warm tears flooded into Tyler's eyes. He turned to the ground so Spencer couldn't see his face. "No, I'm not hurt." He spat the words out. "What are you doing back here?"

Spencer reached down and caught Tyler's elbow and pulled him to his feet. "Been thinkin'. Never been to that part of Mexico." Spencer looked away, hiding his face like Tyler had hidden his. "Hellfire, if a tough old cowhand like Hutt says my father was a good man, I owe it to myself to find out what happened to him."

Spencer handed the Winchester back to Tyler. Tyler wiped a bare hand across his face. And each waited for the other to speak.

Finally, Spencer broke the silence. "Why do you think he wants to send you along?"

"Don't know at all. It's been bothering me." Steam came from Tyler's mouth as he spoke. "Not like Mister Hutt has a stake in anything down there. He said himself that the money's long gone."

"You his kin?" Spencer asked.

"No, sir."

"How long you known him?"

"Just two years now."

Spencer looked over Tyler. "How old are you?"

"Thirteen. Maybe, fourteen. I think."

"You think?"

"Yes, sir. Don't know for actual sure." Tyler bit down on his lip. "Was in a home for foundlings in New York. Don't remember anything but being there. They put a passel of us on a train and sent us west to find folk that'd take us in." Tyler watched the mist from his breath disappear in the shadows of the barn. "Put me with a family in Colorado. They just wanted help on their farm they wouldn't have to pay for. Made me sleep in the barn. Didn't feed me much. After a couple years, one day I just left. They never

39

came lookin'."

Spencer ran his hand down his horse's back. "How'd you end up here?"

"I was sleeping under a pool table in an Amarillo saloon. The man that owned the saloon paid me to carry buckets of beer to the men working the cattle at the railroad during the day and at night, I'd muck out the spittoons and privy." Tyler felt a smile curl the corners of his mouth. "One day Mister Hutt comes to town to buy cattle. He asked me if wanted to be a cowhand. I told him I did. Didn't have nothing but the clothes I was wearing. Put me on a horse and brought me here. Been one of his hands ever since."

"Well, Tyler, for whatever reason, you're going to Mexico with me." Spencer reached out and shook Tyler's hand. His grip was sure and strong. He looked Tyler in the eye. "Reckon Hutt will ever tell us why he wants you to go? He's a hard man to figure."

"Mister Hutt doesn't talk much 'cept about horses and cattle. What he told you about your father was 'bout the most I've ever heard him say at one time."

"Let's see if he has anything to say now."

White sunshine stole through the cracks in the clouds. A rooster crowed. Horses pawed the ground and whinnied for their

40

morning feed.

As Tyler stepped on the porch, the door swung open. A blast of warm steam caught the outside air. Mister Hutt held out two buckets. "Tyler, fill these here —." The old man's eyes opened wide. "Spencer, huh. Came back, did ya?"

The smell of frying bacon hung in the steamy warmth. Hutt handed the pails to Tyler. "Pilar fixin' to give that girl a washin'. Fill those buckets and bring 'em around to the kitchen. She's used up most of what you already hauled. Better bring in some more firewood. And feed those horses while you're at it." Hutt rubbed his chin. "Spencer, come on in."

Tyler set two full buckets near the back door. They were gone by the time he got back with an armload of piñon wood. He scattered hay in the corral, tossed grain out for the chickens, picked up as much wood as he could carry, and headed back to the house. The sun had cracked open the clouds and tossed great shadows on the desert around The Bootheel. He paused and watched the trail to the south for any sign of Miller and the herd. He knew Mister Hutt would ask.

When he brought the wood to the back

door, Pilar cackled at him to stack it there and to come in the front door. He shrugged his shoulders and did as he was told.

Mister Hutt and Spencer had pushed their breakfast dishes out of their way and spread the horsehide map on the table. "Any sign of Miller out there?" the old man asked.

"No, sir."

"It's too early anyway." Mister Hutt's eyebrows arched up his wrinkled forehead. "Pilar's got a plate ready for you. Better get it."

Tyler hurried to the archway that separated Pilar's kitchen from the great room where Hutt and Spencer studied the map. He wanted to get back to hear what they said.

As he stepped into the doorway, Pilar screamed and pushed the dirty end of a broom into his face. Mister Hutt and Spencer laughed. Over the Mexican woman's rounded shoulders he saw the girl. Breath leaped out of him like the time at branding when a calf had kicked him in the stomach.

The captive girl stood in a bucket of steaming water. She tried to turn away and cupped her hands to cover her small breasts. Wet hair hung halfway down her back and shined as blue-black as a raven's wing. As the light played over her bare skin it changed from brown to the color of raw honey.

"No," Pilar shrieked. *"Andale, andale."*

"I'm sorry. I won't . . ." Words spilled from Tyler's mouth. "I didn't . . ." He backed away from Pilar's swinging broom and turned to the table.

Hutt covered his mouth to keep from laughing louder. Spencer leaned back in his chair. "First time I seen a woman full," Tyler sputtered, "naked —."

Spencer tugged at the end of his mustache. "Enjoyable, ain't it?"

The smell of piñon smoke, bacon grease, and gun oil filled the ranch house. Tyler's face burned with embarrassment as hot as the flames in the fireplace. He settled into a chair with his back to the kitchen and tried to listen to Mister Hutt and Spencer as they pored over the map. Too often his mind brought back what he had seen just before the girl had covered herself with her hands. He thought he should be ashamed but shame couldn't muddy the pictures of her in his brain.

The wind rattled the windows and sent a curl of smoke into the room from the chimney. Hutt pushed his chair away from the table. He took a kerchief from his pocket and wiped it over his lips. "Spencer, tell me 'gin about the raiders you rode up on. I want Tyler to hear."

Spencer twisted his coffee cup in his hands. "Followed their tracks near ten miles from where we shot into 'em. They weren't in no big hurry. Just lickin' their wounds and heading on east." Spencer looked at Tyler. "I hung back and watched them through my field glasses. If they knew I was following, it didn't worry 'em none."

"Tell 'im about their leader." Hutt turned his head and coughed.

"Counted fourteen in all. With the three we put down would have made seventeen. That's a big bunch. Anyways, the one that seemed to be givin' orders wore a red beard and rode a milk-white stallion."

"You sure about the red beard?" Hutt's eyes were drawn and wet. "How close you get to 'em?"

"Close enough to tell it was a stallion. And I'm sure about the beard. Red beard."

"A man with a red beard worked for me. Dalton Fox was his name." Hutt drummed his fingers on the table. "Part Cherokee from up Oklahoma way. Always favored long-legged stallions. Most fellas shy away from white horses. Not him. He and your pa never got along. Your pa thought Fox had something to hide."

44

"You think it could be him?"

"Two facts make me consider it. Knew where we'd be pasturin' the cattle this time of year and my brand was on the horse Tyler killed." The old man shook his head. "Fox left here two weeks 'fore your pa took the horses south."

Tyler looked from Mister Hutt to Spencer. The gunman's tongue circled the inside of his cheek and his shoulders dropped.

"I best mull on this awhile," Mister Hutt whispered.

Pilar came to the table. She held the blackened coffee pot in a rag and filled each man's cup. When Tyler looked over his shoulder to the kitchen, she stepped in his way. Her dark eyes scolded him.

Spencer reached out and pulled the leather map into the center of the table. He stood up and bent over it, resting his hands on either side of the drawing. "Just so much scribblin'."

"Not scribblin'. Told you, your pa burned every line of that with the point of a red hot knife. That takes time so he must have had something he wanted to remember. Or that he wanted us to see." Hutt lifted the handkerchief to his mouth and coughed.

Tyler leaned in from his chair and looked at the black lines singed into the leather.

"What's this?" He pointed to the corner.

"Spanish word for desert. That's farther south than he shoulda gone." Mister Hutt tapped the map. "Right here is the Valley of Visions. Part of the reason why every cutthroat scoundrel hides out there is the desert. Climb high enough on the mountains that ring the valley and I'd wager a man could see riders comin' from fifty miles off."

Tyler squirmed in his chair. "Anything else down there?"

"I hear there's some Indians live out there." Hutt drug his yellowed thumbnail across the hide. "Think that's what this mark supposed to be. What's it say?" The old man leaned closer. *"Mesita?"*

"Mesita?" It was the girl. She stood in the archway wrapped in a patchwork quilt. *"Mesita?"*

"What she sayin', Pilar?"

"Señor, that is the first she say." The Mexican woman pulled the quilt up over the girl's shoulders.

Tyler gulped. He wanted to shut his mouth but it hung open. The girl's eyes darted from Pilar to him. She swayed back and forth and then turned to go into the kitchen.

46

"Bring her here, Pilar," Mister Hutt ordered.

The woman put her arm over the girl's shoulders and guided her to the table. Their bare feet padded across the floor.

Mister Hutt pointed at the leather. He traced the lines that drew mountains and tapped the place where the village was burned into the map. "Ask her if she knows these places."

Pilar took the girl's shoulders and turned her so the woman's brown face was just inches from the girl's. Pilar spoke a few words of Spanish that Tyler could understand. Then the Mexican woman's voice turned almost to a song. The notes of each word rose and fell. A lone sunbeam sliced through a windowpane and crossed the girl's face as she leaned over the table to look at the map. Her eyes opened wide and as she breathed out, specks of sunlit dust scattered in her frightened breath.

The girl looked at Mister Hutt and back at Pilar. She nodded and spoke in the same chant that Pilar had used.

"*Mesita* her home," Pilar said. The melody of the girl's voice hesitated. Pilar continued. "The men take her from her village with two other girls. Only she is left." Wetness streaked the girl's cheeks.

47

Mister Hutt moved closer. He reached out and took the girl's chin in his rough hand and tilted her face up to his. "I thought she was Mexican when I first saw her."

Her eyes clamped shut and Tyler could see her tremble. Hutt looked over the girl as if he was evaluating the bloodline of a bull or stud horse.

"No, Indian for sure. Might see some 'pache in her." The old man nodded.

Tyler half-expected him to peel her lips back to check her teeth. He knew Mister Hutt would never do such things to a white girl.

"Good." Mister Hutt looked at Spencer. "Take her with you to Mexico."

"Wait a minute." Spencer whirled to face the old man. "First a shavetail kid, now an Indian girl. Do I have a say in this?"

"It's her home. She can be your guide. Speaks the language."

"Stop." Tyler stood from his chair. "She's a person." He couldn't believe the way he said it. He'd never talked to Mister Hutt like that before. "You're talking like she's just something you can just use." And he said it again. "She's a person." Tyler turned to Pilar. "Ask her, her name."

Spencer's arms fell limp at his sides and he turned to look out the window. A blue vein pumped in the middle of Mister Hutt's forehead. A quiet cough shook his chest and he let go of the girl. Pilar took the girl's tiny hands in hers and spoke.

The girl turned to Tyler and whispered, "Luak."

A hard lump filled Tyler's throat. He tapped two fingers on his chest and slowly said, "Ty-ler."

Mister Hutt moved to a rocking chair near the fireplace. He pinched his eyes with the fingers of one weathered hand. "Pilar, see to it the girl gets plenty of rest." He stared into the fire and began to rock. "Find some clothes for her to wear. We'll buy her new next time we're in town. Feed her all she wants." His voice was thick with phlegm. He brought the cloth to his mouth and hacked until his shoulders shook. When he took the kerchief away Tyler could see flecks of blood on the cloth.

Luak trembled like a frightened songbird. Her eyes darted from Tyler to Mister Hutt. Pilar made the sign of the cross and touched her lips to Luak's forehead. Then the Mexican woman put her arm around the girl's shoulders and led her to the rooms at the back of the ranch house.

"Tyler," Mister Hutt called.

"Sir?"

"I'm going to ride out and meet Miller and the herd. Put my saddle on a fresh horse." And then he said a word Tyler had never heard him speak. "Please."

"You sure, Mister Hutt?" Tyler rubbed his hands on the front of his pants. "You seem a mite tired from all that happened yesterday."

"I'll be fine. Some time in the saddle will help me think things through." The old man combed knobby fingers through his white hair. "Spencer, I'll need your help here with the cattle and chores for maybe two weeks. Weather will start to warm 'bout then. After that, you and Tyler can head to Mexico."

"Still thinkin' that girl should go along?"

Mister Hutt dabbed at the corner of his mouth with the kerchief. "That'll be for her to choose."

CHAPTER FOUR

Orange clouds tinged the west horizon when Tyler heard the cattle. Miller rode to the ranch yard alone and Tyler hurried out to meet him. The cowboy looped the ends of his reins around a post near the front door of the ranch house and filled a metal dipper from a bucket.

"Mister Hutt find y'all?" Tyler asked as the cowhand drank.

Miller dunked the cup into the bucket again. "Rode up on us 'bout noon. Told him we'd have the herd in 'fore dark and to go on back. He told me it was his money and his herd and he'd ride in with 'em if he wanted." He gulped down half the cup and spilled the remainder on the dirt near his boots. "He's feelin' poorly but won't let on."

Tyler's stomach turned sour. He looked out toward the sound of the cattle. "Why didn't he come in with you?"

"That old man's cussed, fought, and bled

over this place and them cows. Pure stubborn, he is. Sent me to get food and fresh horses. Won't get outta his saddle 'til this job's done as he sees it." Miller's lips curled over his tobacco-stained teeth. "I'm damn proud to ride for The Bootheel."

Someday Tyler wanted the men who would work for him to say the same thing.

"I'll get a string of horses to take to the boys. Tyler, see what Pilar's got on the stove."

"You get the food." Tyler's mind flashed to the Indian girl's wet skin beside Pilar's cookstove. "I'll get the horses together."

Miller met Tyler at the corral. Steam seeped out around the lid of a cast-iron pot of Pilar's tamales. The cowboy swung onto the horse Tyler had saddled for him and balanced the pot between his belly and the saddle horn. He never spilled even a drop. Spencer joined them without saying a word.

Tyler wrapped the lead ropes to five cow ponies around his worn saddle horn and followed Miller and Spencer out to where Mister Hutt and the other hands had the herd milling. The air turned crisp and the smell of sage and cattle was all around. Tyler knew the place well. The water in that creek never ran dry and the breaks would shelter the herd if another storm blew in.

"Cows ain't God's brightest animal." Tyler remembered what Mister Hutt had told him. "Point 'em toward water, let 'em find grass and move 'em slow and they don't know anythin' but to be happy. Cows are neighborly animals. Like to be around one another. Let 'em get thirsty or hungry or tired and they can be cantankerous." Tyler remembered how Mister Hutt touched the brim of his hat that day and winked at him. "Cowmen ain't good to be around when they ain't et or had water, come to think of it. But a good hand don't mind bein' alone. Least this one don't."

Night came in a crumb at a time like flyspecks on the barn windows. Cold clung to each gritty grain of darkness. The cattle spread across the trampled bottom ground near the creek. Silhouetted against a cobalt sky, Tyler could pick out four riders. Each lounged on his saddle and watched the herd. Closest to them, Mister Hutt set a short-backed mare. The old man's shoulders drooped and he held a dark kerchief to his mouth.

A bald-faced steer with one busted horn broke from the herd and trotted away. Mister Hutt's back straightened and he touched his spurs to the cow pony. Horse and rider lunged in front of the bawling cow. It swung its head and feinted as it would charge. In a sure motion, Mister Hutt uncoiled his lariat and popped the old cow on the nose with the knotted end of his rope. The steer decided it was time to be neighborly again and retreated into the herd.

Spencer let out a low whistle. He nodded at the old man. "He's good at what he does."

"Told me," Tyler whispered to the quiet, "he was born to it."

Back at The Bootheel, Mister Hutt invited Spencer to sleep in one of the back rooms in the ranch house. Tyler fed and watered the horses and hung Mister Hutt's saddle and gear. Miller and other hands chipped a film of ice from the top of a stock tank and washed in the frigid water. They passed a bottle of mescal from man to man. Tyler thought they seemed satisfied from the work they'd done that day. The men were snoring by the time he slipped into the bunkhouse.

Most nights he would have lit a candle and read from one of his dime novels, or if he was sure the men were sound asleep, read a few pages from his Bible. His body was tired but too many thoughts scurried around in his brain. Wrapped tight in a wool blanket that became his warm safe place, Tyler watched the mist from his breath wisp away in the dark room.

The Valley of Visions. A red-bearded bandit. The map. In two weeks he would ride with Spencer into Mexico. But the shiny black eyes of the Indian girl, Luak, peered at him every time his mind turned.

It was five days before Tyler saw Luak again. And then just for a moment. She stepped from the back porch and gathered the clothes Pilar had left to dry from a rope stretched between the house and one of the outbuildings. Just a glimpse of her black hair. No more.

When Tyler turned back to his chores, Mister Hutt steadied himself on a corral post near the gate. The handkerchief was in his hand almost all the time now.

"Have the Thoroughbred saddled when I get back, boy." His voice was as dry as gravel.

Mister Hutt picked his way around the fence and slowly moved up the hillside to the rimrock.

Tyler led the big horse from the barn and tied him to the gate. When he came back with the saddle, he could hear Mister Hutt's cough on the still air. He tossed the blanket and saddle on the animal and peeked over the horse as he tightened the cinch.

Mister Hutt climbed a few more steps and then sat down on a rock. He took off his hat and rubbed the kerchief over his face. The old man's head bowed and rested in his hands as if he were praying.

Tyler untied the horse's reins and led the animal up through the yucca plants and scattered rocks. He paused in the sagebrush a few steps from where Mister Hutt perched on the gray granite slab.

"Brought the horse so you wouldn't have to walk, sir."

The old man's bony shoulders poked at his jacket and Tyler thought if Mister Hutt moved too quickly they might tear through the cloth. Two days' worth of white whiskers covered his chin. The kerchief in his gnarled fingers was stained with silver-dollar-sized splotches of blood.

"Sir?"

Mister Hutt lifted his face from his hands. He touched the cloth to his lips.

"Tyler, did I ever tell you I went to Alaska when I was not much older than you are now?" Hutt's eyes seemed to focus on a spot above the desert's pale horizon. "There's big mountains and deep rivers that shout at you. They say 'God made me and I'm beautiful.' This here land —" He raised his face. "— it says the same thing in a whis-

56

per." He tried to stand but his legs failed and he eased himself back on the rock.

Tyler stepped forward to help, but Mister Hutt lifted his hand.

"Boy, I talked it over with Spencer last night. You and him are leaving in the morning."

"Sir?"

"Don't 'sir' me." A spark of fire flared in the old man's eyes. "Listen. Get two horses ready and one of our mules. Pick out the ones you think'll serve you on the long ride. You know the horses here better than any man on this ranch. Pick out the best mule."

Tyler started to question Mister Hutt but caught himself.

"Bring the Thoroughbred here and help me up, Tyler." Hutt tapped the rock beside him. "I need to check on things. Won't be gone long. When I get back, rub that horse down and give him extra grain. Keep him in the barn tonight so he gets plenty of rest." Hutt struggled to his feet. "You'll be ridin' him all the way to Mexico."

Tyler wanted to ask why they had to leave in the morning. Why he hadn't been told until now? Would the girl go with them? Words wouldn't come out of his mouth.

Mister Hutt took the reins and reached up for the saddle. Tyler put one hand on the old man's elbow and lifted. He weighed no more than the down from a thistle.

"Tyler, ain't told this to Spencer, but Pilar, she talked with the girl. You'll be takin' her to Mexico with you."

Tyler wanted to scream out his joy and cry all at the same time.

Mister Hutt's worn spurs touched the Thoroughbred's sides. His back straightened. Rider and horse left the hillside at a lope.

In the back of his mind, the hint of thought took shape. The happiness about Luak faded away. Tears filled his eyes because Tyler knew why Mister Hutt wanted him to ride to Mexico with Case Spencer.

The lantern sputtered in the morning dark. Light faded and it hissed for fuel. Tyler pulled the cinch tight on the mule's packsaddle. When he led the animal outside, smoke from the ranch house chimney hung in the air. It was piñon wood from Pilar's cookstove, not the pine Hutt burned in the fireplace to warm the house. Blades of brightness cut around the edges of the front door and sliced through the cracks in the shuttered windows.

Tyler went back into the barn and brought out the horses. Spencer's saddle was on a

58

sturdy buckskin gelding. He had put his own on the Thoroughbred and chosen a black paint with a gentle mouth for Luak.

From the house, Spencer's voice fought to escape through the adobe walls. Tyler was sure the gunman's argument with Mister Hutt about the girl had been decided. But not to Spencer's way of thinking.

After he'd ridden back to the ranch yesterday afternoon, Mister Hutt had sent Miller and the others out to sweep the northern ground and bring in any strays. He had ordered Jesus to ride the high ground west for any sign of the raiders. Only the old man, Pilar, Luak, and Spencer were left at the ranch with Tyler. Mister Hutt always arranged things to suit his purpose.

Last night, the girl had sat silently at the table in the house when they made their final plans. Mister Hutt motioned for Pilar to ask Luak if she wanted to go home. The Mexican woman turned to Luak and chattered a few words in that singsong rhythm. Luak's eyes found Tyler's. She never blinked. She just nodded her head.

"She don't even talk. You can't be sure if she even understood what you asked her." Spencer squeezed the edge of the table until his knuckles turned white. "How she's gonna be any use to us at all? Just another

59

mouth to feed. We don't even know if she can ride."

"How do you think that bunch of raiders got her this far?" Mister Hutt grabbed for his kerchief. Words seemed to catch in his throat between coughs. "She didn't walk —" He hacked into a scrap of cloth. "— 'sides she knows the country down there."

"She don't talk." Spencer's voice was so loud Tyler expected he would jump from his chair. "How she gonna tell us what she knows?"

"I'll teach her," Tyler said, still looking at Luak's black eyes. "It'll take us a week or more 'fore we get to where we'll need her help. I'll teach her a few words each night. By the time we need her, she'll be able to help."

"Sounds reasonable." Mister Hutt huddled back in his chair and struggled to gulp in a mouthful of air.

"So that's how it's gonna be?" Spencer leaned back until the front legs of his chair left the floor. He jammed his tongue in the inside of his cheek and stared at nothing.

"It is. Tyler, pick a horse for the girl," the old man had said. And that was that.

Tyler strained to listen to what might be happening in the house. He thought he could hear Spencer's voice again. There was a pause and Mister Hutt coughed hard.

Part of Tyler wanted the girl to ride with them. He told himself that he could be a knight on some great crusade returning the Indian princess to her home. Though down inside he knew Luak wasn't a princess at all. Most likely her family was dirt poor Indians scratching out a living in a lost village called *Mesita.*

The other part of him put aside all his thoughts of the girl and saw Spencer and him as heroes in the stories he read. Finding treasure. Battling outlaws. Discovering lost cities.

Him on Mister Hutt's Thoroughbred with a six-gun in his hand.

That dream whisked away like dandelion down on a breeze when Mister Hutt's cough shook the rusty hinges on the front door. No matter, Luak needed to go home. And to take her there would mean leaving the only home that Tyler had ever had.

Tyler left the horses tied to the corral and went to get his few things from the bunkhouse. He stuffed extra socks and long underwear into borrowed saddlebags with the wool shirt Mister Hutt had given him at Christmas last. He had decided not to take any books, save the old Bible. Tyler's entire sum of wealth was the thirteen dollars in coins wrapped in a piece of deer hide. He dropped it down the front of his canvas shirt. His eyes swept around the bunkhouse, but there was nothing more of his to take.

The front door of the ranch house opened and spilled light into the gray dawn. Spencer strode to the horses. He patted the neck of the gelding and shoved his big Winchester into the scabbard. The gunman pulled the reins from the corral rail and led the horse out into the yard.

The ends of Luak's black hair flashed in the soft light from the doorway. Her head was capped with a blue bandana and she wore a pair of men's pants and a worn leather jacket that had been Mister Hutt's.

Pilar reached out to steady Mister Hutt but he pushed her hand away. He held one arm tight to his side with the Krag rifle tucked into the crook of his elbow. He caught hold of the fence post near the Thoroughbred, turned, and rested his back on the rough railings. The old rancher reached out with his free hand and stroked his horse's muzzle.

"I told Spencer to take the road over San Augustin Pass." Shadows covered the old man's face. "You'll need to spend a night on the trail and you'll be in El Paso the next day." He took his hand from the horse and fished an envelope from his coat pocket. He held it out for Tyler to take. "That there is the address of a man I soldiered with. Runs a store in El Paso these days. Show him my letter and he'll let you stay with him while you buy supplies and such."

A lump in Tyler's throat grew thick.

Mister Hutt untied the Thoroughbred's reins and handed them to Tyler. "Best get on up."

Tyler wanted to reach out and take the old man's hand. He wanted to tell him thank you for taking him to The Bootheel and teaching him to be a cowhand. Instead, he slipped the toe into the stirrup and swung up into the saddle.

"Boy." A stray beam of lantern light touched Mister Hutt's eyes. "That Winchester is older than you are. 'Bout the only thing its good for is puttin' down a sorry horse or killin' a chicken for Pilar's pot. Take this with ya." The old man reached across time. Hutt's back straightened and Tyler imagined the young soldier he'd seen in the picture with Teddy Roosevelt handing the Krag rifle up to him. Then Hutt's gnarled fingers touched his eyebrow in a half salute.

Tyler could barely draw a breath. "Sir?" seeped from the boy's mouth.

"Adios." Mister Hutt's hand caught the

top rail of the corral and held it as the next cough racked his chest.

A thousand stars speckled the sky over Tyler's head. He felt very small. Spencer's heels kicked the buckskin. Tyler pulled up on his reins and turned the Thoroughbred to follow. The girl fell in between them. Tyler wrapped the pack mule's lead rope around his saddle horn and clamped both hands around it. Saddle leather creaked. Tears filled his eyes.

Tyler knew he would never see Mister Hutt again. Whatever gnawed away at the old man's insides would kill him. Mister Hutt would be dead long before they returned to The Bootheel. Mister Hutt was sending Tyler to Mexico so Tyler wouldn't see him die.

Their horses weaved through the sage and each picked its own path around great slabs of granite where Tyler was sure God's own finger had shattered the rimrock. At the top, the three riders pointed their horses at the red sun and rode east.

CHAPTER FIVE

Case Spencer reached out and let his fingers play over the walnut stock of his rifle. He carried his Winchester tucked in a cutaway scabbard, forward of the right stirrup, so the stock lay above the horse's shoulder and alongside its neck. Others preferred the stock behind the stirrup, angled toward the horse's rump. Other men wanted the motion of pulling out the weapon to be away from the horse's face lest it spook the animal. Spencer wanted his gun where he could grab it in an instant. No turning and looking away from trouble. If seconds mattered, a spooked horse was the least of a man's worries.

His hand touched the rifle again. There was comfort in the feel of the cool metal and smooth walnut.

Spencer let himself enjoy the rhythm of the horse's hooves on the trail. After a while, he slipped his hand into the front of his shirt and touched the envelope the old man had given him. Hutt had told him that there were two hundred dollars in it. There would be no purpose in counting it. If there was less, there was less. If a few dollars more, then more. If Spencer was to wager, there would be exactly two hundred dollars. The firm handshake and the look in his eyes told Spencer that Hutt did what he said he would.

Spencer had known men like Hutt before, though his line of work had brought more of the other kind. Honesty was a special thing. It showed itself as unique as the cadence of that man's own walk. Spencer could trust Hutt.

That meant he could trust the boy. Tyler seemed to have proper wit. He showed to be a hard worker. Knew horses. A bit green when it came to the trouble they were apt to find. But in a pinch, the gunman doubted that the boy would turn and run.

Spencer leaned forward as the buckskin climbed the trail up the pass. The Indian girl was another matter. She had grit. What she'd been through with the raiders showed that. But she had no stake in this adventure other than getting home. Spencer doubted that was enough to let him trust her. He turned in his saddle and looked at her.

Her head was up high and her mouth just an even slash across the brown face. Her lips turned neither up in a smile nor down to make a frown. Only a straight line. Like she had no feelings. She didn't palaver or complain. Leastwise that much was good.

Spencer let his thoughts brew on the two behind him because he didn't want to think about why he had decided to take Hutt up on his offer. When he had ridden away from The Bootheel that first morning, he wanted to be done with the notion that his father had come back from the war. All through his boyhood, he'd promised himself that his father was a soldier-hero. When Hutt told him his father had come to that scrap of desert in the New Mexico Territory instead of back to him in Nebraska, Spencer's insides had burned with hate for the father he never knew.

He had ridden his back trail away from the ranch. With every hoofbeat, his father's old Colt dug into his belly. He had pulled up on the reins, turned around, found Hutt's tracks, and followed them to the raider's camp. He'd got there just when the shooting started. That seemed to be his way. More times than he wanted to remember he had found himself with the Winchester 95 at his shoulder and his sights on some unfortunate.

Laws and civilization were taking over the west. Government trappers were taking out the wolves and mountain lions. Barbwire fences were commonplace. Even the small towns had banks, churches, and schools. A time would come when the need for his kind of gun work would be a thing of the past.

That's why he thought again about what Hutt had told him. If his father was cut from the same cloth as Hutt, Spencer owed it to himself to learn something about him. That meant an old map and Mexico.

Spencer tipped his hat back and wiped the sweat from his forehead with the back of his bare hand. Tyler had picked a good horse. The buckskin hadn't stumbled or missed a step anywhere on the rocky trail up the pass.

The horses stopped in his tracks when the sound of a gunshot rolled down the hillside and echoed back from the valley below. Spencer hooked his hand onto his rifle and slid from his scabbard. Another shot boomed. Tyler jumped from his mount and raced up the trail to Spencer. Luak gathered the reins from Tyler's horse into her hands along with her own pony's.

"Tell her to stay put." Spencer eased open the lever of his Winchester. He glanced down to be sure there was a cartridge in the chamber. "Bring Hutt's rifle."

Tyler turned to Luak. He held his palms down and pretended to pat the ground. "Stay here," he hissed and he snatched the Krag. Luak's eyes widened. She looked up the hill toward where the sound had come from and then back at the two men. She nodded her head in quick jerky motions.

Spencer handed his horse's reins to the girl. "She understand you?"

"I think so."

Spencer looked at Luak. Her lips still made the thin line. She gathered the three horses and the mule around her. "C'mom," he said to Tyler. "Follow me. Walk in the grass beside the trail so whoever's up there won't hear your boot soles on the gravel. We don't know what's up there yet. Could be just a cowhand takin' a shot at a coyote, so don't go gettin' too anxious with that rifle."

The two skirted along the trailside for better than two hundred yards. The pathway crested the hill. Spencer motioned for Tyler to keep low and they peeked over the ridgeline.

Below, where the road crossed an open place in the brush, a wagon with a pair of bay horses had stopped next to the trail. A

69

herd of goats grazed nearby. A man in a flat-brimmed hat sat a saddle horse near the team of horses. It was too far to see the man's face but sunlight gleamed off the pistol in his hand. The driver of the wagon held his head in his hands and rocked back and forth. Sprawled out on the ground by the wagon's front wheels lay a body.

Spencer stood to his feet and called out. "You at the wagon." He held the muzzle of his rifle up so both men could see. "This is none of our concern. Me and two others need to pass with our horses."

The man on the horse jammed the pistol into its holster and then held both hands shoulder high for Spencer to see. "Been havin' words. That one and me." He nodded toward the body on the ground. "He went for his shotgun. Just protectin' myself."

"What started it?" Spencer called to the driver of the wagon. Then hissed to Tyler, "Stand up. Show yourself and that Krag."

Tyler stood and shouldered his rifle like a soldier in a parade march. Spencer bit down on his tongue until it hurt.

The man in the wagon lifted his head. Spencer strained to hear him. "The dead one got too friendly with the whiskey. Caused his own trouble."

The man on the horse lowered his hands

70

and reined his horse to the back of the wagon. "We'll leave him where he lays and ride into Las Cruces to get Sheriff Lucero. I'll tell him my story."

Spencer lowered his rifle only slightly. "What are your names?"

"Jesse Wayne Brazel," the man on the horse answered. "I own the land up the road."

"You in the wagon?" Spencer asked.

"Carl Adamson." The man's voice was stronger now.

"Who's the dead man?" Spencer yelled.

"Pat Garrett."

"Say again." He felt his eyebrows cock.

The man in the wagon shouted, "I said, Pat Garrett. He's the man who shot down Billy the Kid."

"We'll wait for you to pass. Then be on our way." Spencer stepped to the top of the hill where they could watch and kept his rifle at the ready.

Tyler moved to Spencer's side with Hutt's gun still on his shoulder. "He called the dead man Pat Garrett. The man that shot Billy the —"

"If'n it's true, he's just a dead man now." Spencer cut him short and he spit the next words through his teeth. "Next time I tell you to stand up and show your rifle, you get up quick and hold that gun like you're ready to use it. Not like a soldier boy in some main street pageant."

"I'm sorry, I didn't know what you —"

"Listen to me." Spencer never turned his eyes from the men below. "We had the advantage. They didn't know we were here 'til I showed myself. We had rifles. Only saw a handgun down there. I wanted them to be thinkin' about two men with rifles, not just one."

"I'll do better next time."

"See that you do. *Next time* might not be as forgivin' as this one. Now bring the girl and the horses up here."

Spencer held his rifle across his chest as the wagon and rider rode by them. The gun's forestock rested in his bent elbow and Spencer was careful to show that his right hand stayed near the trigger.

"Mount up," he said as the wagon passed. He took his horse's reins from Tyler. "You two go on. I'll wait 'til they're down the trail."

When the two men were out of sight, Spencer climbed into his saddle and loped his horse down to Tyler and Luak. The boy had ridden to where the body sprawled in the dirt near the rutted path. Spencer pulled the buckskin up next to him.

"I thought he'd look different," Tyler said staring at the ants swarming over the bloody stain on the dead man's shirt. "I mean, everyone knows the story of how he killed Billy the Kid. He's just an old man."

"That happened years ago. What he did then don't count for nothin' now." Spencer clucked to his horse and turned. "C'mon. His day to die. Nothin' more."

Tyler urged his horse next to Spencer's on the trail. "That man that shot him didn't seem troubled at all."

"Said he was protectin' himself."

"Still." Tyler turned to take a last look.

"We don't know what happened. Just that a man's dead. One thing for sure, killin' a man leaves a raw spot on your heart that takes a long time to heal."

Tyler's head dipped. "They say you killed a more'n twenty men. I saw you shoot down those two rustlers and walk by their bodies like they was cow flop."

Spencer dug the tip of his tongue into his cheek, then put his spurs to his horse and trotted down the road away from the boy.

At the foot of the pass, the water in a stream played over rocks in a music all its own. Spencer held up his hand and pointed to a cluster of trees.

"We'll camp there." It was his first words since they'd left the body. "Tyler, water and hobble the horses. There's a cookin' pot on the mule's pack. Fetch it and fill it with water. I'll get a fire goin'."

After Tyler took the horses, the gunman scuffed the dry grass away with the toe of his boot and pushed rocks together to build a fire ring. The Indian girl helped Tyler unsaddle the horses and led them to the stream to drink. While Tyler took the pot and went upstream for freshwater, Luak wandered to where Spencer was building the fire.

"Can you get the food?" Spencer said dropping an armload of firewood near the stones he'd gathered together.

Luak squatted on her heels and looked up at him. She tilted her head and lines formed on her forehead.

"Food," Spencer said and pointed toward the packsaddle.

Luak looked at where he pointed and when she turned back her mouth stretched open in a yawn.

"Aw, I'll get it myself." Spencer marched to their saddles. He rummaged through the pack and found a sack of dried beans and the biscuits the Mexican woman had sent. He tucked the blackened iron skillet under his arm. When his head came up, he sniffed the air and smelled a hint of smoke.

Luak bent over the firepit. She held a clump of dry grass in her hands. A single spark glowed in the brown tangle. She held it close to her face and blew into the twisted grass. As flames appeared, Luak laid the bundle into the center of the ring of stones and began to feed in twigs and leaves from a pile she'd gathered. She sat back and placed larger branches near the burning grass. Yellow flames licked higher and Luak added more wood.

Spencer walked back. "Fire," he said.

The girl shook her head. *"Gasa."*

"No, fire," Spencer repeated.

"Gasa."

"Damn it. Talk American, girl. *Fire!*"

Luak shook her head again. *"Gasa,"* she whispered above the crackle of the new flames.

Daylight began to slip away. Tyler came out of the shadows of the trees carrying the kettle full of water. He knelt next to the girl and held his hands out to the fire's warmth.

"Fire feels good," he said.

Luak lips curled into a smile. *"Gasa."*

"Gasa?" Tyler rubbed his hands together.

"Yeah, *gasa,*" Spencer said. "It's an Indian word. Means fire." He licked the inside of

75

his cheek. "Don't you know nothin'?" He tossed the bag of beans to Tyler. "Spill some of that water in this skillet and we'll soak those beans up. Won't be much of a supper tonight, but we'll eat good in El Paso tomorrow."

Luak stood and brushed the dust from the knees of her pants. She picked up a branch as big around as Tyler's arm from the pile of firewood, held it in her hand for an instant, then dropped it and selected another. She looked towards the trees, nodded, and then walked away carrying the piece of wood.

"Where do you suppose she's goin', Spencer?"

"Probably needs to do her business. She'll be back directly."

"Do you like her, Spencer?"

"What kind of question is that? Promised Hutt we'd take her home. Don't matter whether I like her or not." Spencer tossed a twig on the fire. "Them beans ready to put on the fire?"

Tyler turned and looked into the shadows. He cocked his head. "Look, Spencer. Luak's comin' back, and she got somethin' with her."

Where the light of the fire met the night, Spencer saw the girl. Nearly touching the

76

ground, a limp object hung in her hand. The stick she'd picked from the woodpile swung in the other.

"She killed us a rabbit," Tyler blurted.

Luak walked into the firelight and sat next to Tyler. She dropped the rabbit on the ground and held out both her hands. Luak flexed her wrists as if she were breaking something.

"She wants your jackknife," Spencer said.

Tyler dug into his pocket and handled Luak his knife. She opened the blade and in quick motions gutted the animal, tossed the entrails into the darkness, peeled off its hide, and skewered the rabbit on a stick. The aroma of roasting rabbit and simmering beans mixed with campfire smoke.

"Heap better than just beans and dry biscuits," Spencer said as the rabbit cooked.

"You think she killed it with that stick?"

Spencer leaned back into the shadows so Tyler couldn't see his face. "I hear certain Mexican Indians can hypnotize an animal just by lookin' at 'em real hard. Puts 'em in this trance and then they sneak up and knock 'em in the head."

Tyler looked across the fire at Luak.

"Wouldn't be starin' at her if I was you." Spencer bit down on his lip and faked a cough.

CHAPTER SIX

Daylight crowded the stars from the sky. They ate cold biscuits, drank icy water from the stream, and were in their saddles before the orange faded from the sunrise.

Mist drifted from Spencer's nostrils. "Tyler, take the lead. Keep an eye on the girl. I want to check the trail behind us." He turned the buckskin and headed back the way they had come.

Except for deer tracks in the dust, the hoofprints of their stock were the only sign on the roadway. He pointed the horse to the north and rode a wide loop through the broken country. He kept the horse at a gallop and caught up with Tyler and the girl within the hour.

By noon they had left the rolling piñon-covered hills and dropped into the desert flats. The little stream where they had camped by was only a damp mark in the bottom of the sandy arroyo. They peeled off their canvas coats as the sun beat down. The girl twisted her hair into a braid and tied it to the top of her head with a strip of red cloth.

Spencer rolled up the sleeves of his shirt. "Tyler, time to rest the horses."

The boy swung from his saddle and helped the girl down. Tyler held a canteen out for Luak. She sipped and gave it back. After Tyler had drunk, he soaked his kerchief with water and wiped down the muzzle of his horse.

"Wish we had a way to water these horses, Spencer. This day's burnin' hot."

"I thought there'd be water in that creek. Been a dry winter, I reckon. We'll rest here a bit and walk 'em for an hour. Keep your eye in that bottom. Might find a mudhole where they can drink." Spencer dumped water from his own canteen into his hand and rubbed the nose of the buckskin. "Don't find water soon we might need to set tight 'til the cool of the evening. Who taught you about wettin' down a horse's muzzle?"

"Mister Hutt." Tyler splashed more water into the rag and moved to Luak's pony. "He taught me 'bout all I know 'bout horses, cattle, and such."

Luak tugged on the boy's sleeve. "Ty-ler."

79

She pointed to the gully bottom.

"She's tryin' to tell me somethin'." Tyler looked where she pointed.

"Maybe she sees another rabbit."

Luak pulled on his shirt again. "Ty-ler." She dashed to the mule and plucked the skillet from under the canvas. "Ty-ler." Again she pointed to the gully and then slid down the steep bank to the bottom.

"What in the — ?" Spencer shrugged.

She dropped the skillet, bent down, and grabbed a dried bunch of cheatgrass. She wound her fingers into the brittle weed and slowly pulled until the roots came from the ground.

She picked at the dirt stuck to the plant's roots, took up the skillet, and began to scrape away at the sand. In a few minutes, Luak had carved out a saucer-shaped depression.

"Look," Tyler said.

"I see it." Spencer shook his head.

Water, not much at first but then more and more began to seep into the hole that Luak had scratched into the dry streambed. She turned and looked up at the men and for the first time, Spencer saw a smile stretch across her face.

"Ty-ler." The boy's name came out of her mouth like a laugh.

"Get down there, boy, and help her dig that out. I'll bring down the horses. We'll water 'em one at a time. Won't be much but it'll get us to El Paso." Spencer licked his dry lips. *First a rabbit for supper, now this. Maybe the girl will earn her keep.*

For the best part of the next two hours, they let the horses drink. Splotches of mud covered Tyler's pants, but the boy smiled from the work he had done. They enjoyed the clean stream water in their canteens knowing they would not have to share with the horses and mounted up.

"El Paso 'fore night," Spencer told Tyler and Luak.

Tyler hauled up on his reins. "Look there."

Above the flat horizon, a column of black smoke lifted and trailed back in wispy layers of gray.

"I can hear it, too." Tyler cupped his hand around his ear. "Come on." He spurred his horse ahead. Luak followed. Spencer tugged on the mule's lead rope and joined them on the top of a rise in the trail.

"The Southern Pacific Railroad." Tyler pointed at the moving line in the distance. "Headed towards El Paso like we are. I read all about it once, in a newspaper Mister Hutt brought me from Santa Fe."

81

Spencer watched a smile spread across the boy's face.

"Those cars it's pulling are full of copper ore from the mines at Bisbee. Way over in Arizona Territory. They got copper mills in El Paso, you know." Tyler shaded his eyes and squinted. "They stop for water for the engine's boiler at a dozen or more places between here and there. Saw them get water in Columbus one time. From El Paso, they cross all of Texas and head for New Orleans."

"You talk like you know all about it." Spencer's horse sidestepped.

"Told you I read about it." Tyler pointed again. "Luak, train."

The Indian girl tilted her head and studied the movement in the distance.

"She don't know nothin' about trains."

"Tra-in," Luak said.

"Yeah, Luak. Train," Tyler laughed.

"Tra-in."

"See Spencer, she's learnin'." The Thoroughbred turned in a tight circle as Tyler pulled its reins. "Train, Luak," he shouted. "Read that they use all that copper to make wire for electricity. And someday there'll be 'lectric lights in every house in America, Spencer. What do you think of that?"

"We can't sit here burnin' daylight or we'll

never get to El Paso. Come on you two." Spencer took a long draw from his canteen. He spit a mouthful on the ground. "Electric lights in every house. That'll be the day."

Electric lights showed the way to El Paso. Ten miles out they glowed in the sky and by a full mile away the lights melted away the darkness over the town.

"It looks all white and ghosty." Tyler rode the Thoroughbred up next to Spencer's buckskin on the rutted street. "When you get close you can see each light flicker and they're more yellow-colored."

"First time you seen 'lectric lights?"

"Seen 'em in Amarillo. But never this many all in one place." A mix of clapboard buildings and adobe shacks crowded the crooked streets at the edge of the city. Train whistles mixed with the clatter of wagons, and more people than Tyler had ever seen scurried the sidewalks.

"Electricity might be good for towns, I reckon. Where people bunch up together." Spencer reined his horse to the side of the street to avoid a wagon. "I don't like the way all those wires," he looked up, "clutter up the sky." He shook his head. "Don't let that girl get lost."

Luak's head swiveled back and forth. She

never moved her hands from their grip on the saddle horn. Her head jerked and her eyes peeled wide open as a bell clanged and up the street, a vehicle crossed.

"Tell her that's a streetcar," Spencer said, "and explain all about 'lectricity." He hesitated a moment. Tied to a rail with a dozen other horses, his eyes found a milk-white horse in front of an adobe cantina. "Yeah, 'lectric *gasa*."

Tyler looked back at Luak. "I think she's scared."

"What about you?"

"A little bit. Never been around this many folks. The air smells — uh, used. Like sleepin' in a bunkhouse with a hundred dirty cowhands."

"Hang on. Hutt said his friend's store is close here." Spencer took a last look at the white horse and told himself to remember the dirt-walled saloon. "Said to take the side road towards the train yards."

Through the streaked windows, a light showed from the back of El Paso Mining and Industrial Supply Emporium. Spencer pressed his forehead against the glass on the front door and cupped his hands around his face. "I don't see no one." He tried the front door and the knob turned in his hand. "Hello, the store?" He opened the door

84

slowly. Tyler and Luak followed him in.

"We're closed. Come back in the morning. Someone's always here by six." A stoop-shouldered man came out of a room in the back of the shadowy store. "You ain't from the railroad, are you?"

"No, sir. Virgil Hutt sent us."

"Virgil Hutt?" Spencer could see the man's teeth flash in shadows. "Then come on in here."

The man pulled the door behind him open wide and yellow light from a bare bulb flooded into the room. Spencer and Tyler's boots clomped on the wooden floor and they crossed to the counter. Luak hung back in the shadowy dark.

The man reached out his hand. "Oliver Morris. I was just keeping up on my books, otherwise, I'd be gone. My Alice expects me —" His smile glazed over. And even in the little light, Spencer could see the confusion on Morris's face.

"My name's Case Spencer."

"I see your father in you." Morris ran his hand through the fringe of gray hair that hung above his ears. Light glared from the skin of his bald head. "Looking at you makes me feel like I could go to war again and lick the whole Spanish army by myself. As terrible as it all was, your father and Vir-

85

gil Hutt are the two best friends I'll ever have. Boy, there, must be Tyler."

"Yes, sir." Tyler took off his hat and held it in front of him.

"Last time Hutt was in El Paso, we sat in that back room remembering until we were both under the influence of bad whiskey. He told me about you. Said you're going to be one helluva cowman."

Tyler's Adam's apple bobbed up and down. He tried to say thank you but the words wouldn't come and the boy looked at the floor.

Morris pointed at Luak. "Tell your Mexican to take your horses 'round back. There's water and feed. Corral 'em with mine. And then he can find a cantina down the way."

"Sir, ain't no Mexican." Tyler fumbled with his hat. "Indian girl. Named Luak. Mister Hutt sent her with us."

"Oh, a little somethin'?" Morris showed his stained teeth.

"No, sir," Tyler shook his head. "Not like that at all."

"What the boy means to say," Spencer interrupted, "is that Hutt sent her along with us. Said you'd help us get supplies. We're headin' down to Mexico to look for my father. Girl's gonna help guide us."

Morris put both of his hands flat on the

86

counter. He studied Spencer's face. "Your father deserves as much. Now, you boys take care of your horses and then follow me home for dinner. My Alice will want to meet Case Spencer's son."

"What 'bout Luak?" Tyler asked.

"If Virgil Hutt sent her along, I think I can stand a dog eater for a couple of days. Come on, my Alice will make more food than you'll see at a Baptist church supper."

Spencer swung his saddle off the buckskin's back. "Morris said to put ours in the corral with his animals," he said to Tyler. "Have Luak help you and I'll take the gear inside."

He handed his horse's reins to Luak. She wrapped the leather around her fingers and led Spencer's big horse and her pony to the corrals with Tyler.

Spencer hoisted his saddle onto his shoulder and pushed through the door to Morris's back storeroom. He could hear the shopkeeper shuffling through papers on his desk in the next room. As Spencer laid his saddle on the floor he slipped his father's Colt from the saddlebags. He thumbed open the loading gate. The five shiny brass cartridges he'd loaded into the gun showed in the cylinder. The door to Morris's office creaked and Spencer dropped the pistol into

87

the side pocket in his coat.

Morris opened the door to the storeroom. He covered his bald head with a near-new Stetson and slipped his arms into a dark overcoat. "There's a room upstairs my Alice and I lived in when we were getting this business going. Spent every minute of the day here back then." Morris glanced back into his store and then pulled the door shut. "These days I take Sundays off and try to be home by eight 'cause my Alice wants me to."

Morris rattled the doorknob to check the lock. "This business has been good to me. My daughter's husband is starting to take an interest and he'll be —. Oh, you don't want to hear an old man rattle on." He eyed Spencer. "And it's probably a good idea to keep that gun handy." Morris stuck his fingers in his vest pocket. "I keep a derringer close."

Spencer's tongue touched the inside of his cheek. "I didn't want to cause any alarm." He moved his hand away from the pocket with the gun. "I'm carryin' some of Hutt's money."

"No matter. Now get the boy and that Indian girl and let's get going." Morris tilted his head toward a staircase. "The room upstairs. You and Tyler can sleep up there.

88

That Indian can stay in the shed by the corral."

Just then, Tyler stepped into the storeroom and dropped his saddle and the pack from the mule on the floor. "I'll sleep in the shed." Luak scraped her saddle across the doorway. "The girl should sleep inside."

Morris shrugged his rounded shoulders. He looked at Tyler and then at Spencer. "Suit yourselves."

Spencer had to hurry to keep pace with Morris down the city's back streets. He glanced back at Tyler and Luak to be sure they kept up. Luak still flinched at each new sound and squinted her eyes in the glare of the bright lights. Tyler kept close to her side but his head swiveled at the commotion of El Paso.

"Forty thousand people. That's what they say." Morris waved his arms and pointed. "By 1910 they say there'll bc forty thousand people in this town. And twice that many across the river in Juarez."

Spencer nodded and pretended to listen to the businessman. But from the corner, he spotted the flat-roofed adobe cantina he had seen as they rode into town. The white stallion pawed the ground at the rail where it was tied with six other horses.

Morris continued his ranting. "Railroad,

mining, military all have something going on here. But smuggling — guns, liquor, women, you name it — will always be big business whether the town council admits it or not. More money changes hands on the banks of the Rio Grande at night than in all the banks in El Paso during the day." He stopped for a moment and nodded toward the cantina. "Jimmy Six's place there. Give it a wide berth, Spencer. Always some evil bein' conspired upon in that hellhole."

Spencer stopped beside Morris and studied the white horse until he was sure that it was the stallion he'd seen the rustler leader riding. Light spread from the cantina's open door. Sounds of laughter and guitar music drifted from inside. A bearded man staggered into the light and upended a whiskey bottle. The light shone off the spilled liquor on his chin and shirtfront. A dark-haired woman laughed and pulled him back into the shadowy barroom.

"Those shacks out back," Morris said in a loud whisper, "cribs for Jimmy Six's whores."

"Law do anything about it?" Spencer memorized the alleyways beside the building. Barrels and wooden crates were piled as high as the roofline.

"Jimmy built that rattler's nest just outside

the city limits." Morris spit on the ground. "City police keep an eye on it but not much they can do. County marshal is Jimmy's brother-in-law. Might even be a partner in the business."

Alice Morris never said a word. Oliver Morris never stopped talking. Three roast chickens disappeared from the dining room table. As did a bowl of boiled potatoes, two dozen biscuits, a gallon of gravy, and the first green beans Spencer had seen in two years.

"I thought that Indian girl —" Morris untucked the napkin from his shirt collar. "— would eat with her fingers for sure. Who do you suppose taught her to use silverware?" He wiped his mouth with the cloth. "I'd guess missionaries do a respectable job of civilizing the savages, I've heard."

His wife busied herself clearing dishes. She smiled at Tyler but paused before reaching for Luak's empty plate. Then Alice Morris snatched the plate and hurried into the kitchen.

Tyler laid his napkin on the table. Spencer watched the boy's cheeks flush red. He reached out and tapped the boy's boots with his toe. Tyler's glare turned from Morris to Spencer.

Luak watched Tyler's face and Spencer

sensed that she knew his anger. What more she understood he wasn't sure.

Spencer leaned forward and looked Tyler in the eye. He hoped the boy read his look. "Morris, where can Tyler go to buy us more horses? Good horses. Thinkin' we'll need three more for our trip."

Morris pinched his chin. "I'll give you the names of two stables I know of. But you might have more luck at one of the ranches close to town. There's one supplying mounts to the cavalry at Fort Bliss. Might be worth lookin' into. But tell me, why isn't Virgil going with you? Your father was like his own brother."

"Hutt's health is failing," Spencer answered with no more explanation.

"I feared as much." Morris shook his head and looked down at the floor. "What are your plans?"

Spencer twirled a toothpick in his fingers. "We promised Hutt that we'd make a swing towards where my father was last seen. The girl —" He saw Tyler flare. "— Luak. Luak is from a village near where he last sent word. We'll ask around and see what we find." Spencer was careful to add nothing about the map.

"Whereabouts you headed?"

"A village called Mesita. Heard of it?"

92

"Can't say as I have." Morris leaned both elbows on the table. He stroked his chin. "Trouble brewing in Mexico these days. Got 'em a dictator. Portofirio Diaz. Calls himself the Grand Ruler of all Mexico. Just a plain thief. Some say there be a revolution down there in the next two years and folks in El Paso will be able to see the shootin' from their rooftops." Morris shook his head. "Now where's this Mesita at?"

"Valley of Visions."

"Jesus, Mary, and Joseph. Hutt lookin' to get you and this boy killed?"

"No, just find what happened to my father."

"A man you never knew? You got more guts than good sense." Morris picked up a butter knife from the table. He held it like a dagger. "No way to stop you I expect, so I won't try. When are you planning on leaving?"

"If Tyler can find horses he likes tomorrow, we'll outfit the next and start south."

Morris tapped the tip of the knife on the tablecloth. "You know, I just had an idea. Got a letter from a man a couple of months back. Claims he's some kind of geologist or the like. Had his bank transfer money to mine. Wanted me to order some equipment for him. He's wantin' to go prospecting down in Mexico. In this letter, he asked about that valley and said he'd want to hire pack animals and a guide. He'll be here the day after tomorrow. Might be worth talking to. Riding into Mexico as part of a mining expedition might not draw as much attention."

"What do you know about this man?"

"Just that his money is good."

Spencer looked at Tyler. "What do you think?"

Tyler nodded. The boy let a smile sweep across his face.

Spencer knew he should have involved the boy in the conversation earlier. From the look on his face, Tyler was stewing on how he thought the girl was treated by Morris. The boy needed to remember Luak was just an Indian and had a purpose to serve. "Tyler?"

"Don't think one more day won't make no matter, sir."

CHAPTER SEVEN

Spencer stabbed the key Morris had given him into the lock on the store's back door. "Tyler, check the horses, then come on in."

"I told Morris I'd sleep in the shed."

"And I'm telling you to sleep inside." Spencer looked down at Luak. "Both of you." The girl's lips twisted and she turned her face up to Spencer's like a whipped puppy. "Tell her she's sleeping upstairs." Spencer stomped in through the door and left Tyler and Luak outside.

Electric light filtered through a window spotted by moths and streaked with last spring's rains. Spencer always wondered why the glow from electricity seemed cold and hard and so different from the warmth of a wood fire. He spread his bedroll near the door to the stairs. When Tyler came into the dark room, he chose the wall under the lone window and Luak curled in the farthest corner.

Tyler belched from the good food Alice Morris had fixed. He twisted the blanket around him and in a few moments, steady breaths gurgled from the sleeping boy. Spencer imagined bubbles of spittle forming at the corner of Tyler's lips.

Luak cleared her throat and made no more sounds. She never moved. Just lay still beneath a single wool blanket.

Spencer studied the pair for a long moment and then crawled from his bed. He put his hat on his head, scooped up his boots, and slipped out the doorway. He remembered that the third stair from the top creaked under his weight and took a long step over it, careful to keep his footfalls close to the wall.

His canvas coat, with his father's loaded Colt, was on his saddle in the storeroom at the foot of the stairs. He draped it over his arm, opened the back door to Morris's store, and tiptoed into the yard. His buckskin horse snorted and started the other animals milling about the corral. Spencer moved along the hard-packed dirt to the front of the building. Only then did he stop to pull on his boots and coat.

He had seen the white stallion tied to the rail in front of the cantina when they had returned from Morris's home. Spencer

96

needed to know if its red-bearded rider was inside. He took the pistol from the coat pocket, tucked it into the waistband of his trousers, and draped his coat over the gun.

If the red-bearded man was inside, he'd find a table in the back and listen. If the horse was gone, he'd ask a few questions and leave a dollar or two on the bar. Whores found answering questions for money easier than their other work. Either way, before the night was over, he'd know if the man Hutt called Dalton Fox was in El Paso.

The toll of a church bell wafted over the dark streets of El Paso. A horse jerked back and fought the reins that held it to the hitching rail in front of Jimmy Six's cantina. The saddle on its back jostled the horse next to it. Both animals snorted and pawed the dirt. The white stallion tied with them never moved.

Spencer bit down on his tongue. He tugged the brim of his hat down to cover his face and left the shadows from where he had watched the cantina for the past twenty minutes. As he passed the hitching rail, he reached out and touched the nearest horse. His fingers trailed over the brand on the animal's haunches. The horse moved at his touch and stepped into the shaft of dim

97

light from the saloon. In the wisp of pale light, Spencer could make out the Bootheel brand burnt into the horse's hide.

Boot soles scuffed across the wooden floor. Three men filled the doorway blocking nearly all the light. A whiskey bottle hung in the hand of the first. He swallowed the last gulp and threw the empty bottle into the street. The next man grabbed the first's arm and pushed him toward the horses.

"Rosa," the first bellowed, "tomorrow night I come back with more money. *Mucho dinero."* He pulled away from the other's grip and caught hold of the rail near where Spencer waited. Liquor glazed his eyes and its sour smell washed over Spencer's face. The man looked at Spencer. "Rosa, she waits for me, you know."

Spencer turned away when the next man pushed by him. He pretended to stagger and reached out to steady himself on the frame of the open door. As Spencer glanced back towards the street, he saw a second man help the drunk onto his horse. The hands of the third untied the reins of the white stallion.

Spencer's fingers clamped tight on the doorpost. Saddle leather creaked and the horses shuffled away from the front of the cantina. He lifted his eyes. The rider on the white horse kicked his heels into the animal's ribs. In the angled light from the doorway, Spencer saw the rider's beard was the color of rust.

Kerosene lanterns set on stacked beer kegs threw shadows that did not quite touch the corners of the cantina. Here and there, flames sputtered from candles set on the tables. Behind the bar, two bare electric bulbs glared.

A gray-haired man slept on a tabletop. His regular breathing seemed to keep time with the notes that a boy, no older than Tyler, plunked on a guitar. Two men leaned on the bar. Both watched in the mirror when Spencer crossed the floor. Another man in railroad stripes poured two fingers from a bottle into a smudged glass. The trainman absently tapped the half-full glass on the table in front of him and stared at nothing.

Spencer leaned his left side on the bar so he could watch the others in the room and the front door. His father's pistol was tucked in his belt just behind the point of his right hip bone. *"Tequila,"* he said to the stocky man behind the bar.

"Sí." The bartender wiped a glass with a stained rag, splashed it full of a clear liquid, and set the glass in front of Spencer. He held up two twisted fingers. When he smiled, the folds of his wrinkled skin peeled open over one eye as milky as an opal.

"High priced liquor." Spencer tossed coins from his vest pocket onto the bar.

"Only the best, Señor." The sightless eye seemed to study Spencer's hands.

Spencer squinted over his shoulder into a dark corner. Three women sat at a table. One stood and walked from the shadows to the bar. Her face was lost in the darkness. A light-colored dress caught the shimmer of lights. Her legs were as long as a colt's and she was barefoot.

Spencer downed the tequila in one gulp. Its fire torched his chest and when he slammed the glass on the bar, a spider scurried across the floor between his boots. He caught it with his toe and crunched its life away.

As light as that spider's touch, the woman's fingers grazed the back of the hand that held his glass. Spencer turned to her. A nest of curly, brown hair framed her face and touched her shoulders. Despite the cold night, a glaze of sweat made the skin at her throat shine like warm whiskey. Eyes more green than brown looked into his.

"Dey call me Christmas." She flexed her fingers and tapped her nails on Spencer's hand. "What I call you?"

Spencer signaled for another tequila. He nodded at the woman and she shook her head. "Case Spencer," he whispered

The bartender filled his glass until liquor spilled over the brim. Christmas dipped a fingertip in the drops on the bar and touched the tip of her tongue. When her lips peeled into a smile, one of her front teeth was chipped in a sharp angle.

"Lonesome, Case Spencer?"

"Lookin' for someone, Christmas, maybe you can help. I think I saw him leavin' this place."

"Bad man, yes? Only bad men come here." She leaned forward until her round breasts rested on the bar.

"Some say so."

"He know you look for him?"

"No." Spencer let his eyes sweep over her back and hips. He enjoyed what he saw. "Hombre with a red beard. Rides a horse the color of cow's milk. Called Dalton Fox."

Christmas stood straight up. She turned towards the table where she had come from. Spencer caught her wrist. The men at the end of the bar set their glasses down.

"He was here, wasn't he?" Spencer whispered.

Christmas nodded so slightly that her hair

never moved. She looked over his shoulder at the two men. The boy, with the guitar, stopped his music. Then her eyes darted to the bartender. Her head fell back and she laughed loudly.

"Play, *muchacho,*" Christmas shouted to the boy.

She leaned in and let her curls brush Spencer's ear. The boy began to strum. "Put five dollars on the bar and follow me." She pulled away and lifted her arms. Her tongue touched the broken tooth. She caught the hem of her dress, lifted it to her knees, and let her hips move with each note of the music.

Spencer dropped five silver dollars on the bar. Christmas reached out and took his hand. She led him away from the light and out into the alley.

"The men at the bar —" Christmas looked back through the door into the cantina. "— they ride with Fox." She pointed to one of the shacks. "That is mine." She put her hand on the small of Spencer's back and pushed him toward the hovel.

The mulatto whore slammed the door shut behind them and peered through the crack around the doorframe. "If they heard you say his name they will follow us." She turned down the wick on an oil lamp that sat near the makeshift bed on the floor. "Fox come tonight for his business with Jimmy Six. He leave with two others when the business is done. The others, they stay until all their money is no more."

The tiny lamp flame painted gray shadows around the hut. A cracked crockery jar sat next to a tin basin beside the pallet of worn blankets. Christmas took a broken pint whiskey bottle stuffed with a bouquet of dried desert flowers from a three-legged stool. She tapped on its seat and motioned for Spencer to sit. She put her eye to the crack in the door. "They come."

Spencer slipped the Colt from under his coat.

"Ty-ler."

Tyler opened his eyes. Luak face was inches from his.

"Ty-ler."

She dashed to the other side of the room and lifted the empty blankets from Spencer's bedroll.

"What, Luak?" He stood to his knees.

Luak darted back to him and grabbed his arm. She pulled him to his feet.

"Spencer?" Tyler said.

Luak shook her head. She pulled him to the top of the stairs and rushed down. Tyler followed. Luak pulled the long Krag rifle from Tyler's saddle scabbard and pushed it toward him.

"Oh no, Luak." He looked at the gun. "Wait here." He bounded up the stairs and snatched his boots. He took the stairs two at a time on the way back down. "I wish you could tell me what was goin' on." He pushed one foot into its boot and then the next. He took the rifle from Luak.

Luak led him around Morris's store and down the now-dark streets of El Paso. They dodged a line of freight wagons and turned toward the edge of town.

Tyler caught the sleeve of Luak's shirt. "We goin' to Morris's place? It's the other way."

Luak pulled away and raced down the street waving for him to follow. She crawled under an empty spring wagon and flopped on her stomach. Tyler slid in beside her.

Two horses stood tied to the rail in front of a slanting one-story adobe cantina. Notes from a faraway guitar floated from inside. Up the road from the railyard, a quartet of men in overalls and striped caps made their way toward the saloon.

The men elbowed each other to be first through the door. Tyler heard women laugh and the guitar played louder.

"Ty-ler," Luak hissed. She pointed down the side alley. Near a row of wooden shacks behind the *cantina*, a man pressed a finger to his lips and pointed at the door of one of the shacks. The man with him pulled an ax from a chopping block near a pile of firewood.

"I see one of them." Spencer pressed his face tighter against the crack between the door and frame. He rolled his head to one side trying for a glimpse of the other. Spencer depressed the trigger on the revolver and thumbed the gun to full cock, careful not to let the gun make a click. Christmas's breath filled his ear.

"Laugh," she whispered to him.

"Huh?"

"Laugh, like you havin' fun. Maybe they think we just do our business and leave us be." Her hushed voice trembled.

He shook his head. "They're waiting for me to come out. Then they'll jump me." He looked around her room. "Not even a window to crawl out of." Spencer rested his free hand on the doorknob and touched the muzzle of the Colt to the gap in the door.

"You can stay 'til mornin'. Daylight come, dey might not be so brave."

Spencer sensed more than saw. A slash of

metal ripped through the air outside the door. The doorknob burst loose in an explosion of splinters. He slammed his shoulder onto the door to hold it closed. More weight than his hit the other side. For a second that seemed a day long, Spencer wedged all his strength against the door.

Little at a time the door moved inward. Fingertips clawed the opening. The hand jabbed through. Spencer swung the muzzle of his revolver into the palm of the groping hand and pulled the trigger. The blast could not cover the man's scream.

Spencer threw all his weight onto the door pinning the shrieking man's mangled hand. He slammed the butt of the Colt into the blood-splattered wrist until he heard the bone snap. He eased on the door. With a whimper, the man pulled his arm back.

"Blow out that light." He yelled at Christmas. All went black. Spencer cocked the gun, and he burst out the door to face his attackers.

An ax lay in the dirt outside Christmas's door. Three men in overalls stood at the open back door of the saloon. In the dim light, Spencer could see flowery dark splotches in the dust at his feet. Horses whinnied from the front of the saloon and two riders galloped away, headed for the desert west of El Paso.

"Spencer." Tyler ran up the alley. The Krag hung in one hand. Luak was beside him.

"What are you doin' here?"

"Luak came and got me."

Spencer glanced at the girl's face in the darkness. "How did she —" He snatched the rifle from Tyler's hand and jerked open the bolt. "I can handle my own. If I need your help I'll ask for it." When he looked down at the rifle in his hands a rage boiled up from deep in his stomach.

He grabbed Tyler by the shirt collar. "Next time you come runnin' to save my bacon, ya fool kid," Spencer said through his teeth, "bring a loaded gun." He pushed Tyler away. "Now get back to Morris's place and take Luak with you."

Even in the shadows, Spencer saw the color drain from Tyler's face. Spencer slammed the rifle into the boy's hands. Tyler turned. He looked back over his shoulder at Spencer and he stumbled a few steps. Luak ran after him.

"They might be back. Christmas, come with me."

The woman shivered. She looked down at the floor of her crib. With her barefoot, she kicked a severed finger out into the dirt.

She pushed Spencer away.

The boy with his guitar slung on his back joined the men at the back door. Spencer heard their mumbling. Christmas knelt by her bed. She fumbled under the pile of blankets and pulled out a long knife.

"Please come with me. Just 'til daylight." Spencer looked down at the whore. "I don't want them to come back and hurt you."

Christmas rocked back and forth on her knees. She shook her head.

Spencer found the upstairs room at Morris's store empty. From the only window, he spotted Tyler's silhouette on the top rail of the back corral. The boy's head was bowed and the Thoroughbred rested its face on Tyler's legs. Luak sat at the base of the same fence post and she crossed her arms over her chest to ward off the cold night.

Spencer scuffed his boots through the gravel to be sure they would hear him coming, but only Luak raised her eyes. The gunman climbed up onto the top rail of the corral next to Tyler. His hand reached out, found the Thoroughbred's mane, and tugged on a tuft of hair.

"I've been thinkin' mules might be better than horses for where we need to go." Tyler never turned to look at him. "We got good

108

horses. Need mules to carry the supplies." Tyler stroked the Throughbred's face. "I'm not sorry for what I said back there. You coulda got yourself killed. Luak, too." He tangled his fingers in the horse's mane. "Ah, damn it, Tyler. It was brave of you to come after me. I mean, not knowin' what you were gettin' into takes grit."

Spencer drew a big circle on the inside of his cheek with his tongue. "Shoulda told you what I was up to."

Still, the boy refused to talk.

"Always," Spencer raised his voice, "check and double-check to be sure that rifle's loaded if you expect there might be even a small chance for trouble." He pulled his hand away from the horse. "Damn it, Tyler."

"It was Luak." The boy whispered. "She musta followed you and seen what was happenin'. I was asleep. She came back and got me."

Spencer looked down at the girl. Luak's eyes shined up at them like burnished stones in a rich woman's bracelet. Spencer blew out a long breath. "When we rode into town, I saw a stallion tied up in front of that cantina. A white stallion. Remember me telling Hutt that bunch of raiders that tried to run off his herd was led by a man ridin' a white stallion? Man with a red beard?"

Tyler turned to Spencer and nodded. "The same bunch that had Luak?"

"Yeah. The white horse was there when we came back from Morris's house. I waited 'til you two was asleep and went to see what I could find out. Wasn't lookin' to make trouble."

"You took your gun."

"That I did. In case misfortune found me."

"The man with the beard? Was he there?"

"Yup. Luak musta recognized those men and knew I was in for trouble. This time I got myself out of it. Next time, I'll need to know I can count on you. You ain't no fool. You were comin' to help. I respect you for that." Spencer pulled a sliver of wood loose from the fence and tossed it into the corral. "I'll never go off again without tellin' you. You got my word on that."

Spencer let Tyler think about what he'd said. Finally, the boy spoke. "I want a gun."

"You got that Krag."

"No. I want a Colt. You know, somethin' I can always have with me. And I want you to teach me to use it." Tyler rubbed the front of his pants with both hands. "I have money."

Spencer nodded his head. "Tomorrow after we buy the mules, we'll find a gunsmith and you can get yourself a gun. I'll take you down in the *bosque* and show you how to use it. You just remember. Havin' a Colt on your hip don't make you ready for trouble."

"I want you to teach me that, too. I don't ever want you to be worried 'bout me in a fight again."

"It's not somethin' you just learn by talkin', boy."

"I think I know that."

"I think you do." Spencer swung off the fence. "Better get some sleep. Lots to do tomorrow. Tell Luak to come in with you." He started for the building.

"Spencer, damn it." Tyler dropped off the fence and balled his fists. "You don't treat her any better than Mister Hutt or old man Morris. Luak was the one that brought me. You know how scared she musta been when she saw the men that did those things to her? She's the brave one here."

Luak stirred at the mention of her name but didn't stand.

Tyler stepped toward Spencer. "You always say, 'Tyler tell Luak this er tell Luak that' —. She's as much a part of what we have to do as you or me. Just cause she's Indian you think she don't count. I'm tellin' you now she does."

Spencer held out his hand to Luak. She took it and he helped her to her feet. "Luak," he said in his loudest voice. "Let's go get some sleep." And he turned his back so Tyler couldn't see the smile on his face.

CHAPTER EIGHT

Morris unlocked his store at five o'clock the next morning. Spencer and Tyler helped him harness two teams and manhandled full loads into the delivery wagons. Morris offered fresh biscuits his wife had sent and brewed stout coffee on a mesquite-fired stove that sat next to the front counter. Tyler and Luak took their meal and went out to see their horses.

One by one the store's employees wandered in through the back door. Morris shared the coffee with each and assigned the workday's tasks.

The bell over the front door rang for the first time. A stocky man hooked his thumbs into the vest pockets of a gray suit and ambled into the store.

"Oliver," he said pushing back the brim of his straw sombrero.

"Earl," Morris returned the greeting. "What brings you out so early?"

113

Earl drew himself to full height and haughtily sucked in his belly. His coat drew back over his chest. Over the rim of his coffee cup, Spencer saw an ivory-stocked Colt pistol holstered on the man's hip and a badge pinned to his vest.

"Is that Virgil Hutt's Thoroughbred out back in your corral?" the man asked.

"It is," Morris answered.

"Where is that old man? I'd like to say hello."

"Ain't here. Sent the horse with two of his hands."

"Didn't think he let anyone ride that high-dollar horse but him."

"You thought wrong and you didn't come in here to talk about horses." Morris filled a tin cup with coffee and set it on the counter for the man. "Spencer here rides for Hutt." Morris nodded. "Meet Earl Santos. Earl is an El Paso city policeman. Works the night shift. Ain't that right, Earl?"

Santos tipped the cup to his lips and set it on the counter. Oily strands of hair hung from beneath his hat and stuck to his forehead. A shiny pink scar crossed his cheek and disappeared behind his ear. "There was trouble last night at Jimmy Six's place. A real mess."

"Thought that hellhole was outside the

city limits and didn't concern you." Morris filled his cup again.

"Professional courtesy, amigo. I told the sheriff I'd ask around." Santos smiled at Spencer. "Someone heard gunshots and a man scream. There was blood in the alley. We found someone's finger in the dirt. A real mess, you know." He picked up the cup and took another drink. "A real mess. Like a soft turd dropped by a tall horse." Santos grinned, like he was proud of what he had just said, and showed his teeth.

"Anybody see anything?" Spencer asked.

Santos never took his eyes from Spencer. "Oliver, you know how it is at that place. Men with wives don't remember much if they've been dippin' their wicks at Jimmy Six's."

"Far as I'm concerned the whole place could burn down and most of this town will never shed a tear." Morris ran his hand over his head. "Now just what can we be doing for you, Earl?"

"Like I said, I saw Mister Hutt's horse and wanted to say hello to the old man. The rest was just talk." He drank the last of his coffee. "Gracias, amigo." He started for the door and then turned and looked at Spencer. "Oliver, I forgot to mention. One of Jimmy's whores got her throat slit early this

115

morning. That mulatto wench. It was a real mess, you know."

The policeman closed the door behind him. Spencer's knees went weak. He caught the edge of the counter, spilling his coffee.

Tyler walked in the back door. Spencer turned to the boy.

"I heard," Tyler said.

Morris mopped up the coffee with a rag. He looked at Spencer and then at Tyler. "You two don't know anything about what that man was talking about, do ya?"

"No, sir," Tyler was quick with the answer. "No, sir. Don't know nothin' about it at all."

Tyler looked over the mules. Spencer thought about Christmas. When the boy was satisfied, he picked out three and Spencer paid the man forty dollars to hold the mules until the next day. When they rode back into town, Spencer took care to watch Jimmy Six's cantina. There were horses tied out front. The white stallion wasn't one of them. In the alley, the door to Christmas's hovel swung open on the day's little breeze. From inside the cantina, a woman's laugh floated. A man's voice answered her. When Spencer heard the lift of guitar music coming from the saloon, his stomach turned.

"Morris said the gunsmith's store is down

116

that street."

Tyler turned in the saddle.

"We'll leave the horses and walk." Spencer reined his horse towards Morris's store. "Tell Lu—" He caught himself. "Luak, we're going to take a walk uptown."

The Indian girl tilted her head at Spencer.

"Uptown, Luak." Tyler gathered his reins in one hand and pointed towards the city. "Uptown."

"Uppp-tonn," Luak repeated.

"Let's go in here a minute." Tyler stopped in front of the open door of a brick building on the corner.

"What for?" Spencer stepped out of the way of a woman pushing a baby buggy. The little boy she had by the hand stared down at Spencer's spurs.

"There's just somethin' I promised myself I'd buy next time I was in a town. Come on." Tyler took Luak's hand and pointed his chin at the open door. She shook her head. "It's all right, Luak. Come on."

Tyler stepped in front of a table covered with jars of penny candy. The boy bent forward and studied each one.

Luak turned away from Tyler and looked up at a headless mannequin wearing a woman's dress. Spencer guessed she knew

117

what the dress was for but she wondered why the woman had no head. The Indian girl stood for a long moment looking up and then spotted a display of bright-colored ribbons. With one finger she reached out, touched a piece the color of the sky, and just as quickly pulled her hand back.

"You want it, Luak?" Tyler stepped up beside her. He picked up the ribbon and held it next to her hair. "I'll buy it for you."

Spencer was wrong. Against the girl's shiny black hair the ribbon changed from the color of the sky to cornflower blue.

Tyler held out the ribbon. A smile curled Luak's mouth until white teeth gleamed in her brown face. She snatched it from Tyler's hand.

"Help you there, son?" a man in a white apron behind the counter asked.

"I'll take the ribbon and a nickel — no, a dime's worth of licorice whips." Tyler dug in his shirtfront for his coins.

The shopkeeper filled a bag with the candy. He held out his hand for the ribbon but Luak wrapped it tighter in her fingers.

Thank you, sir," Tyler laughed. "Some licorice, Spencer?" He hung a black string in his mouth and gave one to Luak.

"I believe I will." They joined Spencer on the street in front of the store. "Tell her not to get —" He caught himself. "Luak, don't get candy on that new ribbon."

Spencer bit into the black candy and in that instant, the faces of the twelve dead men he carried in his brain melted like the sweet. Christmas was alive. And he remembered what it was like to be a boy.

The gunsmith's shop was in a narrow building wedged between a hotel and a laundry. Like Morris's store, a bell over the door jingled when they entered. Two dozen rifles and shotguns sat one next to another in a rack behind a counter that ran the length of the building. Tyler went to a case near the end and knelt to look at a collection of handguns behind the glass.

"Be there directly," a voice called from a back room. An oily hand pushed back a stained curtain and the gunsmith walked in, wiping his hands on a red rag. "He'p ya?"

The curtain moved again. A man, a head and a half taller than the gunsmith, ducked through. Leather suspenders crossed a starched shirt and his khaki pants were tucked into knee-high calfskin boots. The long legs and dark boots made Spencer think of a giant grasshopper. In the man's hand hung the shiny steel and polished wood of a new rifle.

"Need ammunition and the boy wants to look for a belt gun," Spencer said to the gunsmith.

"A Colt," Tyler added.

The smith tossed the rag on the case next to Tyler's fingers. "That one with ya?" He pointed at Luak.

"She is."

"Know her place?" the old man grumbled.

Spencer shook his head.

Luak fumbled with the gift Tyler had bought for her. She pulled the new ribbon across her forehead and tied it beneath her thick black hair.

Spencer looked over the counter at the stacked boxes of cartridges. "Four–oh–five Winchester. Better give me 'bout a half dozen boxes."

"Heard good things about that round." The long-legged man pushed his small rimless spectacles up his nose. "A real stopper. Roosevelt ordered one for his trip to Africa. Says it's big medicine."

"Killed everything I needed it to." Spencer held out his hands. "Whatcha got there?"

"It's the new Savage lever gun." He passed the rifle to Spencer. "Only the female form is more beautiful to touch than a fine rifle."

Spencer put the rifle to his shoulder and sighted on an imaginary target. "A little long for my taste, but a tall fella like you should be able to handle it. Case Spencer's the name. The boy lookin' for a handgun is Tyler and the Indian girl is Luak."

The tall man took Spencer's hand in a firm grip. "Leland Bowie. From Michigan."

"Far piece from Michigan. Whatcha doin' in El Paso?"

"I'm a geologist headed into Mexico."

"Prospectin' for gold?"

"Heavens, no. It's oil I'm after. Someday it will be more valuable to this nation than gold. Mexico has it. And I intend to find it and become filthy rich." Bowie laughed at his words.

"You buy some equipment from a man named Morris?" Spencer squinted at Bowie. "Owns El Paso Mining and Industrial Supply."

"I ordered some things from him."

"He told us you might be looking for a guide and packers." Spencer handed the rifle back to Bowie. "Tyler and me are headed into Mexico. The girl is from there. She knows the trails and speaks the language." Spencer looked at Luak. He hoped she did know the way.

The bell over the front door jingled before Bowie could say anymore. In through the door marched Earl Santos.

"Amigo," Santos called. "Spencer, what brings you here?"

"After hearin' 'bout the trouble last night Tyler there decided to buy a handgun." Spencer turned his back to the policeman and pretended to study the guns on the display rack. Bowie followed his lead and turned his face.

Santos walked to the counter where the gunsmith and Tyler stood. "Thought you should know —" He leaned close to the gunsmith. "— someone broke into the hardware store on Fifth street last night. Stole guns and ammunition."

Tyler stepped away from the display case. The gunsmith looked Santos in the eye and then hacked a glob into a tarnished brass cuspidor behind the counter. Tobacco juice dribbled from his lips into the stubble on his chin. "Saw Tommie at the post office. Told me what happened. Said they cleaned him out of .30-30 and .45 Colt ammo and took six new Model 94's still in the crate. Musta knowed what they was after."

"Maybe somebody will try to sell them to you?" Santos found a toothpick behind his ear and tapped it on a gold front tooth.

The gunsmith shook his head. "You know darn good and well that those guns grew fins and swam the river soon as they left

122

that store. They're deep in Mexico by now."

"Still —" Santos worked the toothpick into his teeth. "— let me know if you hear anything. And keep your doors locked at night."

The gunsmith lifted a shotgun from a hiding place behind the counter. The gun's barrels had been sawed off just an inch in front of the forestock. "I can take care of my own. Anything else you want to tell me, Santos?"

"No, sir." He tucked the toothpick away where he had found it. "But, Spencer —" The policeman started for the door. "— the whore. Doctor sewed her up. She's gonna live. Won't be as pretty as before, though." The door shut behind him.

Spencer buried the tip of his tongue in the side of his cheek and fought not to show even the smallest hint of emotion.

"What was that about?" Bowie turned and looked at Spencer.

Spencer shrugged his shoulders. "He thinks I know somethin' about a barroom fight last night."

"Do you?"

Spencer only lifted his eyebrows.

"Ask me, Santos knows more than he lets on." The gunsmith tucked the shotgun away. "He probably knows who stole those guns if he didn't do it hisself. Half the police

123

department are thieves. And that one —"
He spit again. "— is as crooked as a dog's
hind leg." He mopped his chin with the
back of his hand and looked at Tyler. "Boy,
this ain't no museum. You gonna just look
or you ready to spend your money?"

Tyler left the store with a used Frontier
Model Colt and ten dollars gone from his
savings. The gunsmith threw in a box of .44
caliber cartridges and a used gun belt and
holster. The previous owner of the gun belt
was a bigger man than Tyler. To wear it, the
boy would have to wrap the belt around his
narrow hips twice. And he would have,
except the gunsmith reminded him that
there was an ordinance that forbid carrying
guns openly within the city limits of El Paso.
Tyler tucked the Colt and holster away in a
burlap bag with the ammunition Spencer
had purchased.

When they left the store, Earl Santos
leaned against the doorway of a building
across the street. The policeman sucked on
a toothpick. Santos followed Tyler, Luak,
and Spencer, and the tall man named
Bowie, but stayed half a block behind. When
they turned down the road to Morris's
store, Santos paused. The policeman took
his hat from his head and fanned his face

despite the chill in the afternoon air.

Tyler took three quick steps to catch up with Spencer and Bowie. "You been watchin' him?" he asked.

Spencer turned over his shoulder. "Yup." He never missed a step. "Keep Luak close."

Spencer slipped his hand inside his jacket. Spencer's fingers adjusted the Colt stuffed behind his hip. Across the street, between faded gray warehouse buildings streaked with bird droppings, two men on horseback eased onto the rutted road from an alley.

"Think there's gonna be trouble?" Tyler stopped for a half step. He reached back, grabbed Luak's arm, and moved the girl between him and Spencer.

"Not real sure." Spencer moved the pistol around his belt so the grip was above his belt buckle. "Bowie, you carrying a gun?"

The tall man nodded. "Thirty-two automatic. Pocket gun. People can hardly tell I have it."

Spencer licked his lips. "Sometimes it's best if folks know you have a gun."

Bowie's head swiveled to look back at the two horsemen, but he kept pace with Spencer.

"Tyler," Spencer said. "Slip that new pistol of yours out of that feed sack."

"But it's not loaded."

"They don't know that."

Tyler lifted the long-barreled revolver from the bag. He mimicked Spencer and stuffed the gun into the front of his belt.

He slung the heavy sack over his shoulder and hooked the thumb of his right hand in his belt next to his gun.

Tyler's world slowed and his senses stood strait-razor keen. In the air, he tasted the smoke from the copper mill. It mixed with the smell of the rivers of filth that ran into the Rio Grande on the Mexican side. Pigeons cooed in the deserted buildings and he heard the birds waddle on the rafters like old men with sore feet. From behind him the clop of the riders' horses' hooves on the street thundered in his ears.

Luak half-turned around as she walked. Her eyes fixed on the men behind them. Her skin flushed and her eyes stretched open.

A freight wagon pulled by four mules rattled up the rutted road from the other direction. Through the dust, Tyler could make out three men on horseback behind the wagon. The first pair road side by side. A long quirt hung from the wrist of the rider that trailed the first two.

As the lead mules passed, the riders clucked to their horses and touched spurs to the animals' sides. Tyler wrapped an arm around Luak's waist and moved the girl behind his back, and as he turned to face the three, a coil of rope hissed through the air.

The hemp slapped across his face. As his eyes filled with water, a gloved hand smashed into the side of his head sending him sprawling to his knees. "Luak," he called out as mules squealed and horses trampled around him.

Tyler rubbed the stinging welt on his face. Through foggy tears, one of the riders leaned from his saddle and caught Luak by the front of her shirt. The blue ribbon she had tied in her hair fluttered free. Luak's head snapped forward and she buried her teeth into the bare skin of the man's forearm.

The rider tried to shake her off as one might try to free himself from a biting lizard. His skin clamped in her teeth stretched and tore away in a splash of bloody droplets.

In a long overhand motion, the rider with the quirt brought his whip down across Spencer's shoulders. The gunman's arms shot forward. One tangled in the end of the lash, while the other found the horse's bridle and jerked down on the wide-eyed animal. Dust roiled up from the street. An unholy shriek of fear came from the horse at Spencer's hand.

Tyler tried to stand. The horse fought Spencer's grip. Its hind legs kicked out and knocked Tyler back to the ground. The boy lifted himself on an elbow; he clawed for Luak, and pulled her to him. Flecks of the man's blood smeared her lips.

Bowie's long arms grabbed one rider by the collar and pulled him from his saddle. Still gripping the outlaw, Bowie smashed the man's face with his fist

A crack as loud as a pistol shot made all the other noises fade. Spencer had wrestled the quirt from his attacker. With the leather braid tangled in his fingers, Spencer brought the wood handle down over the man's face.

The man crawled away, dodging the flailing hooves of his horse. Spencer jerked the Colt from his belt. Bowie, with a palm-sized silver gun in his hand, moved to Spencer's side.

"Tyler —" Breath heaved from Spencer's lungs. "— you and Luak alright?"

Tyler scrambled to his feet and pulled Luak tight against his side. "Yes, sir." He struggled to pull his gun from his belt.

"Bowie?" Spencer thumbed back the hammer of his gun. Their assailants scrambled

128

into their saddles and rode away down the street.

"That was rather exciting," Bowie said. "Did you know those men?"

"I've got an idea who they might be. You held your own."

"Boxing team. University of Michigan." He lowered his gun and pushed his eyeglasses up his nose. "Any idea —"

"Some kind of warning, I reckon. If they wanted to do real harm, they woulda jumped us at night. And with guns — not whips and fists."

Tyler bent down and picked Luak's blue ribbon from the dirt. He brushed it off as best he could and pressed it into her fingers. "I'll get you another one." He knew she didn't understand him, so he touched her cheek as gently as he could.

Over the top of Luak's head, Tyler spied Earl Santos on the boardwalk a block away. He stepped in front of Luak and tugged his new pistol from his belt. "Spencer," a tremor shook every fiber of who he was. "Look."

Near the El Paso policeman stood a man with a red beard. Afternoon sun flashed off Santos's gold tooth. The man with the beard pointed a finger at their little group and snapped his thumb forward. Santos laughed and the two men turned and walked away.

"Put the gun down." Spencer lifted the pistol from Tyler's grip. "They just wanted to give us a scare."

"I ain't scared." Tyler clenched his teeth.

"Then you're a fool."

CHAPTER NINE

"Came in two, three days ago." Morris opened the door to a shed near the back of his property. "Did just what you told me. Signed for 'em and had 'em put in here. Didn't try to open 'em up and check for damage. Left that for you to do."

Bowie took a crowbar from Morris and hurried to the wooden crates. "Open the doors and let some light in here," he said as he knelt by the first box. "Give me a hand with this, please."

Tyler swung open the door. Dust floated in the beams of sunlight around Bowie. In the shadowy light, the two wooden crates reminded him of coffins.

Spencer found a hatchet inside the door. As Bowie lifted with the pry bar, Spencer wedged the flat of the ax blade between the box and its lid and twisted up with the blade. Bowie freed the bar and hooked it into the wood near the middle and pushed.

Nails screeched as they pulled free from the wooden slats.

Spencer caught the lid in his free hand and heaved upward. Splinters snapped loose. Bowie caught hold and the two men tore the top off of the crate.

"Just as I ordered." Bowie rested the crowbar on his hip. "The other crate should be packed just the same way. Take a look, Tyler."

Tyler expected some strange scientific instruments or at the very least shiny brass and polished glass. Instead, two sheet metal boxes nested in the crate. Tyler figured they'd been made to fit a mule's packsaddle.

"Two more just like these in the other." Bowie tapped the other crate with the toe of his boot. "My equipment shall require two mules. Our food and other supplies will take two more."

Tyler cocked his head at Bowie. "So you're gonna hire us? After the trouble on the street?"

"I know you and Spencer handle yourselves well."

Tyler thought how he'd been knocked to the ground and hadn't been able to help fight off their attackers. Even Luak had bitten a man. Tyler had pulled his unloaded revolver after the fight was over.

"Bowie and I talked." Spencer lifted his foot and toed the edge of the open crate. "He's headed pretty much where we want to go. He's not payin' nothin'. I just agreed to ride with him and help with the pack animals." Spencer licked his lips. "Wolves run in packs. It'll be better for all of us if we stick together for a piece."

"When do we leave?"

"Tomorrow," Bowie said. "There's a late afternoon train leaving from Juarez. I've arranged for a boxcar for our supplies and animals. Three days on the train and then we strike out cross-country for the Valley of Visions. And my fortune." Bowie's wide easy smile spread over his face. "Maybe you'll change your minds and we'll all be rich men."

"Don't know about that, sir." Tyler looked at Luak. "We promised that we'd take her home."

"Another reason I trust you," Bowie laughed out loud, "integrity."

Oliver Morris stepped into the shed and looked down into the box. "Oh my hell, you three have work to do if you're gonna be leavin' tomorrow. Food and such to buy. Mules to get."

"And a saddle horse for me," Bowie said.

"Make it a long-legged one." Morris eyed

Bowie. "Or you'll be draggin' those fancy boots in the dust all across Mexico." He spit into the dirt outside the shed door and his face went dark. "Make up a list and I'll take my wagon to get your supplies. And I'll send one of my men to get your mules."

"Tyler, you go with him. Pick out mules to haul Bowie's gear," Spencer told him.

Morris nodded. "No need for you to be walkin' the streets. Bowie, there's a good horse in the back corral I'll make you a deal on."

Morris leaned on the doorframe of the shed and pinched the skin between his eyes. "Plan on dinner at my place. I'll let my Alice know you'll be comin'. Might be the last good food you'll have for a spell." He turned to leave. "Part of me wishes I could go with ya'll, but I'm too damned old."

The first cool hint of evening slipped around the corrals at the back of Morris's store. While Tyler checked the hooves of the new mules, Luak watched from the top rail. The trampled and stained ribbon hung from her hair. Light from a lantern brightened the shed where Spencer and Bowie oiled the packsaddles and loaded the food that Morris had brought from town into bundles to be strapped onto the mules come morning.

Bowie and Spencer finished their work. When the men came to the corral, Spencer had his saddle over his shoulder.

"Good animals, Tyler," Spencer dropped his gear onto the ground. "You chose well."

"That girl ever talk?" Bowie asked.

Tyler set the mule's foot on the ground. He brushed the dirt from his pants with his gloves. "I've been teachin' her some words." Tyler walked to the fence and took hold of the rail near where Luak sat. "*Gasa* means fire in her language."

"*Gasa*," Luak said.

Tyler looked up at her. "And water is *acone*, right Luak?"

He raised a hand towards the trough. "And what you call that, Luak?" He pointed at one of the mules.

"*Sata*." The girl's teeth glistened in the dusk.

"See there," Tyler looked at Spencer. "Mule is *sata*."

Spencer turned to Bowie. "Which one's the teacher?" He dug into his jacket pocket. "Here Luak." He fished out a long shiny blue ribbon. "Had Morris pick this up in town. Girl like you oughta have a clean ribbon."

Luak plucked it from his fingers. "*Cat-tay*," she said.

"I guess *cat-tay* means thank you." Spencer nodded to Tyler.

Luak touched the new ribbon to her cheek and her laughter blended with the men's.

Bowie reached out and took Luak's hand. Luak shook her head and pulled away.

"Whacha doin', Bowie?" Tyler asked. "You're scarin' her."

"She's been around you two saddle tramps too long. She needs to know how a gentleman treats a lady." He faced the girl and bowed at the waist. "Please," Bowie said to her. He pushed his eyeglasses up his nose. "Come with me. I'm warming some water — *acone.*" He pretended to dip his fingers in a pot. "So we can wash." He rubbed his hands together. "For dinner." He touched his lips and moved his jaws up and down.

Luak nodded and jumped from the fence.

Bowie placed his hand on her shoulder. It was scarcely higher than his hip, Tyler thought as they walked to Morris's store.

"I'm hungry, too," Tyler said. "Hope Morris's wife fries up more of that chicken like last night."

" 'Bout dinner." Spencer picked up his saddle. "Bowie and I been talkin'. I'm going to take my horse and do some scoutin'. I plan on meeting you two and Luak the day after tomorrow at one of the railroad's water

136

stops down in Mexico. I looked over a map and showed Bowie where I'll be."

"Spencer?" Tyler dropped from the top fence rail.

"Wasn't goin' to say anything but I promised no secrets." He rubbed his chin on the saddle that rested on his shoulder. "There's a warrant out for me."

Tyler stopped. His arms hung at his sides and he stared at Spencer.

"Somethin' I didn't do." Spencer looked away. The burnt glow from the setting sun hid his face in the shadows. "I don't want to take the chance of gettin' caught at the border. Bowie doesn't know. 'Sides, I think it's best if we had an idea if Fox and his bunch are following us."

Tyler swallowed hard. He saw the pistol in Spencer's belt. "You're goin' off like you did before?" His fingers found the raw welt on his cheek. "Let's just get over the border and look for what happened to your father." Tyler felt his voice grow louder with each word. He grabbed the fence with both hands.

"Tyler?"

"Let me go with you."

"Bowie needs your help gettin' the mules loaded on the train." Spencer took the quirt he'd wrestled away from the attacker from his saddle horn and handed the whip to Tyler.

Tyler turned the quirt over in his hands. He ran his fingers over the braided horsehair and stout mesquite handle. "Promise me you'll start no trouble."

"My word."

Spencer was gone before Tyler, Luak, and Bowie locked up Morris's warehouse for the night. They saw him turn the buckskin away from the city and ride out into the desert.

The smell of fried chicken drifted from Alice Morris's kitchen. Her husband asked about Spencer when they sat down to eat.

"He said he had things to do," Bowie told him. "He'll meet us in Mexico."

"Spencer," Morris said, "might be better off slippin' across the Rio Grande where no one's watchin'. A man like him never can be too careful."

The fork fell from Tyler's hand and clattered onto his plate.

Spencer followed the tracks of a half dozen riders toward the setting sun. He pulled the buckskin up and turned back and picked a different road into El Paso. One that wouldn't take him by Jimmy Six's cantina or Morris's store. He paid a dollar to a peg-legged man at a livery stable to watch his horse and set out across town for the hospital Morris had told him about.

The low building was built of adobe like most of the homes near it. Winter bare trees crowded a grassy courtyard the hospital shared with a church. The smell of alcohol and urine hung in the halls and bleach stung his nose. A tired woman in the gray habit-clothes of a nun pointed towards the end of the hall. A baby squalled. Weak moans mingled with throaty snores.

He found Christmas in a room with eight other beds.

Clean sheets and blankets covered her. In the dim light, her skin that seemed so golden at the cantina was the color of candle wax. Damp hair plastered against her forehead and an eyelid drooped over one of her eyes, making a white crescent that touched the red rim.

"You know this woman?" A hand touched Spencer's shoulder. A white priest's collar showed at the man's neck.

Spencer could only nod. His eyes found the enflamed gash on the woman's neck. Dark threads, sticky with dried blood, held the wound closed.

"The doctor said the knife missed her

jugular by no more than the width of a match head. Angels they watch over her, no?"

"Will she be alright?"

"She lost a great deal of blood. They've given her something so she can sleep. And sulfa drugs to keep away infection." The priest reached out and touched her hand. "If God is willing her life will be saved. It is her soul that concerns me."

"Father, I want to leave some money to help take care of her until she's —" Spencer licked his lips. "Do you have something I can write with and a piece of paper?"

"I can find something."

"I want to leave a letter for her. When she's well enough, can you give it to her?"

The priest nodded. "Find me on your way out." And he left the room.

Spencer pulled a straight-back chair close to Christmas's bedside. Her skin felt cool when he touched her arm and he wondered if she'd have the strength to draw her next breath. A hatred he'd never felt burned in his chest until tears flowed. He sat there in the dark willing his strength into each rise and fall of the whore's chest. The bell in the church tower chimed twelve times before he left her.

He found the priest sleeping on a cot in a

140

small room near the front door. Spencer left five twenty-dollar gold pieces and scribbled a few words on a piece of paper. "Promise me, Father?" He folded the paper and handed it to the man.

"I will pray for you. What is your name?"

"Save your prayers for her," Spencer told him as he left.

CHAPTER TEN

Tyler hopped backward. The mule side-stepped away from him and hitched up one hind leg. "Watch 'im, Bowie. He's fixin' to kick."

Bowie gave one more tug on the rope that lashed the metal box of equipment to the animal's packsaddle. He turned away from the mule's rump and eased back a step. As quick as a snake strike, the mule's lips peeled back and its head snapped around, clamping its yellowed teeth on the meaty part of Bowie's backside just below his suspender buttons.

Bowie bellowed in pain and jerked away but the mule nipped again catching the cloth of the tall man's shirt, pinching into the layer of skin under it. The next noise Bowie made was a screech higher in pitch than Tyler thought any full-growed man could make.

Tyler threw himself over the mule's neck,

grabbed its ear, and twisted. The animal huffed in a breath and brayed a terrible reverberation that had the sound of victory to it. The other mules joined in. Ragged hee-haws filled the corral.

One of Bowie's hands rubbed the slobbery mark on the seat of his britches and the other found the tear in the back of his shirt. As he backed away, Bowie looked over his shoulder as if he expected to find his blood seeping from the wounds. The sole of his new calfskin boots slipped in a mound of still steaming mule manure and he tumbled onto the ground.

A rooster crowed, mules brayed, and a cur dog joined in. With his belly to the sky, Bowie crab-walked away from the stamping hooves of the pack mules. He dodged the next flailing foot but found the next pile of droppings with his left hand. His right clasped the bottom rail of the fence and he pulled himself under just before the mule wrenched away from Tyler and snapped at his heels.

Ivory-white teeth flashed in Luak's mouth. Both hands shot to cover her lips, and laughter that rippled like a mountain stream quieted the sounds of the animals.

Bowie glowered up at the girl. "She pretends she doesn't understand, but she laughs in English." He lay back in the dirt and shook the green from his left hand. He looked at his hand. "Will it be like this every morning?"

"No, sir, I was thinkin' this was one the easier times I've had loadin' mules." Tyler hid his face behind the packsaddle and ground his teeth to keep from laughing out loud.

Bowie looked at his fingers, shook his head, and then wiped them across his pants.

"If'n you want to clean up some, I'll get the horses."

"No, we'll have to unsaddle them and load them into the boxcar when we get to the station. I'm sure that will be an adventure also. How long will it take to get across the bridge?"

"Morris said to figure on two hours. And another two after that to get to that Mexican train and get loaded into the boxcar."

"We best get a move on." Bowie lifted himself from the ground. "And Tyler, don't mention how the mules and I got along to Spencer."

Tyler gave the last mule a swat across the rump with the horsehair quirt Spencer had wrestled from the man that had attacked them. The animal sauntered up the wooden

144

ramp into the boxcar with the others.

Blood dripped from Bowie's smashed knuckles as he slammed the gate shut behind the mules. He sagged against the chute fence. "I'm just going to stand here a minute and rest." Bowie's eyes closed and he let out a deep breath. "How long until the train leaves?"

"Mexican trains never leave on time."

Tyler looked through the fence boards at the man who had just spoken.

"Most leave *mañana*. If you're lucky this one will get out sometime today." The stranger's scuffed boots and dusty clothes showed he was a working man. Sweat stains darkened the crown of his hat, and the seat of his pants had worn through and was patched with leather. "Did I see the Bootheel brand on that long-legged thoroughbred horse when you were loading? Virgil Hutt's place, right?"

"You're right on both counts." Tyler climbed over the fence. "You know Mister Hutt?"

"Can't say as I've had the pleasure. But I'm looking for a man that was riding a horse marked with his brand."

Tyler thought of the Bootheel brand burnt onto the hip of the dead horse at the rustler's camp. And Spencer had said one of the horses outside Jimmy Six's cantina wore Mister Hutt's brand. He threw a sideways glance at Bowie and waited for the stranger to say more.

"Man was riding a buckskin geldin'. Folks saw him on the other side of the river" — he nodded toward the American side — "with a couple of fellas. Had an Indian girl with 'em."

Bowie lifted his head. Tyler swallowed hard.

" 'Fore I say more I need to know who I'm talkin' to." Tyler's fingers tightened on the handle of the quirt.

"Name's J.T. Sadler." He held his right hand up with the palm toward Tyler. "Let me show you somethin'." Slowly he unbuttoned the flap on his shirt pocket and poked his fingers inside. His hand came out holding a star-shaped badge. "Texas Ranger." He let the badge drop back into his pocket. "Don't see that buckskin horse here."

"He was with us, but had his own business to attend to." Bowie took a step toward Tyler. "I've hired the boy to handle my mules and the girl is our cook. Going on a bit of an expedition into Mexico."

"This 'he' you said had business, his name Spencer?" Sadler's eyes were icy clear and they found Tyler.

"Yup. He don't ride for Mister Hutt." Tyler spoke before Bowie. "Just bought a horse from him."

"Will you be seein' Spencer anytime soon?"

"Wouldn't think so. Like we said, he had his own business to attend to. What's this about?" Tyler remembered the warrant Spencer had told him about.

"Last night, a man that looked like Spencer left some money at the hospital to care for a whore that got herself cut up."

Smoke from the train clung to the sweat beads on Tyler's forehead.

"Texas Rangers want to thank him?" Bowie licked his skinned knuckles without taking his eyes from Sadler.

Sadler smiled. "Not at all. Just that sometime after Spencer or whoever it was left the hospital, two men got beat senseless in the alley behind Jimmy Six's place. Thought this Spencer might know who did it."

"What did the men say?"

"One's havin' a might of trouble talkin' with a busted jaw and most of his teeth gone. The other ain't come to yet." Sadler's cool eyes found Tyler again. "Doc says he might never. Barrel of a handgun can make a terrible weapon."

Tyler mopped his face. His mind saw the

pistol in Spencer's belt.

Bowie stepped in front of the boy. "They sent a Texas Ranger across the border to ask about this goings-on? These men must be important."

"No, sir. Some men get what they have comin'. Let's just say these two won't be missed at the church choir practice." He plucked a tobacco pouch from the same shirt pocket that held his badge and tucked a pinch behind his lip. "I had to deliver a prisoner to the *Federales.*" He nodded over his shoulder. A barrel-chested man with a drooping black mustache stood between two Mexican soldiers. "When I saw the brand I thought I'd ask." Sadler pushed the dust into a mound with the toe of his boot and dribbled tobacco juice onto it.

Tyler felt his fingers relax on the whip handle. The breeze tickled the gritty dampness on his forehead. The livestock noises that Sadler's voice had hidden came back to life.

"First trip into Mexico?" The ranger bobbed his head towards the train.

"It is," Bowie answered.

"If'n they run behind schedule — and they will — they'll try to make it up at the water stops. Won't give you time to care for your stock. Won't do no good to complain.

148

If you need more time, gringo silver in the engineer's palm will do the trick." Sadler swallowed back the fluid in his mouth. "Bribes is 'bout the only way things happen on this side of the Rio Grande." He kicked the dirt he'd piled. "And if you run into this Spencer, might mention that El Paso might not be a good place for him to visit. Good luck, hombres, you'll need it."

Sadler turned on his heel and walked away. The ranger tipped his hat to the prisoner he'd left with the soldiers.

"Adios, Pancho," he said.

Over the noise of the mules in the boxcar, Tyler heard Sadler whistle the first notes of "Dixie."

Four hours later the train chugged away from Ciudad Juarez. Tyler sprawled out on the floor of the boxcar with his head on his saddle. Shafts of light danced in and out of the gaps in the wood slats of the car's siding. Black smoke snaked back from the engine, speckling animals and people with cinders and grit.

The engine belched at each hill. Steam hissed. Through half-open eyes, Tyler watched El Paso across the river. For the first time, he let himself think of all he was leaving.

Tyler had never owned more than the clothes he wore. He sat a borrowed saddle on a borrowed thoroughbred horse. About the only thing that was his was the Colt he'd bought with the little money he'd tucked away. Mister Hutt had handed him the Krag rifle when they left The Bootheel and Tyler intended to give it back. If Mister Hutt was still alive.

When he swallowed he could taste the smoke on his tongue.

Tyler had never thought of Mister Hutt not being at The Bootheel. And he couldn't bring himself to think of being anyplace except herding stock for the old man. Now he was on a train heading into Mexico to follow a map to . . . ?

He didn't know that either.

Luak plopped down cross-legged beside him. The new blue ribbon was knotted in her hair and the trampled, bloodstained ribbon that he'd bought for her was around her neck, sort of like a necklace those women in El Paso wore.

Bowie sat against the side of the boxcar. His eyes eased shut despite the rhythm of the rails and the pulse of the light on his face.

Spencer had promised that he wasn't looking to make trouble. From what the

150

ranger had said, Spencer hadn't kept his word. Maybe the gunman had broken his other promises. Maybe he wouldn't be waiting for them in Mexico. Could a man with the law after him be trusted?

The mule that had sunk its teeth into Bowie's hind end stamped its foot on the boxcar floor.

Maybe Spencer'd been hurt. Could be he was licking his wounds somewhere and couldn't get to Mexico.

Then what?

Luak watched the country roll by through the open door. The skin along her jaw quivered with the bouncing train. Her hair swirled in the smoky wind. She smiled back at him and touched the ribbon at her neck.

If Spencer didn't meet them, then he and Luak would ride with Bowie far as they could. When Luak recognized her country, he'd take her to her village. Then he'd ride back to The Bootheel. That settled that.

But, it didn't. Spencer would meet them where he promised.

Tyler would bet his new Colt pistol on that.

The train moved out through the edges of the dusty, squatty town, nothing like the Spanish palaces Tyler had read about in his dime novels. But for the first time since

Mister Hutt had asked him if wanted to be a cowhand, Tyler was choosing for himself. It gnawed at his stomach like the hunger after a long day with the herd.

Shacks, not much more than piles of wood, crowded close together on the hills around the Mexican city. Gaunt-faced brown women with hollow eyes watched the train move by. They gathered children with bulging bellies around their skirts. Hordes of flies swarmed around every face.

"The choices we make, boy," Mister Hutt had told Tyler one scalding hot afternoon at The Bootheel, "are like ripples on water." The old man plunked a pebble into the last puddle from yesterday's rain. "When you first decide to do somethin', it makes a big splash. Waves spread out and trouble the still all around it. But as your choices play out they become part of who you are until they gentle down and lose themselves in the still again. Careful, Tyler, with the things you choose."

Luak's black eyes met his and he turned away.

Outside the train, a mother hugged a little girl to her side. Both raised their hands to wave at the passing train. The child's legs were so spindly that Tyler was sure he could span them both with his thumb and finger.

A twisted old man, whose ripples had long ago reached the edge, stared at the train with filmy eyes that could not see. Another mother clutched an infant, who had yet to toss its first pebble, close to her breasts.

Tyler wanted his bunk at The Bootheel. Not the dirty floor of a train car. He wanted to smell sage on the rimrock hills. Not dirty smoke and mule dung. He wanted Pilar's *frijoles* and *tamales*. Not tinned beef. Most of all he wanted to be sure.

And he wasn't sure of anything.

He checked to see if Bowie's eyes were shut, then Tyler's hand found Luak's.

CHAPTER ELEVEN

It was the black of night when the train made its first stop. Tyler struggled to his feet and nudged the sleeping Bowie with his toe. Both men brought buckets of water to their horses and mules. Tyler shoveled out the car and Luak spread fresh straw.

Outside, three men loaded new firewood on the flatcar behind the engine. Sputters, snaps, and Spanish curses filled the air as cold water from a tower funneled down a wooden chute into the boiler. Steam slipped from every rivet head and seam in the old locomotive, until with a great jerk, the boiler belched and the train moved again.

Luak found a can of peaches in the supply packs. She motioned for Tyler and he tossed his jackknife to her. She hooked a blade into the rim of a can and worked her wrist up and down until she could bend back half the lid. In the sputtering light of a lantern, she speared a half peach with the

154

knife and gave a piece to Bowie and then another to Tyler.

It tasted cool and sticky and wonderfully sweet. They ate with their fingers and never said a word to each other. Peach syrup dripped down the front of Tyler's face. When he tried to wipe it away, he felt the grime of the day smear over his chin. Luak smiled and he wondered how her face could be so clean and his feel so dirty.

Bowie curled up on the floor. His breathing fell in rhythm with the rattle of the train. Luak laid her head on Tyler's shoulder and in the rocking, dark boxcar, Tyler felt brave and strong.

The buzzing of a horsefly woke Tyler. The vibration of its wings tickled his chin. When he tried to whisk it from his face, he found the insect glued to last night's peach syrup. He plucked it from his face and tossed it out the open door. Just sneaking over the crest of the eastern horizon, the sun looked like the sunny-side yolk of morning eggs and great shafts of light, just as golden, painted the clouds in the sky. Each bounce and tussle of the train changed the color of the new day from gold to red to orange.

The round part of Luak's hips rested against Tyler's legs. Both her hands tucked under her head and her shiny hair curtained her face, hiding her eyes and mouth from him. Bowie let out a ragged snore and Tyler was afraid Bowie would wake and spoil it all. But the tall man's eyes never opened. Instead, his pink tongue lolled from his mouth.

As quietly as he could, Tyler slipped away from Luak. He found his scuffed Bible in his saddlebags and sat in the open doorway with his boots hanging above the moving ground. He left sticky dark marks on the page corners until he found the passage he wanted. Even then, he looked at the sky between each verse he read.

The ball of the sun had inched above the horizon when the shriek of the train's whistle broke into Tyler's morning world. He craned his neck and spotted a water tower and a smattering of adobe huts on the flat desert floor. As much as Tyler wanted to spot Spencer's buckskin horse, only chickens and goats spooked at the train's noise.

Luak stirred. She sat up and rubbed her eyes.

"We stopping?" Bowie groused.

"Looks like a village comin' up."

"Any sign of Spencer?"

Tyler's heart jumped. "Don't see him."

"No matter." Bowie stood from the floor

and reached out to steady himself in the rocking car. "He said it would be sometime tomorrow before he'd find us."

Tyler climbed out of the doorway and went to his saddlebags. When he pulled back the flap to tuck his Bible away, the desert morning turned blizzard cold. Though Tyler hadn't seen it earlier, there with his belongings, Spencer had left his father's map.

Breath caught in Tyler's chest.

Maybe Spencer wasn't going to meet them.

Steam whooshed from the locomotive. Steel wheels on steel rails strained. The whistle blew three blasts.

"Agua," a voice shouted. Men in the other train cars jumped from the slowing train. Tyler pulled the flap closed and tied the thong tight.

"We're supposed to stop here for a half-day." Bowic crossed the car. He stumbled as the train clanked to a stop but caught himself. "After we get the stock unloaded and fed, I'll go into the village and see if I can find something hot for us to eat."

Tyler lugged the wooden ramp into place and one by one Bowie and Luak led the horses and mules to a small enclosure near the railroad tracks. From a spicket at the water tower, Tyler hauled pailfuls, until he filled the corral's trough. Then he helped Bowie toss out hay for the animals.

The sun warmed the day and both men stripped out of their shirts. Bowie hung his hat on a fence post, but Tyler left his on and the two washed their faces and chests in the trough as the horses drank.

Luak dangled her legs from their open boxcar door.

"I'm gonna get her a fresh bucket so she can clean up." Tyler snatched a pail from the ground, tossed it in the air, and caught it by the bail. "*Acone,* Luak." He winked at her.

"I'll see what I can find in town." Bowie flicked the water from his hands. He slipped his long arms into his shirt and gathered up his hat.

Tyler rinsed out the bucket at the water tower, wiped the mud from the pail's rim with his fingers, and then filled it with clean water. He skimmed a floating splinter of wood from the surface and took the water to Luak.

Tyler set the bucket into the car doorway next to her. He dipped his fingers in the pail and splashed a few drops on Luak's face. Her cupped hand shot into the bucket and she dowsed Tyler's bare chest.

Tyler pretended to dip his hands in the

158

water and scrub his face. "Wash, Luak." He rubbed over his chest.

Luak shook her head and frowned. She crossed her arms in front of her.

Tyler remembered the glimpse of her naked body in front of Pilar's cookstove. "No, Luak. Go in there." He pointed with both hands into the boxcar. "Wash your face." He motioned with his hands. "And fingers." He rubbed his together. "I won't look." He turned his back to her and covered his eyes. But his mind brought back her brown skin shiny with the water. "Honest."

When he turned, Luak pointed to the corral.

"All right, I'll go over there."

She made a circle in the air with a finger.

"Yeah, I'll turn around."

"No," she said loudly and covered her eyes.

"I told you I won't look." Though part of him wanted to very much.

Luak pulled the pail into the car and motioned to Tyler as if she were chasing flies away.

"I'm goin'." Tyler walked away. When he got to the corral, he pulled off his hat and tossed it on the ground. He pushed a mule's face away from the trough and dunked his head into the water. He pulled it out with a great splash that caused the black mules to bray. Tyler swept the water from his hair. He enjoyed the streams that ran down his chest. The sun and desert air whisked the dampness dry in a second. He found his hat, jammed it on his head, and put on his shirt.

The ping of the water drops tapping the bottom of the pail became as soft as the music made by distant church bells. Luak's voice hummed a song — as soft and distant as the very tips of blades of grass stirred in a warm wind.

He stole a peek over his shoulder.

Shadows played over the girl's figure and flecks of sunlight outlined her through the slits in the board siding. She bent down, filled her hands with water, and then raised them over her head so the water fell over her hair and shoulders. Tyler's bottom lip curled over his teeth and he bit down hard, but he couldn't turn away. Luak's crumpled shirt lay on the floor. She stretched upward until her back arched. From her out-stretched hands, drops of water drizzled onto her face and breasts.

Tyler's breath caught in his throat. He knew he should turn away but he needed to drink in the sight like a thirsty man. If he turned away he might never see anything so beautiful again.

The black mule stretched out its hind legs and peed a great pool in the dusty corral. One of the soldiers who had been with the ranger's prisoner leaned against a corral post. He cradled his rifle in the crook of his arm and a stalk of straw hung from the corner of his mouth.

"Heh, heh." The man grinned at Tyler with stained teeth. He raised his eyes toward their train car. *Bonita. Muy bonita.*

Anger boiled with Tyler's shame. He felt no better than the soldier. Though he cared for Luak more each day, he'd broken his promise to her.

No different than Spencer's to him.

Tyler unwrapped the corn husk from the last tamale that Bowie had brought back from town. He shoveled the mush and spicy meat into his mouth with his fingers. Bowie paced by for the fourth time in the last hour. The tall man stopped, put his hands on his hips, and looked down at where Tyler sprawled in a spot of shade.

"They just look at me and shake their heads when I ask when we'll be leaving." Bowie pushed his glasses up his nose and shifted his weight from one foot and then to the other. "At noon they said, *una hora*. It's nearly three now and they just said *una hora* again."

"Figure they must be waitin' to load that car they hitched to the train." Tyler leaned back, put both hands behind his head, and looked up at Bowie. "You might want to set a spell and rest. You've walked back and forth to town a half a dozen times."

"Aren't you anxious to move on?"

"Yes, sir. I'm just as anxious as you are. But I don't have no say over when this train is gonna leave so I don't fret on it so."

"You sound just like those Mexicans. *Una hora*."

"We're in Mexico, sir."

Bowie shook his head, turned, and paced down the tracks. Behind the stock car that held their saddles and supplies, a rickety open-top had been hitched to the train. The car had seen better days, Tyler thought. Nearly all the paint had worn from the wood and rust decorated every piece of metal. The wheels creaked as the car rolled into place. When one of the railroad workers saw the questions on Tyler's face, the man had shrugged his shoulders.

The two soldiers had found a place in the shade of the water tower. They sat cross-legged on the ground and played cards with

162

their prisoner. It seemed that the winner of each hand was rewarded with a drink from the bottle that sat between them.

Luak slept in the open doorway of their train car. Tyler gathered himself, stood, and moved between the car and the soldiers, to block the men's view. The prisoner won the next round and lifted the bottle to his lips. For the first time, Tyler saw that the prisoner's hands were no longer shackled.

Bowie stomped back. He took off his hat and mopped the sweat from his forehead.

Tyler sniffed the air. "Bowie, I smell somethin'."

Bowie's eyes grew wide. "What do you mean you smell something? I smell mules and horses. Smoke. This village reeks like a sewer." He drew air in through his nose. "What do you mean you smell something?"

"I smell cattle."

"Cattle. How can you tell cattle smell from horses? Or mules?"

"Spent most of my life around cattle. When I'm around 'em I don't notice 'em. When I'm not I can smell 'em a long ways off." Tyler sniffed again. "I'm tellin' ya I smell cattle." Tyler turned an ear toward the village. "Listen."

Bowie cupped his hands around his ears. "I hear something too."

163

A din rose from the desert beyond the village and grew louder. Dust lifted in a cloud. Goats bleated. Dogs sulked between the adobe buildings and barked. More people than Tyler had seen the whole day crowded onto the dirt streets. Women grabbed small children and tucked them tight to their skirts. Chickens cackled and scurried away.

People scrambled for doorways. The soldiers ended their game and ran for the train. Then the street filled with cattle. Hurried by two vaqueros, the herd funneled through the village. Carts overturned. Water jugs smashed. Running at the sides of the moving horde of animals, six boys in loose-fitting pants and shirts shrieked and waved their straw hats.

The tallest boy sprinted ahead. He ran to the train and leaped up on the open-top car. The boy caught hold of the side gate and shoved it open. Workers in the train yard threw a wooden ramp to the opening and jumped away. The boy waved his hat over his head.

"He's signalin' to the others to load 'em up," Tyler called out to Bowie.

Three of the boys ran to one side of the ramp. The tall boy jumped down and joined the other two on the other side. They spread their arms and made a loading chute with

164

their waving arms and legs. Cattle channeled through, onto the ramp, and into the car.

"I ain't never seen anythin' like that." Tyler hollered. "Those boys are gonna load forty head in less time than it took us to load four mules. Mister Hutt saw this, he'd hire those boys on the spot."

Bowie touched Tyler's shoulder. "Look."

Tyler turned. On the other side of the train, away from the commotion of the cattle, two men on horseback, one leading a saddled horse, rode up to the two soldiers. One tossed a small sack to the soldier who'd watched Luak. The soldier dumped the bag into his hand. Silver coins glared in the sunlight. The prisoner jumped from where he'd been waiting and vaulted into the empty saddle. Then, the three galloped out into the desert.

Tyler raised a hand to shade his eyes. Near a stand of paloverde trees, the three riders met a group of men. Tyler squinted. The freed prisoner reached out and shook the hand of a man on a white horse.

Bowie plucked his glasses from his face and wiped the dusty lenses on his shirt. "Those the same men that jumped us in El Paso?"

"Can't tell for sure." Tyler's tongue rubbed

the roof of his dry mouth.

Bowie jammed his glasses back on his nose. "I wish Spencer was here."

The band of riders moved away.

Bowie stepped closer to Tyler. "He'll meet us like he said he would, won't he?"

"Been havin' an argument with myself about that."

Cattle squalled. Hooves banged on the wooden ramp. The high-pitched screams of the herder-boys snapped at the afternoon. The train's engineer ran up to Tyler and Bowie. The man waved his hands in the air. "*Andale amigos.* The train. We leave. Load your mules. We no wait."

The wheels of the train began to turn as soon as Tyler pushed the loading ramp from the door of their stock car. He opened the gate that separated the livestock from the rest of the car and walked among the animals. He took time to touch each neck and run his hands over the muzzle of the horses and mules. Tyler felt the steel-hard muscles in Mister Hutt's Thoroughbred relax as he stroked the big horse. Even the black mule that had bitten Bowie calmed when Tyler's fingers scratched its mane.

Daylight seeped away. Desert air chilled. The sun dropped away like a toy rolling from a child. A white stripe of cold light traced the horizon, touching black clouds that piled in the sky and the train rumbled south.

Through the gaps in the car siding, Tyler could see one of the Mexican boys who had brought the cattle to the train. He perched on the corner of the ancient open-top railcar. His legs dangled above the cattle. One hand clamped his straw hat to his head. The other gripped the rough wood. Smoke and soot swirled around him.

"What do you suppose he's doing there?" Bowie asked when Tyler pointed at the boy.

"Got sent to watch the cattle, I'm guessin'." Tyler pushed by the animals to the back of the car and peered through the gaps in the siding. The boy's hat slipped away and dropped onto the cattle below him. He caught hold of the wood sides with both hands and wedged himself into the corner of the car. The boy's eyes squinted as the dust and cinders whipped his face.

"My God, he'll like to freeze out there." Bowie snugged the collar of his jacket around his neck.

"If he don't fall off first." Tyler shook his head.

The kerosene lantern, hung from the roof

of the stock car, vibrated as if each railroad tie the train crossed sent a special message through the steel and wood. The black mule's eyes glared like tarnished marbles in the dim light. Bowie slumped against the pile of saddles. It amazed Tyler how easily the man could fall asleep. Luak huddled in her blanket and watched the moonlight wash over the desert.

Through the openings in the wood siding, Tyler could see the top of the Mexican boy's head. The little vaquero had wedged himself into a corner of the open cattle car where he could keep watch over the cattle.

Orange specks of burning ash swept past and disappeared behind the moving train. Tyler took one more look at the boy and then leaned back and closed his eyes.

A sound that seemed to scream its way from the very pit of hell shattered the night. Tyler bolted to his feet. He found Luak first. She tossed her blanket aside and the two scrambled to check the horses.

The Thoroughbred's eyes peeled wide and he reared. In a jolt from the moving train, the horse lost its footing. It stumbled and it screeched out in fear. Tyler threw himself over the makeshift partition that separated the animals from the storage space and he caught the big horse's halter.

168

"Luak." Tyler wrapped her fingers around the bridle. "Hold him tight. Don't let him loose."

Wide-eyed mules stamped their feet and bashed their bodies against the side of the train car. The black animal bared its teeth and snapped at Tyler's face. He caught the black mule around the neck and held its head tight to his chest. "Settle." Tyler forced evenness into his voice.

"What was that sound?" Bowie shouted.

"Hush, don't spook 'em any more than they already are." Through the openings between the boards, Tyler saw the Mexican boy balancing himself on the edge of the open-top. One of the steers had reared up and caught both front legs over the side of the car. The animal thrashed to free itself. It tossed its head back and forth, narrowly missing the boy with the tips of its horns. Unable to free itself, the animal screamed again. The Mexican boy reached toward the frightened animal, but lost his footing and tumbled into the cattle.

Tyler let loose of the mule, pushed his way through the other animals, caught the edge of the open door, and swung outside the moving train.

"Don't be a fool," Bowie yelled.

Tyler's fingers wedged into the gaps of the

board siding. The soles of his boots caught the metal edge near the floor. He inched along the side of the moving car. His foot lost its grip on the manure-slick strip of wood and in that instant, all his weight hung from his fingertips. Pain shot through his forearms. He tried to pull himself up. Tyler willed air into his lungs and fought for the next handhold. The toe of his boot reached out, found the sliver of space that would hold him, and he edged on a few more inches.

Boards snapped as the injured steer floundered to escape. Its cries stabbed into Tyler's ears.

One more arm span brought Tyler to the corner of the car.

Through slashes of moonlight and the gray glow of the lantern, Tyler spotted the boy huddled on the floor on the cattle car. His skinny arms shielded his face from the hooves of the animals.

The steer flailed around trying to free itself. The top board splintered. The confused animal lurched upward again as if trying to throw itself from the moving car. Over the rattle and rush of the speeding train, the jagged edge of the broken rail impaled the animal's soft stomach. The animal bellowed with a terror that it couldn't understand.

Tyler pressed his feet into the side of the train above the hitch and hurled himself over the gap between the speeding cars. He caught the rough wood and he pulled himself up to his waist.

The injured steer swung his head. The curve of its horns smashed into Tyler's head above his temple.

Dizzying waves swam through his skull. He clung to the boards and bent forward. Tyler caught the boy by the back of the shirt and lifted him from the bottom of the car. Again the steer slapped his head towards Tyler. Dark, salty blood sprayed Tyler's face.

A rooster tail of sparks flared from between the cars. The train racked from side to side. Tyler clung to the boy's shirt praying it would not tear away. Fire burned in his cramped muscles. Dragon breaths of sooty, steam slipped from the locomotive. Bells clanged. Wind slipped by his face. Long seconds slowed until, inches at a time, the train settled to a stop.

Lantern light bounced around him. Bowie caught him by the back of his belt. Other hands lifted until Tyler and the boy lay on the ground.

The trapped steer thrashed and moaned, still caught in the splintered sideboards.

Blood spurted from its nostrils. A rifle shot cracked and all went quiet. Smoke drifted from one of the soldier's rifle. The cow slumped in its death trap.

"Tyler." It was Bowie's voice. "You saved him." His hands pried the claw that was Tyler's fingers from the boy's shirt. "Let him go, now. Let him go."

Tyler's stomach heaved. His head throbbed. The blood in his veins turned icy.

"Ty-ler."

Blackness settled like a dark blanket all around him.

CHAPTER TWELVE

Spencer picketed his buckskin horse in a hidden arroyo a half-mile from the rail line's water tower and corrals. Wind across the desert whined like a frightened child crying for her mother. He climbed the low hill that shielded the pocket from the train tracks. He bellied the last few feet and lay on his stomach peering through the sagebrush. With the wind in his face, he studied the desolate tract beyond the place the train would stop for any sign that he might have been followed.

The tips of the sagebrush moved in the breeze. The midday sun traveled halfway across the afternoon sky. Finally satisfied that no one waited, he slipped down the hill, stopping every dozen steps to watch and listen. Dusky-blue quail darted through the brush ahead of him. Grains of sand skittered across the wind-polished dirt near the corrals.

Three times he circled the place where the train would stop for water, but Spencer found no tracks except his own.

A curl of black smoke from the coming train marked the distant sky. Spencer hurried back to where he had hidden his horse.

The train set its brakes and dragged to a stop. Only then did Spencer swing into the saddle and rode to meet Tyler, Luak, and Bowie.

The Thoroughbred horse tossed its head as it stepped from the darkness of the train car onto the ramp that led to the corral. Bowie's horse and Luak's pony followed. Bowie dodged the snapping teeth of the black mule. The gangly man swore and cracked it across the rump with a cinch strap from the packsaddle. Luak snapped a blanket in the air over her head. The other three mules snorted and clomped from the railcar into the corral with the horses.

Tyler sat in the open door of the stock car. A dirty bandage was wrapped tight around his forehead. Dried blood spotted the cloth above his right ear.

Spencer slid from his saddle and walked up to the boy. A purple half-moon bruise colored Tyler's cheekbone. Tyler tried to stand but slumped back on the rough boards.

"Bowie," Tyler said. "Look who's here."

Spencer put two fingers under Tyler's chin and tipped his face up. "You say somethin' about Luak's cooking she didn't like?"

"Got tangled up with a steer, that's all." Tyler pulled away. "Beginnin' to wonder if you were goin' to join us like you promised."

Bowie jumped from the train car and offered his hand to Spencer. "Tyler's lucky it's just a few bruises and the cut on his head. The boy here is quite a hero. Middle of the night, a Mexican kid fell into the bottom of a car full of cattle. Tyler shimmied along the side of the movin' train and then jumped to the next car. Reached down and pulled the rascal out before he got trampled."

"Wasn't nothin'." Tyler stood and swayed. He reached out and grabbed the side of the train car. "You'd've done the same thing."

"Might have." Spencer clucked his tongue against the roof of his mouth. "Or might not. You did, that's what counts. Gonna be all right?"

"Ground moves around a mite under my boots." Tyler steadied himself on the car and then let go. "Bowie helped. He got the engineer's attention and stopped the train or else I fear I'da got tore up worse." Tyler pointed to a boy lugging a bucket of water to the animals in the corral. "Got Eloy out of the fix he was in."

The Mexican boy stopped and when he saw Tyler pointing, his mouth opened in a toothy grin. Eloy set the pail on the ground and pushed the sleeves of a too big denim shirt up his skinny arms.

"That one of your shirts, Tyler?"

"Yes, sir. His got all torn up by the cattle."

Spencer let out a low whistle. "Climbing the side of a moving train is foolhardy enough. Giving away a good shirt? Now that's plain stupid."

"You got your opinion on 'bout everything I do." Tyler scowled up at Spencer. "Some take care of their friends."

Spencer turned to Bowie. "Let's get the mules loaded and horses saddled. I want to get away from here 'fore nightfall."

"We should camp here. Tyler needs the rest." Bowie looked from Tyler to Spencer. "It'll be dark in a few hours."

"I can ride." Tyler climbed to his feet and stared at Spencer.

"I cut the tracks of a dozen riders this mornin'. Smaller bunch been trailin' me since I crossed the Rio Grande. Figure they joined up with some others." Spencer caught the top corral rail in both hands.

Bowie spoke in a whisper. "I'm pretty sure we saw Fox and his riders before we pulled out of the village last night. Two of Fox's men gave those *federales*" — he tilted his head toward the soldiers — "a bag of money, I guessin', and rode off with their prisoner."

Spencer's knuckles turned white on the fence rail and he rammed his tongue into his cheek. "What'd he look like? This prisoner, I mean."

"Big in the chest. Black mustache."

"Francisco Villa." Spencer spit on the ground next to the toe of Tyler's boot. "Horsethief when he's not runnin' guns."

"I heard the ranger call him 'Pancho.' " Tyler kicked dust on the spittle and locked his eyes on Spencer.

"Ranger?" Spencer turned full-face to Tyler.

Bowie moved between the two men. "Texas Ranger brought him over the border and handed him off to the soldiers."

Spencer leaned his back on the fence and hooked the heel of his boot over the bottom rail. "Makes sense. Heard Villa had crossed the border. Musta got crosswise with the law up there and they sent him back. If he's riding with Fox —"

Tyler cut in. "Ranger asked some questions 'bout you."

Spencer pushed his hat up his forehead.

"Said a couple of men got theirselves pistol-whipped in an alley near Jimmy Six's place."

"I don't owe you no explanation."

"You gave me your word. No trouble." The muscles in Tyler's jaw bunched.

"Listen." Spencer returned Tyler's stare but spoke to Bowie. "It's near as flat as a tabletop all around here and a fresh-born baby's hind end has more cover. We camp here and they can see our fire for ten miles. I'm speculatin' if we ride due south 'til dark we'll find sweet water in the edge of those hills. Now every minute we burn here puts us that much further from a spot to hide and them that much closer to us. We gonna get those mules loaded or not?"

Tyler blinked first. "I'll get the packsaddles."

"No." Spencer licked his lips and held the stare. "You rest your head. Bowie and I'll load the mules."

Spencer hopped the corral fence and caught the black mule by the halter. When the animal bared its teeth, he jabbed a knee in the animal's ribs. The air left the mule's lungs like a blacksmith's bellows. "Just can't

178

let 'em try to give ya trouble."

"It's how you treat people sometimes." Tyler pushed the words out under his breath.

"What's that?" Spencer pretended not to hear.

"Nothin' "

Spencer knew there was truth in what Tyler said. It was his way. He didn't know any other way.

The Mexican boy brought the pail to Tyler. Tyler cupped his hand into the water and splashed it onto his face. He reached out and rubbed the boy's head. "Take care, little amigo. You'll be on your own now."

Eloy set the bucket down and wrapped both arms around Tyler's legs. "Gracias. Muy gracias."

"You done said that a hundred times. Don't thank me no more."

Spencer wrapped the lead rope to one of the other mules around the rail next to Tyler. "Best tell him to be on his way."

Tyler pushed the boy's arms down and looked at Spencer.

"He can't come with us. The boy's *patrón* sent him to watch those cattle. He's got a job to do. Like we have to do ours. Gettin' Luak home." Spencer went to the next mule.

"What about findin' what happened to your pa?"

"Yeah. That too." Spencer buried his tongue in the side of his cheek.

Bowie spurred his horse up next to Spencer's. "I'm worried about Tyler. Look how he has both hands on the saddle horn. You ever see the boy ride that uneasy in his saddle?"

Spencer handed the lead rope to the mules to Bowie. "I'm keepin' a close eye on him. Luak is too."

The Indian girl kicked her pony up beside the Thoroughbred. She reached out and placed her hand on Tyler's hip and steadied him when his horse missed a step.

"See there," Bowie said.

"I'm thinkin' the grit he learned workin' for Hutt will keep the boy on his horse. And he wants to show me how tough he is. That'll clamp his legs all the tighter to that saddle." Spencer tapped his heels on the side of the buckskin horse and rode away.

They followed a dry riverbed south. Just at dark, near the hills, they found pools of muddy water in an arroyo. Further on, a trickle of clear cold water threaded through the gravelly bottom.

"We'll camp here." Spencer swung off his

180

buckskin horse. "Bowie, let's get the packs off the mules. We'll take 'em down below so they won't foul our drinkin' water." He picked up a twisted piñon branch. "Luak, *gasa.*" He pitched the wood onto the bare ground near the creek. "Tyler, climb on down and find a place to sit and rest."

The boy took a deep breath. It took two tries before Tyler could lift his leg over the saddle. Finally, he slid from his horse. Luak gathered the reins from his hand. Tyler rubbed the bandage on his head and slumped forward.

Luak dropped the reins and tried to hold him up.

"Ty-ler."

Spencer vaulted from where he stood, caught Tyler under the arms, and lowered the boy to the ground.

Tyler sputtered to speak. His eyes rolled back and he became dead weight in Spencer's arms.

"*Acone,* Luak." Spencer laid Tyler on the ground and pushed the horse away.

Luak scrambled for a canteen slung from Spencer's saddle horn. She pulled the stopper and poured the water into Tyler's mouth. Spencer took the canteen from her and let the water dribble on Tyler's lips. Tyler gulped down the liquid and his eyes opened.

Luak turned to Spencer. She stood, shoved both her hands into his chest, and stomped away.

"It's all right," Spencer said. "I shouldn't have pushed him so hard. He can sleep now."

CHAPTER THIRTEEN

Tyler told his eyelids to move. They peeled open no wider than the edge of a knife blade. Sunlight jarred his brain and he clamped his sticky eyes shut again. He heard himself moan.

"Tyler?"

A small hand touched his shoulder.

"Ty-ler."

He knew Luak's voice.

"Go slow, now."

It was Bowie talking.

"Water, Luak."

Tyler lifted his head.

"Easy, boy."

Cold water touched his lips. Tyler felt his throat gulp it down.

"Not too much, Luak."

Tyler wanted more. Luak's face was close to his.

"Ty-ler."

He lifted himself on an elbow. The earth

swirled. His stomach knotted. He made himself sit up.

Luak's fingers pulled at the front of his shirt. Bowie held his shoulders.

"Tyler, you okay?"

"My head hurts." He commanded his eyes to open.

Luak squealed. A happy sound.

"Take it easy. You had us worried."

Tyler lifted one hand from the ground and rubbed his eyes. "More water."

Luak held a tin cup to his mouth.

"She and Spencer sat up most of the night with you. You thrashed around something fierce. You feeling okay?"

"I think so." Tyler let his head fall back. Warm sunlight washed over his face.

"That old steer must have walloped your head harder than we thought."

Bowie leaned close and blocked the sunlight. When he moved away Tyler squinted and the pain stabbed his head.

"And the way Spencer made us ride —"

"Where is he?" Tyler turned his head and tried to look.

"He's down with the horses. He wanted to know when you woke up." Bowie motioned at Luak and pointed down the arroyo. She stood and ran away. "He won't admit it but I think Spencer was more concerned about you than he wants to show." Bowie let out a deep breath. "But not as worried as Luak. She sat with you the whole night. Don't think she ever slept."

Tyler raised his face when Spencer's shadow hid the sun. Spencer knelt and Tyler shielded his eyes as the gunman's shade passed over him.

"You decide to wake up?"

"Yes, sir."

"How's your head?"

"Hurts a mite but I can ride."

"No. We'll rest here another day. Two if we need." Spencer lifted Tyler's face and looked into the boy's eyes. "You're lookin' better since last night. We'll get some food in ya and you'll get your strength back."

Luak pushed Spencer's hand away from Tyler's face and dropped onto her knees. Strings of willow bark, stripped from a green tree, filled her hands. She raised a piece and pretended to put it in her mouth. She worked her jaws up and down and then pushed the bark into Tyler's hand. Luak lifted Tyler's hand so that the fibers touched his lips.

"I think she wants you to chew on that." Spencer hunkered back on his bootheels. "Must be some kinda Indian medicine or the like."

Tyler pushed the woody strands into his mouth and began to chew. "Bitter tastin'."

Luak pressed another piece into his hand. Tyler looked to Spencer.

"Don't see no harm in tryin' it," the gunman said. "Rest and food is what ya need now. But go ahead and do what she wants."

Tyler spit the pulp on the ground, took the next piece from Luak, and put it in his mouth. Luak touched his forehead. Her smile crept over her dark skin.

Spencer rubbed his fingers over his jaw. "Remember how Luak brought in that rabbit that first night on the trail? She disappeared right after sunup this mornin' and came back carryin' a stick and four of the plumpest quail you've ever seen." Spencer pointed to the tops of the piñon trees around their camp. The tips of the branches swayed in the breeze. "We got enough of a wind to spread the smoke if we keep the fire small. What say we cook 'em up?"

Tyler took the next piece of bark from Luak. "Sounds good."

"When she brought the quail in, I told Bowie about the rabbit. He thinks if we let her take the hatchet, we'll be eatin' venison tomorrow night." Spencer put his hand on Luak's shoulder. She squirmed and moved away from his touch.

Tyler tore the last scrap of meat from the bone and flipped the gristle into the fire. "That was good. I feel better. My head hardly hurts at all. Think it was that bark Luak had me chew on?"

"Could be." Spencer shoveled beans from a tin plate into his mouth with his fingers. He held the plate out. Tyler shook his head. "Or maybe that crack from the steer's horn is wearing off." He offered the plate to Luak. She shook her head, never taking her eyes from the fire. "I'll save the rest for Bowie. He's up burying his equipment. I told him to hide it here for a spell."

Tyler tossed a twig on the coals and watched it melt to nothing. "What ya plannin', Spencer?"

Spencer moved the skillet with what was left of the beans away from the flames. "First, I'm gonna let this fire burn out. I don't want to risk someone seein' our smoke. We'll sit tight the rest of the afternoon. Tonight, I'll take Bowie and ride the ridge to the west. From the high ground, we should be able to see any campfires out on the flat." He lifted his Winchester from where it leaned on his saddle. "On my way here, I came across an old man and his woman on a little farm. Watered my horse in their well. First light, we'll swing that way. They'll tell us if they've seen anyone. Be back here by nightfall. If things look good, we'll head out towards Luak's village the next morning."

"Leave Bowie here. I'll ride with you." Tyler started to stand.

"No. You and Luak stay here and take care of the mules. You need your rest."

"Spencer, you promised me you'd teach me how to use my gun. If I have to wait here I should be ready."

"Someone could hear the gunfire and know where we're hidin'."

"I need to know."

"I'll show you some things. Won't make you a gunhand but it'll do for now. Then Bowie and me'll ride out."

Tyler found new strength from the weight of the Colt pistol in his hands. It shined silvery blue in the morning light with tiny flecks of rust on the barrel.

Spencer knelt beside Tyler on a saddle blanket they'd tossed near the dying campfire. Bits of sand and dried leaves skittered across the ground. A hawk perched on the branch of a dead tree and watched. Spencer laid the belt and holster next to an open box of cartridges. "While you were asleep last night, I cut a hand span of leather off that gun belt. It should fit around your middle now." He picked up the cartridge box. "Open the loadin' gate."

Tyler caught the gate with his thumb and flicked it open.

"You know how to load it, don't you?"

"Mister Hutt showed me. I tried his pistol once. Mostly I shot rifles."

"Just make sure —" Spencer handed him five cartridges. "— that the firin' pin rests on an empty chamber. They call it a six-shooter, but only a fool carries a Colt with all six. Load one, skip one, then load the other four."

Tyler did as he was told.

"Remember that if you're facin' a man that knows guns, he'll be doin' the same thing," Spencer told him. "Count his shots. There'll only be five. Now bring it to full cock, catch hold of the hammer tight, squeeze the trigger, and ease the hammer down on the empty chamber. Gentle like. Pretend you're squeezin' a woman's —" Spencer looked at Luak. "Aw. Just go easy."

Tyler eased the hammer down. "Is it that dangerous to load all six?" Tyler hefted the loaded gun and sighted down the barrel at the hawk on his perch.

"Knew an old boy once that had all six chambers loaded. End of his lariat got hooked on his belt while he was workin' cattle. It pulled the gun free and when it hit the ground, it went off." Spencer touched the tip of his tongue to his dry lips. "Gutshot his horse and damn near gelded him."

Tyler squeezed his legs together.

"Listen Tyler, just carryin' a gun don't make you brave. If anything, you should be more scared."

"Scared?"

"Scared about what it gives you the power to do."

Tyler thought for a long minute. "How do you aim it?"

"If you got to aim you better be usin' that Krag rifle. That hogleg —" Spencer tapped the Colt in Tyler's hands. "— is for when you're real close to trouble and it's all you have left. Don't be believin' what you read in those dime books. Nobody ever shot the eyes out of a grizzly bear a quarter mile away from the back of a gallopin' horse."

"Were the men you killed close?"

"Most of the men I killed never knew I was aiming at them."

Pain stabbed Tyler's head again. He wanted a handful of Luak's bark to grind between his teeth. He looked down at the pistol in his hands and swallowed hard. Spencer's words rumbled in his sore brain. Tyler tried to keep the thought from forming. But he knew what Spencer was telling him.

Spencer had shot men in the back.

Spencer stood from his knees. "Keep that gun belt close. But be sure the Krag's always at arm's reach. Trouble could be close from now on."

Loose dirt and stones cascaded down the hillside trail from where Bowie had gone to hide his supplies.

"Spencer. Come quick." It was Bowie.

Spencer ran from the creek bottom up the hill. Tyler looped the gun belt around his waist and followed. At the top of the hill, Bowie straddled the worn pathway. Sweat streamed from the man's face. His rifle trembled in his grip. One shaking hand pushed away from his body and a finger pointed toward the middle of the trail. "St-stop," Bowie stammered.

Before Tyler could see what he was pointing at, Spencer said, "Bowie, you're a greenhorn fool."

"It — it's a snake."

"I know it's a snake."

Tyler spied the brown coils on the smooth-worn trail. The rattler lifted its head and hissed. Its tail jangled and made a noise like the wind chasing dry leaves over smooth rocks. The serpent showed its fangs and its head bobbed and circled in a slow dance, never moving its cold eyes from Bowie.

Bowie gulped, "Should I shoot it?"

"No," Spencer barked. The snake hissed louder. "A rifle shot will tell the whole world where we are. 'Sides you're more apt to hit me than that snake."

"What should we do?"

"Any other time you just walk around it. But —" Spencer took two quick steps forward. He pinned the hissing serpent to the ground with the butt of his Winchester, pulled a knife from his boot, and in a quick jerk of his hand, severed the snake's head. The thirsty dust on the path clotted into small knots as it gobbled up the snake's blood. Spencer snatched up the writhing body and stuck it in Bowie's confused hand. "We might need something to eat on the trail. Put that in your saddlebag."

Any color that was left in Bowie's face blanched away. He balanced his rifle in one hand and held the still twisting headless rattler as far away as he could with the other. As Spencer turned to walk back to camp, he kicked the snake's head into the brush. Tyler heard Luak giggle. When he turned to look, her eyes were bright and both hands were clamped over her mouth.

Tyler and Luak watched Spencer and Bowie until they were specks that disappeared on the far ridge. Sunset brought cool air. They sat side by side, wrapped in a single blanket, staring at charred logs that Spencer had ordered them not to light. For the first time all day, the hurt was gone from his head. His belly was filled with *tortillas* and peaches from a can Luak had dared to open. The Thoroughbred snorted and pawed the ground. Mules groaned in answer.

Luak rested her head on his shoulder. The Colt on his hip gave Tyler comfort.

Maybe, Tyler thought, when all this was over, Luak wouldn't want to stay in Mexico. Maybe she'd come back to The Bootheel with him. They'd raise horses. Mister Hutt said that keeping horses was more trouble than they were worth. Mister Hutt had said that a hundred times. A man just needs horses to work cattle. The old man was too set in his ways.

Tyler and Luak would raise horses. With the big Thoroughbred at stud, they could start their own line. Tyler would train them himself. Folks would come from three states and two territories to buy horses with the

Bootheel brand.

Luak leaned heavily on him. He knew she had drifted off to sleep. As gently as he could, he laid her on the ground and wrapped the blanket around her. Tyler checked on the horses, found another blanket, and stretched it out on the ground next to Luak. He lay on his back and rested his head in his hands. The Krag rifle was just an arm's length away. Just like Spencer had said. And the Colt lay tucked in its holster at the edge of his blanket.

They'd find out what happened to Spencer's pa. Luak would come back to The Bootheel. They'd raise a whole pasture full of thoroughbred horses.

Like spots on an Appaloosa pony, a million points of light speckled the night sky. Tyler reached out his hand and touched each star.

Mornings always brought a surprise. Tyler marveled at how the black of night melted away after sunrise. Which bird's song would he hear first? What tracks would he find in the dust to show an animal had stalked close during the night?

Luak's blanket was empty. He guessed she'd gone to rustle up something for breakfast. If she took the hatchet, they'd be eating venison. They'd have to save some for Bowie.

Then he heard her cry. He reached for the Colt. Its holster was empty. He went for the Krag.

A boot crushed down on his chest.

"He's one of Hutt's all right," the voice said. "This is the one I saw shoot the horse out from under Spade 'fore that Spencer killed him."

"Luak," Tyler screamed.

The boot moved from his chest to his throat and pinned Tyler tight to the ground.

CHAPTER FOURTEEN

Spencer reined the buckskin horse to a halt at the top of a mesquite-covered rise and peered toward the thread of black smoke in the morning sky. Bowie's horse short-stepped in a tight circle around the buckskin. Bowie caught his saddle horn to keep from falling.

Bowie jerked his head toward the smoke. "It's not a campfire at all." He swiveled his head as his horse passed in front of Spencer. "You knew it all along." He spit the words at Spencer. "It's a house. By all, that's holy, Spencer. Is that the old man's farm you told me about?"

Spencer jerked the big Winchester from its scabbard, touched his spurs to the buckskin's ribs, and loped off the hill.

Bowie smacked his reins on his horse's rump and followed.

A bony rooster pecked at the bloody wound

on the dead dog's ribs. It flapped its wings and scurried away as Spencer's horse clomped into the farmyard. Yellow flames flickered on the thatched roof of the adobe hovel. A calf bawled, but would not leave the side of its bloated mother. Flies swarmed and dark blood stained the dirt around the dead cow.

Bowie pulled his horse at the edge of the carnage. He touched his spurs to his horse's ribs and entered the farmyard like a man walking into a chapel. "We're too late," he whispered.

Spencer slammed his big rifle back into its place on his saddle. He guided his horse around the charred remains of a wagon. The gunman wiped his mouth with the back of his gloved hand and stared down.

"What is it?" Bowie called.

"Stay back."

Bowie dropped his reins and ran to where Spencer sat his horse. The old man's hands were bound to the wagon wheel. Still smoldering mesquite branches lay piled on his stomach and crotch. Flames licked at the man's clothing. The flesh on his face hung from his skull like overcooked meat. Vacant eyes stared at everything but saw nothing.

Bowie doubled over and gagged.

"I told you to stay back."

Bowie raised his hands to shield himself from the horror. "I hope he was dead when they did that to him."

Spencer turned his horse and walked it to the door of the burning house. "If he was dead, they wouldn't have bothered." He leaned from his saddle and looked inside.

Bowie emptied his stomach on the dusty ground. "Spencer, you said he had a wife." He wiped his mouth. "They might have taken her with them."

Spencer kicked his boot out from its stirrup. He caught the door of the house with his foot and slammed it shut. "She's in there."

"Is she — ?"

"What do you want me to do? Draw ya a picture?"

Bowie dropped onto his knees. Tremors shook his body. He pulled his glasses from his face and clamped his eyes shut.

Spencer climbed off the buckskin. He snatched away a wooden pail from in front of the crumbling adobe house. Near the corral, he lowered the pail into a hand-dug well and filled a trough. He gathered Bowie's horse with his own, unsaddled both, and let them water. He caught the frightened calf and tied it close to the horses. When he was done with the animals, he took a full pail to Bowie.

"Get some water in ya." He sat the bucket next to the other man.

Bowie shifted on the ground, not wanting to see the terrible scene when his eyes opened. He dipped his fingers into the pail and wiped them across his face.

"Drink it." Spencer pushed the bucket with the toe of his boot.

Bowie filled his hand with water and brought it to his lips. "How could anyone do that to another person?"

"There's a breed of man that doesn't feel. He'll do anything to help him get what he wants."

"This Fox, he's that kind of man?"

"He is. And he's got worse ridin' with him."

"What about you, Spencer? Are you that kind?"

Spencer turned away. "Listen, there's tracks of a half-dozen shod horses headed away from the corral towards the mountains. Looks like the bunch that was following me split into two groups. I'm guessin' they'll try to meet up at the base of the mountains where they can find water."

Bowie's head snapped up. "Tyler and the girl." He climbed to his feet. "They need us. We've got to hurry."

"We rode most of the night. We ride now we'll kill the horses."

Bowie grabbed Spencer's arm. "Spencer."

"They need rest and feed. We need the same."

"We need to go now."

Spencer slapped Bowie's hand away. "Whatever's gonna happen on that mountain, we can't change." Spencer pulled his knife from his boot. "You build up a cookfire. I'll get us somethin' to eat."

At the corral, Spencer caught the calf and cut its throat.

Rawhide thongs cut into Tyler's wrists. Another strip of the leather across his forehead held his head into the trunk of a tree. Drops of blood mixed with his sweat. Rays of midday sun scorched his face and cracked his lips. His tongue thickened and stuck to the roof of his mouth. Luak shook free of the Indian near the fire and ran toward where Tyler was tied. Water splashed from the tin cup in her hands with each running step she took.

"Stop her," the red-bearded leader shouted.

A shaved-headed outlaw lunged after Luak. He caught her by the hair two steps before she reached Tyler. Before the man pulled her from her feet, Luak threw the water from the cup into Tyler's face.

In that instant, the liquid cooled his skin and he sucked what few drops he could into his mouth. The precious sweetness could not wet his rage.

Luak's tormentor dropped her onto the ground. He turned to the four other men near the fire and flashed a toothless smile. Luak's foot shot upward smashing into his groin. The man screamed and crumpled to his knees clutching himself. He lashed out with his fist and caught Luak in the stomach. Air whooshed from her lungs.

"The girl." Dalton Fox pointed for the biggest of his men to bring Luak. The man picked up his rifle. "No, don't hurt her. I like her."

A scar the color of flattened worm crawled from the corner of the man's mouth to his ear. One hand was wrapped in a filthy bandage. The scarred-face hulk moved on cat-quick feet and snatched Luak from the ground with his good hand. Luak hung from his hip like a bundle of rags. He turned to Tyler and held out his bandaged hand. "Your friend, Spencer, did this to me." Tobacco juice dribbled from his lips. "I'll get even with him. 'Til I find him, you'll have to do." He kicked a spray of sand into

Tyler's face.

Fox came where the man held Luak. He reached out and tangled his fingers in her hair. "I remember this little one. She cooked for us." He let go of Luak's hair and knelt to look into Tyler's eyes. "And kept my men warm at night. But you know that. She keep you warm last night?"

Tyler strained at the thongs that lashed his hands around the tree behind his back. They only cut deeper into his wrists.

Fox leaned closer. His foul breath filled Tyler's nose. "I'll make this easy. Tell me where Spencer is and you'll die quick. Keep quiet and the girl will watch my Indian scrape your skin from your bones with a dull stone." The flat of his hand shot out and smashed into Tyler's face.

Luak twisted in the big man's grip. She snapped her head forward and bit down on her captor's wrist. He slapped her face as if he were striking a pesky bug.

"If I tell you, will you let Luak go?" Tyler croaked.

"No." Fox shook his head. "I like her too much." Yellow teeth showed in his smile. "That one, she likes to bite." Fox peeled open the front of his shirt. Scabbed-over inflamed blotches just below his collarbone marked the man's chest.

Tyler's heart stopped when he thought of what Fox and his men had done to Luak.

Fox stood up and looked down at Tyler. "Think about what I said. Will it be quick or will you scream for death to come?"

He turned his back. "Tie the girl so she can't get away," Fox said to the big man. He raised his voice. "Miguel, tell the others to gather up their horses and mules. They won't have any use for them."

Tyler's anger burned hotter than the sun that scorched his face. He curled his fingers and fought to tear away the leather with his nails, but the thongs refused to give. His anger turned to tears that could not fall.

The bald man that Luak had kicked gathered up Tyler's saddlebags and dumped them out on the ground. He sorted through Tyler's belongings and stuffed the shirts and ammunition back in the pouch. He held Tyler's Bible in his hands for a few seconds, shrugged his shoulders, and tossed the book in the weeds.

The black mule bellowed. Mister Hutt's Thoroughbred cried in fear.

Chapter Fifteen

"How much longer, Spencer? It's been four hours." Bowie paced from the corral to the spot of shade where Spencer rested.

Spencer lifted a scrap of meat to his lips and slowly chewed. "Saddle the horses."

CHAPTER SIXTEEN

Fox's men returned with the horses and mules. The man with the bandaged hand tugged on the lead rope and fought the black mule each step of the way. The mule bared its teeth and snapped. The man snatched a piece of firewood from the ground. He clubbed the mule across its face. The mule reared and flailed at the sky with its hooves. The outlaw jerked hard on the rope until the animal stood at an uneasy calm.

Fox cut the cords around Luak's ankles and lifted her to her feet. She fought to pull away but Fox wrapped his fist in her black hair and led her toward where Tyler sat roped to the tree. "Natalia," Fox called to a bowlegged Indian with a long-ago broken nose. A bowie knife hung from the squat man's pistol belt. The blade was as long as Tyler's forearm. Fox's other men gathered a few steps behind.

"Time's come, amigo." Fox moved Luak in front of him. Her head was barely past his waist. "This Apache is good with his knife. I've seen him cut the guts outta live deer and never trouble its beatin' heart." He lifted Luak from the ground by her hair. Sounds came through her clenched teeth, but she refused to scream. The tip of Fox's tongue circled the girl's ear.

The strength that had melted away surged. Tyler strained against the thongs that held him to the tree. The word "no" formed in his mouth and he screamed it.

"It's simple, amigo. Where do I find Spencer? Tell me now and spare yourself the pain." Fox twisted his fingers deeper in Luak's hair. "You'll die anyway. How long you suffer is up to you." He shook Luak like a rag doll. "She'll watch each stroke of the Apache's knife."

A stream of words spilled from Luak's mouth. The Indian turned to her. She babbled again.

"What's she sayin'?" Fox asked.

"She say if you no kill the boy she take you where you want."

Luak chattered again.

"She say no kill boy. She be your woman forever."

Fox laughed. "Ask her about Spencer."

The Indian spewed a series of grunts at Luak. Her head moved up and down. More words babbled back.

"Sí, she will tell you all she know about Spencer. Again she say, boy must live."

"Then cut him loose." Fox's head reared back and a great howl of laughter filled the morning air.

CHAPTER SEVENTEEN

Spencer rode up next to Bowie and caught hold of the man's reins. "Pull up."

"It's nearly noon, Spencer. We got to get back to that mountain."

"This rough country is hard on horses. Wear them out and we'll both be afoot and do no one no good."

CHAPTER EIGHTEEN

"I won't let my Apache hurt you, boy." Fox pushed Luak away. The big man with the bad hand caught her and held her tight to his side. "I promised. My word is good."

Tyler felt the Indian's knife wedge between his head and the tree. With a quick motion, the blade cut through the strip of leather that bound his head.

"Cut him loose. Then tie his hands tight."

The Indian sliced Tyler's hand free. Rough hands jerked him to his feet and forced his hands together behind his back. Another strip of rawhide wrapped around his wrists.

Fox smiled at Luak. "Ask her about Spencer."

Tyler could make out Spencer's name in the string of singsong the Indian gibbered at Luak. Luak pointed at the eastern ridge — away from where Spencer and Bowie had ridden. "Tra-in," she said.

"She say they ride east to meet the train.

Get supplies."

Fox held Tyler in a stare. The bearded outlaw nodded so that only Tyler could see. "Boys, get your horses. The girl will ride with me. And bring that black mule for the boy here."

The big man held Tyler while the others gathered their horses and supplies. The Apache led the mule to where Tyler waited under the tree.

"Best blindfold that mule, he's a mite jumpy. Wouldn't want the boy to get hurt now."

The Indian covered the mule's face with a scrap of canvas and tucked the edges under its halter. The animal stamped its foot once and then stood still.

"Put the boy up on its back." Fox spit on the ground.

Tyler stiffened. One man caught him under the arms. The Indian took his feet and lifted him onto the mule.

Fox climbed onto his white stallion and reined it close to where Tyler sat. "That girl thinks a powerful lot 'bout you. I promised her I wouldn't kill you. But that girl is a black liar. Spencer didn't go to no train. You've got supplies for a month here." Fox lifted his rope from his saddle and shook out a loop. "I promised her I wouldn't kill you. Gonna let this mule do it for me."

Fox tossed the coils of his lariat over a tree limb above Tyler's head. He leaned from his saddle and slipped the loop over Tyler's head. Luak gasped. The Indian caught the loose end and wrapped it around the tree trunk where Tyler had been tied. As he knotted it in place, the rope dug into Tyler's throat.

"We're gonna ride off and leave you and the mule. Even with that blindfold that mule can only stand so long. When it walks away you'll swing from the tree and hang there chokin'." Fox took his canteen from the saddle and took a long swig. "Mule might need water and wander off. Or might just get hungry and take a step or two so it can get a bite of grass. Might shake that blindfold free and decide to go explorin'. How long do you think you can talk gentle to that mule and keep it standin' still?" Fox took another drink and slung the canteen back on his saddle. "Maybe you'll just give up and kick it hard in the ribs and get it over with."

Tyler's insides turned watery. Every muscle in the mule's back rippled against his legs. From down deep inside sweat beaded on his forehead. Any drop that fell from his face could spook the mule.

"I'll have this Indian girl's tooth marks in me tonight." Fox turned the stallion and walked it away.

The wind teased the hair on the mule's mane, horse hooves shuffled in the dirt, and Tyler's blood pounded through his veins. Each of Fox's men took time to look Tyler in the eye as they rode away.

CHAPTER NINETEEN

A breath of wind stirred the weeds. The cover of Tyler's Bible resisted, then opened in the hot gust. Pages shuffled in the breeze. At the ragged edge of his brain, Tyler found the book's words.

Yea though I walk through the valley of
  the shadow of
Death
  I will fear no evil
  for thou art with me.

Tyler yearned for that comfort, but he was alone, and fear he'd never known before choked at him. Dust clung to his lips. The sun burned down. He dared not swallow. The fall of his Adam's apple could spook the mule.

The black animal filled its lungs. Its ribs ballooned between Tyler's thighs. Tyler shifted to keep from losing his balance. The rope grabbed his throat.

"Whoa, black mule." He pushed the words through the tightness around his neck. "Easy there."

The mule stamped its foot.

"Settle down, now."

During calving season, the spring before last, a coyote had got to killing fresh-born calves. Mister Hutt told Jesus to bait a snare with afterbirth and set it to strangle the killer. Tyler and Jesus found the coyote the next morning. Bailing wire tangled around its neck. In its last minutes of torment, the coyote had snapped at itself and torn chunks of skin and fur until death claimed the animal. Its blue tongue hung from its open mouth. Eyes bulged in the last gasp of air.

"Easy mule." Even Tyler's eyes starved for moisture.

Spencer knelt on the dusty trail. He held his horse's reins in one hand and touched the marks in the dirt with the other. He looked up the mountainside.

Bowie jumped from his horse. "What do you see?"

"Here —" Spencer pointed at the path. "— the six we've been following met up with some others. Looks like eight more." He stood up and stabbed his tongue into

the side of his cheek. "Those eight are leading five animals. Without riders."

Bowie's face wrinkled in thought. "I don't
—" He looked up the hillside. "Tyler and
Luak? What they did to the man — you
don't think —"

Spencer turned to his horse and his boot
caught his stirrup. "Come on."

One night in the bunkhouse, the other
hands had talked about a horse thief they'd
seen hung in a trail town. Miller had said
that the criminal didn't choke to death if
the hangman did his job right. The foreman
had said the drop from the gallows broke
the victim's neck. A good hangman used
new rope. He weighed the condemned and,
depending on the man's weight, calculated
how far a drop it took to snap the man's
neck.

If the hangman figured wrong, the culprit
would strangle at the end of the rope.
Sometimes it took close to an hour for the
man to die.

A blowfly landed on the top of one of the
mule's ears. The insect rubbed its tiny front
feet together. The fly's red eyes stared up at
Tyler. The mule's ear twitched. The fly
circled towards Tyler's face. It perched in
the not-quite whiskers on his upper lip.

215

Hurrying wings brushed Tyler's nostril.

Tyler wanted to shake his head. To shoo the tickling speck away.

The mule shuffled forward. The fly buzzed away. Tyler shinnied back towards the mule's tail. The rope dug deeper into his throat.

Did he weigh enough or would he . . . ?

Tyler mashed his eyes shut. The face of the strangled coyote was painted on the back of his eyelids.

"Oh, Luak." More of a thought than a whisper.

Spencer took the reins from Bowie's mount. "We'll leave the horses here. I figure we're still a mile or better from where we left Tyler."

"And the girl," Bowie added.

"Yeah, and the girl."

"Spencer, I've been adding things in my head. You said they were leading five animals. Luak's pony, the Thoroughbred, and four mules make six. What happened to the last one?"

"Don't know. You saw what happened at the old man's place." The dead cow and abandoned calf flashed in his mind. "Life don't mean much to this kind of man. Get your rifle. When we get to the top of the hill, I'll slip down to where we hid the horses. You stay on top and cover me."

Bowie tugged his rifle from his saddle as Spencer led the horses away. "I'll bet they shot that black mule. That devil sure could make anybody mad enough." He rested the rifle on his shoulder and followed.

It could have been five more minutes or five more hours.

Tyler couldn't be sure. How long until it would be dark and Luak would be alone with Fox and his men, Tyler didn't know.

Despite the heat of the day, a chill moved down Tyler's spine.

Flies swarmed around the canvas that covered the mule's eyes and buzzed around Tyler's lips and nose. In the weeds, the pages of his Bible fluttered in the wind.

He maketh me to lie down in green
   pastures
He leadeth me beside the still waters.

The mule had to be as thirsty as he was. Tyler twisted his head in the noose and looked at the sky. For the hundredth time, or maybe the thousandth, he struggled at the thongs that bound his wrists together. But it was no use.

I will fear no evil
For thou art with me.

The mule stepped forward. Tyler's legs felt each notch in the mule's spine as he scooted back. His legs touched where the mule's haunches curved down to his hind legs. He felt the base of the mule's tail through the seat of his pants.

In the sand along the little stream, a puff of air stirred the ashes of the fire. Soot and sand twisted together in a spinning funnel no taller than a calf. The dust devil grazed the ground and swept towards the thatch of weeds where Tyler struggled to stay on the mule.

The black mule bobbed its head. Tyler bent forward to keep his seat on the mule and each fiber of the rope dug into his throat. The mule tossed its head and the canvas slipped down so that half an eye showed.

Tyler sucked in a breath. "Whoa, black mule."

Spencer crouched down and peered over the mesquite brush on the hill above where they had camped with Tyler and Luak.

Bowie crawled in beside him. "My equipment is still where we left it. No tracks. It doesn't look like anyone came close to where you had me bury it."

"I found boot tracks where we left the stock last night. They were here, all right."

"Any sign of Tyler or Luak?"

"Nothin'." Spencer raised his head and studied the creek bed in the arroyo below. Blades of grass bent in the wind. A cone of dust and soot swirled around the blackened ring where their campfire had been. It bounced like a child's top across the sand and crossed into a patch of weeds. Sunlight glared off a white blur stirred by the whirlwind.

"Bowie?" Spencer pointed with the barrel of his rifle.

"I see it. It looks like that wind is whipping the pages of a book."

Spencer's body stiffened. "God in heaven."

The mule shook its head. Through the brush and shadows Spencer picked out its legs, then head and neck. Then the image took shape. "Tyler." A taut rope stretched from the boy's neck over the crooked branches above his head. Spencer squinted in the bright sun.

"They hung Tyler." Bowie had found the same sight as Spencer.

"No, but if that mule takes one more step
—"

"What can we do?"

Spencer hoisted his rifle to his shoulder.
"Maybe I can bust that branch with a
bullet."

Just as quickly as it had come to be, the
whirlwind was gone. Tyler let the breath
seep from his lungs and, though every fiber
of his body cried for water, his eyes made
tears.

Miller had said that a man could twist and
choke at the end of a rope for more than an
hour.

Then Fox's laughing words thundered in
his head. "Maybe you'll just give up and
kick that mule hard in the ribs."

That's what he would do. When the mule
took one more step, Tyler would kick the
mule and try to push up and off. If he tried
hard enough it might just be enough of a
jolt to snap his neck.

He looked at his Bible in the weeds.
Perhaps he could find some words of comfort. But the last gust from dust devil had
shut the book's cover.

"Easy mule." Tyler couldn't hear his voice.

Spencer steadied his Winchester across a

boulder. He drew a breath and eased the hammer back. A bead of sweat ran from his hatband and pooled in his eyebrow over his right eye.

"No." Bowie's fingers fastened around the barrel of the rifle. "It's more than four hundred yards. If you miss, the shot will spook the mule and Tyler'll be dead. We have to get closer."

Spencer thumbed the hammer back to safe. "Can you pray?"

"I think so."

Spencer stood up and started for the trail. "Then pray I'll try to get there before the mule takes its next step." He placed his rifle beside the path.

And Spencer left at a run.

Each stride down the hill jostled Spencer's hips and knees. He loped by the place where he had killed the rattlesnake. Tyler and the mule were hidden in the tangle of branches and shadows. He could only make out the branch with the rope. Bowie's footsteps fell hard on the packed dirt behind him. With each running step, Spencer formed a plan.

Come up from behind where neither Tyler nor the mule would see him. Grab the boy. Hold him up and cut the rope as the mule ran away. Not much of a plan, but all he had. No time to explain it to Bowie. Spencer was in a race. Second place meant Tyler would die.

"Whoa, now."

The canvas slipped down the mule's face another half inch. The white rim around its eye showed and the animal shook its face side to side trying to free its eyes from the stiff fabric. Tyler slipped to one side. Each fiber of the rope tore into the skin on his throat.

He told the cramped muscles in his legs to be ready. Ready to kick the mule and throw himself upwards with all his might.

The mule shook the canvas away from its face. It tossed its head upwards.

Tyler lifted his tired legs. He aimed his heels at the mule's ribs.

It was too late to go for the rope. Spencer tossed his knife away. Tyler's boots smacked the mule's side. The mule bellowed and reared. Spencer lunged for Tyler's legs.

He caught hold around the boy's thighs. Spencer stumbled with the jolt of Tyler's weight in his arms, but he kept his feet. He lifted the boy trying to keep the noose from drawing tight.

Bowie was there in the next instant. A

knife was in his hand. He sawed at the rope, it gave way, and all three tumbled to the ground, Spencer's arms still wrapped around Tyler's legs.

The mule brayed. It kicked its heels and pranced into the creek bottom.

The dust hung thick in the air. Spencer scrambled to his knees. He pulled the loop free from Tyler's neck. Tyler's eyes opened and the boy gagged for air.

CHAPTER TWENTY

"Cut his hands loose."

Tyler knew the voice. He felt the straps around his wrists break free. His fingers went to his throat and clutched the raw burn on his skin. He tried to make words come but could only croak.

Tyler dragged himself across the sand to the trickle of water in the creek. He pressed his face into the current and sucked in the cool water until the silt from the bottom filled his mouth and clung to his teeth. When he raised his face, he saw the scuffed leather cover of his Bible in the weeds. His prayer had been answered and the angel was Spencer.

He jabbed his hand into the middle of the stream and pulled himself through the water and snatched up the book.

"Luak." Tyler rolled onto his back with the Bible tucked to his chest. "They took Luak." He struggled to his knees. "Spencer, we gotta —" He fell back onto the ground. "— help her."

Spencer rolled from his stomach onto one hip. He crossed one boot over the other and flicked the rowel of one of the spurs with his finger so that it twirled.

Tyler waited for Spencer to curse him. To tell him he had failed again. That Luak's capture was his fault.

But Spencer didn't tell Tyler he had just saved his life. He didn't remind Tyler that when one of Fox's raiders had charged up the hill at the Severed Finger, Tyler had shot the horse and Spencer had saved him there too. Spencer didn't remind him that Tyler had brought an unloaded rifle to the alley behind Jimmy Six's. Or that he'd lost Mister Hutt's Krag rifle and that Fox had the Thoroughbred. Or even that the handgun he'd bought with his own money was gone.

The grit Tyler had sucked from the creek bottom coated his throat. He knew tears would show Spencer how weak he was but he couldn't stop them. Tyler pulled himself to his knees. "We hafta save Luak."

Spencer spun his spur again. Sunlight, reflected from each blade of the turning star, flashed over Tyler's eyes. "What happened here?" he asked.

Tyler let it all spill out. How'd he been

asleep when Fox's men first came, that Luak had traded herself for his life. That Fox had caught her in the lie and left him to hang.

Bowie squirmed at each part of the story but Spencer never moved.

Tyler finished and let the last words dribble from his mouth. "We hafta, Spencer. We hafta go after them."

The line at Spencer's lips parted for the first time. "No use. If they haven't wrung her neck already, by the time we find them Fox will have sold her for a pull on a whiskey bottle to any man that wanted her. The leavin's won't be worth the sweat you wipe off a horse."

Tyler bolted to his feet. "Don't you say that." He wiped the drying sand from his face. "If you won't help, I'll go by myself."

Spencer flicked his spur. "Go ahead." The gunman picked a piece of firewood from the ground and held it out to Tyler. "Here's a stick to fight 'em with. You got nothin' else."

"What are you sayin', Spencer?"

"No use following 'em. We need to study the map Hutt gave us and Bowie's charts and make our best guess where they're headed. We'll catch up to 'em and hurt 'em as much as we can."

"What about Luak?"

"If she's alive —"

"Don't say that."

Spencer raised his voice. "If she's alive, we'll do what we can."

Tyler balled his fists.

Spencer turned to Bowie. "This here is none of your concern." He tapped a vest pocket. "I'll pay you for the loss of your mules and what supplies you have left. You can ride back to the railroad and catch a ride to the next village. Tyler and I'll do this ourselves."

Bowie jammed Spencer's knife into the sand. "I'm staying." He stood up from where he sprawled on the ground. "I'll go with you. For no other reason than to keep you two from killing each other."

"Your choice," Spencer said to Bowie and then turned to Tyler. "Better go catch that mule."

Tyler slapped the dirt from his pant leg. "You go catch the mule."

When Tyler got back with the black mule, Spencer and Bowie knelt over Bowie's maps. Bowie's fingers traced across the paper. Spencer pointed and Bowie tapped a place near the center of the map. Spencer lifted the leather his father had burned with his knife. The gunman nodded.

"Tyler." Spencer folded the leather and dropped it into the front of his shirt. "I got an idea where they're headed. You're gonna need to ride that mule 'til we can find another horse. Can you do it?"

"I can ride anything with four legs."

"Rig yourself some sorta saddle. We need to get Bowie's gear dug up. We'll get what sleep we can and light out at dawn."

"Can't we leave now?"

"At dawn, I said."

Tyler tugged on the mule's lead rope. "I'll need a gun."

Bowie stood up. "There's a shotgun buried with my equipment. I brought it for hunting. Tyler can use it."

Spencer shook his head. "Let's see what else you've got. We'll take what we need and hide the rest here. Better get to diggin' 'fore the sun goes down."

Tyler balanced the double-barreled shotgun across the mule's withers. The sun's first light of the day cracked the horizon behind him. The muscles in his thighs ached from his hours on the mule the day before. He tried to push away those thoughts but the morning air on the raw welts around his neck reminded him of it all again. But when

228

he thought of Luak and the night she'd spent with those men, it was as if yesterday's rope squeezed his life away.

Spencer led the way on the big buckskin. Tyler and the black mule followed and Bowie trailed behind. Spencer had told them they would follow a dry creek bed. If they kept to the bottom of the little arroyo their chances of not being spotted were better. That was all the gunman had said.

Tyler stuffed a bit of old biscuit into his mouth. His throat hurt as he swallowed the dried lump. Another reminder of yesterday. And another reminder of how far they were from Luak.

They rode all day and into the night. They camped without a fire. Thoughts of Luak haunted Tyler's sleep. Darkness still hung thick in the air when they saddled up the next morning.

"Tyler —" Bowie forced his horse up alongside the black mule as they padded down the next creek bottom. "— do you know what month it is?"

"Not really all that sure." He shifted on the blanket he used for his saddle. "Seen a dove sittin' her nest last night when I went for water. Doves nest out in May back on The Bootheel. We're farther south so I reckon it could be April."

229

"In Michigan, April is when winter melts away and things turn green." Bowie's horse matched the mule's steps. "Tyler, I'm amazed how you observe the things around you."

"Just do, I guess. Don't think about it much." Tyler whisked a swarm of gnats away from the welt on his neck. "Learned from watching Mister Hutt mostly and doing what he does. We get up while it's still dark so we can be in the saddle come first light. Work 'til it's too dark or we're too tired to do more or the job's done."

"I would like to meet your Mister Hutt someday."

"Don't think you'll be able. He'll be dead by the time we get back if he's not already."

"I'm sorry."

Tyler turned his head away from Bowie and pretended to study a single puff of clouds in the desert sky. "Mister Hutt says there'll be a time when men'll need watches and calendars to decide what needs to be done, not the dawnin' of the day. Might even be a machine that does some of the thinkin' for 'em." He scratched the mule's neck. "Thoughts like that tends to complicate your mind, don't it?"

"Sometimes I forget you're only fourteen, Tyler."

230

"Spencer don't." Tyler touched his spurs to the mule's sides.

When it was night, they ate chunks of beef, slick with grease and as warm as the day, from a shared tin can. Spencer allowed no fire. Tyler shivered in a blanket spread on the ground and fought sleep, lest the visions of Luak and Fox's men would come again.

But the dreams came.

Spencer was on his horse when Tyler first stirred. "You and Bowie sit tight. I'll scout ahead."

Bowie wiped the dust from his glasses and watched the buckskin horse disappear down the wash. "He's like a panther on the hunt."

Tyler shook his head. "Or a whole pack of killer wolves in one body. The only reason he stops is to rest his horse. He could go on for days at a time."

"Is it Fox he wants?"

"Can't be sure. But I don't have any chance to get Luak back without him."

Tyler took the mule and Bowie's horse to the only water they'd found. Chalky stripes stained the soil around a stagnant puddle no bigger than the lid of a rain barrel. He kept the mule back so the horse could drink first, then pulled the horse away so the black mule could drink its fill.

Bowie hurried down to the water hole. "Spencer's coming in fast."

Tyler passed the horse's reins to Bowie and pulled the mule from the water.

Spencer had his Winchester in his hand. He loped the buckskin up to where they waited. "Four riders coming in. Bowie, give your rifle to Tyler and take the shotgun."

Tyler felt his insides go tight. "Fox's men?"

Spencer pulled his hat off and studied the high ground above the arroyo where they had camped. "Sure of it."

"Is Luak with them?"

"No."

"How can you be sure they're Fox's men?"

"Four men on horseback and they're leading the pinto pony the girl rode."

The barrel of Bowie's rifle turned white-hot in Tyler's hand. If they had her horse, then what had they done with Luak?

"Listen to me." Spencer knelt and made four spots in the sand with his finger. "Bowie, you're gonna wait right here for them to ride up on you. Wave for them to come in. All friendly like."

"Why me?" Bowie's lungs rattled as he sucked in a breath.

"Might recognize me or Tyler. Just let

them come to you, but load that shotgun with buckshot and keep it handy." Spencer pointed to the ridge above where they stood. "Tyler, you're gonna scramble up there and hide where you can watch what's goin' on. I'll do the same on the other side." He pointed to the opposite hill.

Tyler eyed the steep slope Spencer wanted him to climb.

Spencer saw where he was looking. "Hide yourself good but be sure you can see." Spencer touched the marks he had made in the sand. "They'll come in single file. Only the leader will do the talkin." Spencer looked at Bowie. "Big man. Hand's wrapped in a rag."

Spencer caught Tyler by the wrist. "Pick a place where you can see Bowie. The others will spread out while the leader talks." He drew lines in the dust. "When the big man goes to get off his horse, he'll turn so his back is to Bowie. As his right leg comes over the saddle, Bowie won't be able to see his gunhand. Put all your hate over Luak in one spot. The second his hand touches his pistol —" Spencer's tongue found the center of his cheek and traced a tight circle. "— put a bullet twixt his shoulder blades."

Tyler supped in his breath. "In the back?"

"If you don't, Bowie's a dead man. I'll deal with the other three."

CHAPTER TWENTY-ONE

A hot, angry sun blazed the rock under Tyler's hands. He scrambled up the side of the ravine and wedged himself into a jagged crevice no bigger than a saddle. A clump of soapjack bulged from the side of the rock face, like the giant from a child's story had stuffed a bit of green in the side of the drab cliff.

Tyler tucked the barrel of Bowie's rifle through the dagger-shaped leaves and rested his face along the stock. Lines of tiny ants trooped up each stalk to the waxy yellow flowers. Rough rocks stabbed his hips and when Tyler turned a bit to find comfort, the toe of his boot touched a fist-sized stone. The stone rolled loose from its place. Tyler reached out to steady it but his fingers only grazed the stone. It slipped over the side of the depression where Tyler hid and tumbled down the slope.

Tyler froze. He searched for Bowie in the

shadows below. The rock bounced once on the rocky sides of the canyon wall and catapulted into the air. All was quiet. Seconds stretched before the echo of the stone striking the sand below found Tyler's ears.

A honeybee buzzed past his ear. The insect lit on the yucca's pale flowers. Grains of pollen clung to the whiskery hair on its legs. Tyler clicked off the safety on the rifle and trained its sights on the dry wash bed below.

The bee left the flowers. It circled as if examining the sweat on Tyler's face and landed on the barrel of the gun.

Spencer knew the steep canyon walls would hide the riders until they were below the pocket in the rock face where he'd sent the boy.

The gunman studied it in his mind again. The riders would come in single file. Spencer was sure of it. The big man with the bandaged hand would see Bowie as an easy target. He'd pretend to be friendly, wanting to lull his prey into thinking there was no harm. The riders behind him would spread out, each ready to strike if needed. The leader would turn his horse a bit. He'd talk and when he moved to swing from his horse's saddle, his holster and gun would be hidden from Bowie. The man's right hand would find the gun and as his foot touched the ground, the bullet from a Colt would tear into Bowie.

It was up to Tyler. A task no more difficult than killing a skunk caught in a leghold trap. But this skunk was a man. Now Tyler had grit, but he'd come up short before. Spencer was banking that Tyler's feelings for the Indian girl would sharpen him for the job. One pull of the trigger when the big man's hand touched his pistol was all the boy needed to do.

The others would turn to see where the shot came from. Their backs would be to Spencer.

He would kill the first in his saddle. The next would die before his foot left the stirrup. The third would wheel his horse and try to escape down the narrow gully. It would be an easy straightaway shot. Spencer planned on killing the fleeing horse with his fourth bullet.

Most likely, the other three horses would run towards Bowie. They'd catch them, pick out the best for Tyler, and kill the others. No reason to take a chance the horses would find their way back to Fox.

Spencer knelt behind the crest of a jagged sandstone outcropping and peered down into the valley. From the corner of his eye, a stone clattered down the opposite canyon wall. He lifted his head and glared at Tyler.

If the boy failed this time, Bowie would die.

The line of horsemen came down the narrow path at the bottom of the canyon. Bowie sat on a rock and lifted a canteen to his mouth. His horse and the black mule were tied close by.

"You there," the first rider called. "Riders comin' in. We be friendly." He turned to the three behind him and touched the brim of his hat.

Bowie stood. He rested the shotgun on his shoulder and his mouth moved but the deep valley swallowed up the sounds. The first rider's head rolled back and his mouth hacked open like a laugh should roll out from somewhere deep inside him.

The pink scar of the leader's face made Tyler's stomach twist. He remembered how the big man had hoisted Luak like a bundle of limp rags and for the first time, he was sure he could do what Spencer had sent him to do.

One of the followers, on a chestnut horse, moved his mount to the left. The next reined his horse up to the right. The last rider looped the lead rope to Luak's little pinto around his saddle horn and trotted up beside the chestnut. The scarred man touched his spurs to his horse and the animal turned away from Bowie.

It was just like Spencer had said. *He'll turn in the saddle so Bowie can't see and reach for his gun.* Every muscle tightened and Tyler's toe slipped on the ledge. A walnut-sized pebble bounced off the rim.

The big man raised his head to look up at the noise.

Tyler's finger pressed the trigger.

Everything moved at once and from all directions. It was as fast as light and as still as ice on a frozen stream. As the rifle's recoil slammed back into Tyler's shoulder, the honeybee flew a crooked line away from where it had perched on the gun barrel. The spikes of the yucca plant whipped apart with the muzzle blast.

Tyler's world boiled with hate. Time paused as if the bullet might fall from the sky and never reach the man. Then vivid red sprang from the wound in the center of the man's back. His head jerked backward. His arms flailed and a gun dropped from his limp hand. The sound of a bullet slapping flesh would live in his dreams until the day he died. Not a scream. But the last sliver of life leaving a body.

Over the terrible noise, Spencer's first gunshot tore through the morning.

Dime novels told of gunfights filled with honor. Men looking each other in the eye. There was nothing noble here. It took no courage to kill the unsuspecting. Gunsmoke, screams of frightened horses, and men's death groans filled every inch of the little canyon.

Spencer racked the lever of the Winchester and jacked the third cartridge into the chamber. The last raider leaned over his horse's neck and slapped his fleeing horse's rump again and again with the ends of his reins. Spencer steadied his rifle on the boulder in front of him and aimed.

At the bark of the rifle shot, the horse folded in mid-stride. Its shrill cry of terror and pain echoed off of the valley's walls. The animal rolled, throwing its rider, and came up pawing the ground with its front hooves, dragging its useless hind legs behind it in some pitiful effort to escape the pain.

The taste of death filled Tyler's throat and bubbled into his mouth. Screams of the crippled horse stabbed into his ears. The

240

last raider, the one who led Luak's pony, scrambled away from the flailing horse. He clawed for the gun at his hip. His empty, fearful eyes found Tyler on the hill.

Spencer's next shot smashed into the man's head. Like a dream in the blackest night, crimson mist haloed his head, and bits of white bone and hair flew into the air.

Tyler raised Bowie's Savage and pressed the rifle to his cheek. His stomach turned over as the sights steadied on the thrashing animal. He took up the trigger slack but hesitated. A blast from Spencer's Winchester put the horse down. Tyler mashed his eyes shut.

Bowie's chest moved up and down like a panting dog's. All the color had drained from his face until the white of his bones showed through.

Red droplets splattered Bowie's round glasses. His tongue touched his lips and Bowie gagged at the trace of taste he found there. "It happened so fast."

"You're alright, aren't you?" Tyler asked.

"When the man turned his back to me, I —" Bowie looked at Tyler through his smeared eyeglasses. "— I don't remember. Something warm hit my face. Then I was on the ground."

"It's over now. You best sit there another minute." Tyler found Bowie's canteen. "Drink some water."

Spencer touched the first body with the toe of his boot. The big Winchester still hung ready in his hands. He dug two fingers into the dead man's vest pocket, then looked into his cupped hand and tucked the silver coins into his pants pocket. He grabbed the next dead man by the shirt collar and turned him onto his back, and rested the muzzle of his rifle on the corpse's throat.

Spencer pulled the gun belt loose from the limp body. "You two did well. And Tyler, no matter how many times I've heard that noise, it still chills my insides. I had to put that horse down." He checked the dead man's pockets. "Pick whichever of those horse you want —" He pointed his chin at the dead man. "— and take anythin' you fancy, they won't be needin' it."

The shadow of a circling vulture swept over the blood-streaked sand. Bowie shaded his eyes and looked up. A half-dozen black shapes, called by some harbinger of death, floated on the thermals above.

"We gonna bury 'em?" Tyler knew the birds and other animals would feast on the bodies.

"If things were the other way, they wouldn't put you in the ground. They'd leave you where you lay." Spencer poked the last body with the barrel of his rifle. He tucked the man's pistol into his belt. "Look here." He knelt by the downed horse and wrestled a rifle from the saddle scabbard. "Mister Hutt's Krag rifle. It found its way back to you."

Tyler looked at the dead man's face. "I don't remember him with the ones that took Luak."

"They look different when they're dead. 'Sides he probably traded for the gun like they traded for the girl."

Two running steps brought Tyler to Spencer. Hot tears boiled in his eyes. "You don't know that." He turned and stared at the dead horse. "Why do you have to say that?"

Spencer tossed the Krag through the air to Tyler.

Tyler snatched the rifle with both hands before it touched his chest. He turned it over in his hands, wrapped his finger over the trigger, and leveled the muzzle at Spencer's belly.

Spencer's back went ramrod straight. "I was you, boy —" His tongue circled the inside of his cheek. "— I'd check those saddlebags for ammunition."

The wind stammered. The air all around grew heavy like a storm was coming in. But, no clouds filled the sky. Just the shadows of birds that waited to feed on the dead.

The whole world rested on the barrel of the Krag and weighed on it until the muzzle pointed at the ground. Tyler leaned the rifle on the dead horse and untied the saddle-bags. He kept his face down. Tears welled up. Not for Luak. Not because he'd killed a man.

Tyler wanted to be back at The Bootheel. He wanted things to be the way they were the day before Spencer rode down that hill. Before Mister Hutt got sick. Even before Luak. But it would never be that way ever again.

"You did well today, boy." Spencer touched Tyler's shoulder and walked away to find his buckskin horse.

CHAPTER TWENTY-TWO

Spencer lashed the bedroll he'd had taken from the dead horse to the back of his saddle. "Tyler, the chestnut looks to be the soundest, but it's your choice. The ones you don't choose, put down. Don't want to take a chance they find their way back to Fox."

"What about Luak's pony?"

"What about it?"

"When we find her, she'll want her horse."

"That's *if* we find her. And *if* we find her alive, what horse we put her on won't matter."

"Why you keep sayin' that, Spencer?" Tyler ground his teeth together. Blood streaked the sand between his boots like butchering day at The Bootheel. Three men, who minutes before breathed free air, now were lifeless shells swarming with rust-colored ants. "You think they killed her, don't you?" Anger had left him. "Then say it, Spencer.

Luak's dead. Say it."

Spencer turned from his horse. "That girl had one chance in a hundred — no, ten thousand." He tapped the barrel of his rifle across his thigh. "You told us the way Fox and his men looked at her. She's less than nothin' to them. They'll use and cut her up coyote bait." He turned back to the buckskin and slammed the Winchester into its scabbard. "You gotta know what we might find." It was as if Spencer wanted all the hate in him to take hold of Tyler.

Tyler fought hard to keep it away. Without even the smallest piece of hope, Tyler knew he would become as dark as the gunman. Or no different than Fox.

Bowie stepped between the two. "Maybe we could use the pony as another pack animal. And we might need a spare horse if one of ours goes lame in this God-awful country."

Spencer tipped his hat back on his forehead. "Bring the pony. And only the pony. Strap everything you think we can use of theirs on the mule." He looked down the wash over his horse's back, grabbed the saddle horn, and swung up without touching the stirrups.

Bowie moved in front of Tyler. "Except for the man with Tyler's Krag, the others were carrying new Winchesters." He looked up at Spencer. "Why do you think they were out here? Looking for us?"

"Fox is like the meanest dog in town. He's gonna piss on every post he can to let everybody know what's his. 'Spect he sent those boys to look for us."

"Then he'll be waiting for them to report in?"

"Yup."

"And when they don't?"

"Yup."

Bowie's shoulders dropped.

Spencer turned his horse. "Down the wash aways —" He tilted his head. "— the trail splits. You two stay to the high ground. I'll follow their backtracks a piece and see what I can figure. Find a place to camp come dark. No fire. I'll find you. Kill those horses like I said. Use your knives, hear?" Spencer put his spurs to the buckskin and rode off.

Tyler grabbed the legs of one of the dead men and dragged the body down the gully.

Bowie cocked his head. "What are you doing?"

"I saw a place where the last water through here undercut the bank. We'll push the bodies in under there and cave it in on 'em. Ain't right to leave 'em for the vultures."

247

"What about the horses?"

"We'll take 'em with us."

"But, Spencer said —"

"There's been enough killin' for one day." Tyler shifted his grip on the corpse's legs. "We'll bring the horses with us. Things change, we do somethin' then."

"Tyler, you got more guts than a slaughterhouse floor."

Wet marks in the shadows of the canyon wall led to a trickle of water that seeped from the sandstone. Sprigs of grass and weeds formed a ragged circle around a puddle no bigger than a frying pan. The water was as clear as crystal and so cold that Spencer's head hurt from the greedy way, he gulped his first mouthful. He filled his canteen and then let the buckskin horse drink and graze on the few morsels of green. With his back on the rock wall, the shade cooled him from the harsh day's sun.

The story Spencer didn't want to know was shown in the tracks in the sand. Five horses and riders milled on the valley floor. One of the horses, most likely the Indian girl's, smelled the little bit of water. They tied the five horses to the brush along the rock face opposite the spring. Scuffs in the dust showed how the pony fought its tether but was unable to pull free and go to the water.

When the five horses left, the hoofprints of the pony did not cut as deep into the sand as they had when they entered the valley.

In the tangle of brush and weeds, Spencer found a scrap of a satin ribbon on a cactus thorn. And the ribbon was cornflower blue.

After Tyler watered the horses in a hidden stream that a man could step across without changing out his pace, he picketed them in a draw surrounded by scrub brush and piñons. He found a place to sit and watch. A stone on the ground caught his eye and Tyler pretended it was a time when death did not rule his thoughts. He picked up the pebble, intending to toss it in the brush for the pure joy of throwing a stone. When his fingers clawed it free of the dry clay, he held an arrowhead as perfect as the day it was made. The white flint had been chipped by an ancient hand and made to kill. He let it drop into the dirt.

The marbled clouds at sunset fast turned from orange and purple to gray. Dusk settled around. The black mule stamped a foot and pulled on its rope. Tyler stroked the stiff hair along the mule's mane and patted all along its back to soothe the animal. The mule's nostrils sniffed at the air and the faintest scent of woodsmoke drifted up from where the hill gave way to the valley floor.

Bowie would not be foolish enough to build a campfire. Spencer had told them to camp and wait. No fires, the gunman had been clear on that. This smoke came from below. Not from the rim of the rocks where Tyler had left Bowie and their gear.

Tyler slipped through the brush, careful to keep his footfalls on rocks and hard ground. Where the high ridge sloped away, he spotted a yellow glow of a small fire in the valley below. In the speckled darkness, dim shapes he knew were cattle grazed on bunchgrass. Not more than two dozen and no horses he could see. Just the figures of one or two men by the fire.

Like day had turned to night, a chill moved down his neck and all the small hairs along his backbone stood on end.

More of Fox's men with stolen cattle? Camping for the night before they head back to meet their leader?

The Krag rifle felt awkward in his hands and the nervous place in his stomach rolled over. Tyler backed away from where he hid and picked his way up to the rimrocks to find Bowie.

On the night air, Tyler recognized Spencer's horse's throaty nicker. The gunman sat with his rifle across his knees and feet wide apart. When he saw Tyler, he slipped the long-bladed knife from his boot and dug it in the dirt between his knees. Bowie sliced a strip of meat from a smoked ham they'd found in the goods they'd taken from the dead men.

"Cut that thin, Bowie, we might need to make it last." Spencer turned the dirt over with his knife.

Bowie held the piece to Spencer. "If I cut it any thinner, it will only have one side."

Even in the darkness, Spencer's skin seemed as white as milk. His shoulders bent forward and he looked at the meat for a long time before he lifted it to his mouth.

"Campfire in the valley. Might be Fox's men with a dozen steers." Tyler dropped onto his heels and took the next strip of meat from Bowie.

Spencer shook his head. "No, couple of Mexican boys trailing cattle. I slipped by them on my way to find you." He looked at the food in his hand but didn't take another bite.

"Somethin' happen out there, Spencer? You look like you rode hard."

"No." The meat dropped from his fingers into the dirt.

"Spencer?"

The gunman lifted his head. In the gray light, Tyler could see the veins that etched Spencer's eyes. "Would you take care of my horse? Put him with the others."

Tyler couldn't remember the last time Spencer had asked him to do something. Always before Tyler had been told. He caught the buckskin and turned to lead it away, glad it was two boys in the valley, not men with guns. "Spencer —" Tyler looked at the back of the saddle. "— that bedroll you took from the deadman's horse is gone."

"Musta come untied and fell off somewhere." He stabbed his knife deep into the dirt. "No need to go lookin' for it."

Tyler found his Bible at daybreak. He propped his back against a flat rock and stared at the open book until it was light enough to read the words. The Book had no mention of cowhands, but Tyler always took to the story of David, the shepherd boy. Tyler knew nothing of tending sheep. But he felt a kinship for the boy in the Book who took care of livestock and killed the bear and lion that threatened his flocks.

The feeling was stronger this morning.

David had killed the giant with a stone and sling. Much like Tyler had killed the big man that took Luak with a bullet from Bowie's rifle. That had been only yesterday. But so long ago.

"Somethin' I need to tell ya." Spencer walked up. Much of the color had found its way back to the gunman's face. Bloody threads still webbed his eyes. He leaned his hip on the rock near Tyler's shoulder. "Readin' your book?"

"Yes, sir."

"Never did take to that myself. Heard a preacher tellin' his people to pray for the soldier boys. For their protection and that they'd win the war." Spencer rammed his tongue into the inside of his cheek. "Figured somewhere else, another preacher was tellin' the folks of the boys on the other side to do the same thing. Now, how's God supposed to choose who's to win?"

"Don't think it's about all that." Tyler closed his Bible. "Alotta folks think prayin's all about askin' and gettin'. I figure the Good Lord wants us to respect Him and appreciate all He's made. If He's mighty enough to keep all this in order —" Tyler tipped his head toward the new day over the valley. "— He's able to know what's good and right for us. Folks want to understand God. When you think you understand Him, it makes Him smaller. I don't want to believe in a small God."

Spencer plucked a blade of dry grass and hung it in his lips. Golden rays of sunlight washed over the valley, and in the brush, a bird sang a morning song. "What's your book say about all this?"

Tyler fumbled with the pages. "Right here —" He touched the center of a page. "— Habakkuk, chapter two and verse twenty. 'The Lord is in his holy temple; let all the earth keep silence before him.' "

Spencer looked up at the sky. The bird hushed its song. After a long minute, he whispered, "Lofty words, Tyler. Lofty words."

"Somethin' you wanted to tell me, Spencer?"

Spencer curled his lip over his teeth and bit down. "Yeah, Bowie's cuttin' up that ham. Better get up there 'fore he eats it all hisself." The gunman took a last look at the valley below and left Tyler alone with his Bible.

The men ate scraps of smoked ham. Tyler kept a close eye on Spencer, but the gunman scanned the valley below and never looked Tyler's way. It took a mouthful of water from his canteen for Tyler to wash down each bite of the dry meat.

Spencer wiped his fingers on his shirt. "Tyler, that buckskin horse of mine needs rest. I'll ride one of the others today." Before Tyler could speak, Spencer added, "Knew you'd brought the horses with you." Spencer stood and dusted off the seat of his pants. "If they get in the way —"

"I'll handle it then." Tyler got to his feet and looked Spencer in the face, but the gunman turned away. Tyler's hands clinched into fists.

Bowie scrambled up and stepped between Tyler and Spencer. "I've been studying the maps. If I'm right, that notch in the mountains out yonder is the entrance to the Valley of Visions."

Spencer nodded. "Those mountains are more than a day's ride from here. We need to cross more desert and that ridge of foothills."

"The village — Mesita — will be just this side of it." Bowie looked at Tyler. "Spencer thinks that Fox and his bunch are using Mesita as their base. That way when trouble comes they can slip into the valley and hide out. Isn't that what you said, Spencer?"

The first hot breath of the day teased the dust at their feet.

Spencer nodded. "That's my guess."

Tyler licked his lips and tried to see Spencer's face, but the gunman turned away. "Mesita is Luak's homeplace. Remember, she told us."

"I remember."

"Reckon if nothin' else she's back with her people." Tyler edged closer to Spencer.

Spencer took another step. "What I reckon is that those four we killed yesterday are supposed to report back sometime. If we're goin' to have surprise on our side, we need to get to that village 'fore Fox is expectin' them back." Spencer worked the lever of his Winchester just enough to be sure there was a bullet in the chamber. He pointed the barrel of the rifle at the valley floor below. "They know we're here."

The two boys Spencer had seen last night with their cattle stood beside a campfire far below. When Tyler squinted, he could see the tallest raise his hand and point up the hillside to where he stood with Spencer and Bowie.

Spencer spit between his boots. "Get the horses. We're going down there."

"Then what?" Tyler stayed rooted to the place he stood. "Kill those boys?"

Spencer never turned. "Might have to."

Spencer jerked the reins out of Tyler's hands. He vaulted into the saddle and never tucked the big Winchester into its scabbard. The horse turned in a tight circle. Spencer raked his spurs across the horse's sides. Horse and rider plunged off the hillside to the valley below.

Tyler dropped the saddle he was about to put on his horse. He caught hold of the animal's mane and jumped onto its back. "Bring the horses, Bowie." Tyler kicked his heels into his mount's ribs. "Spencer's liable to do somethin' to those boys and their cattle."

Tyler let the dead man's mare pick its way down the steep slope. They cut through the dust Spencer's horse had raised. His mount skidded on the loose rocks, nearly tossing Tyler from its back. Through the piñon trees, Tyler saw Spencer reach the valley floor and kick his horse toward the cow camp.

The smaller boy hid behind the taller. Neither moved as Spencer rode to them. Clamping his knees tight, Tyler urged his horse into a gallop, not sure if he would hear Spencer's Winchester blast in the next seconds.

The rifle still hung in Spencer's hand like he was holding a pistol. The weapon's muzzle pointed at a spot inches in front of the tall boy's feet.

The boy's eyes were wide, but he'd set his jaw trying to hide his fear. He held the other boy behind his back. The fingers of the little boy twisted in his big friend's shirttail.

Tyler swung his leg over his horse's back and tossed himself to the ground. He stumbled, but kept his feet under him and stopped between Spencer's rifle and the Mexican boys.

Spencer lifted the Winchester and pointed the barrel at the sky. "Tyler, there's good in you I'll never have."

Tyler tilted his head and looked up at the man on the horse. Spencer's lips pulled together in a tight line. His trigger finger tapped the rifle's receiver. Then like some dark smear on Spencer's soul released its hold on him, the gunman climbed from his horse and tangled his reins in the branches of a tree near the campsite. He hunkered down onto his bootheels, a few steps from Tyler and the boys. The rifle lay across his thighs, pointed away from the camp. He snapped up a piece of grass, motioned at the boys, and then tucked the blade between his lips. "See if they'll talk to you, Tyler."

The black mule brayed from the hill above. Tyler could make out Bowie and the string of horses zigzagging their way off the mountain. His mouth went dry. He pumped his hands open and shut.

Spencer sucked on the grass.

Tyler felt hands tugging on the back of his shirt. He could not make himself turn away from Spencer.

"Señor Tyler?"

It was a boy's voice. And one he recognized.

"Señor?"

Too afraid to look away from Spencer, Tyler reached back for the hand that pulled on his shirt.

"Tyler?"

Tyler remembered the pitch of the voice and glanced over his shoulder.

Shiny, dark eyes flashed up from the bantam-sized vaquero. Black hair fell across the boy's forehead.

"Eloy?" Tyler kept one eye on Spencer. "Eloy, is that you?"

"Sí, Señor."

The boy's fingers wrapped around Tyler's belt. "Tyler." And then in a string of gibberish Tyler could not understand, Eloy spewed words to the tall boy who stood nearby.

The boy bobbed his head up and down. "Señor, Eloy told me how you save his life. At the train."

"You speak English?" Tyler took a quick look back at Spencer.

Spencer's fingers drummed the side of his rifle just above the trigger.

Slowly Tyler faced the tall boy.

"*Un poquito,* Señor. At mission, I learn me a little bit." He looked past Tyler to Spencer the whole time he spoke.

"You got a name?"

"Señor?"

Tyler thought of the few words of Spanish he'd learned from Pilar at The Bootheel. *"Como — ah — como se llama?"*

The boy tapped the front of his shirt. "Paco."

"Well, Paco," Spencer scrambled to his feet. "You hear tell about a man calls hisself Dalton Fox?"

Paco bowed his head. *"Hombre muy malo."*

"What's that?" Spencer stepped up beside Tyler.

"I think he means —" Tyler put his arm over Paco's shoulder. "— he knows Fox is a bad man."

While they waited for Bowie to make it down the hill with their supplies and the other horses, Tyler took the boys to a spot

260

of shade under the piñons. In the cool air, the smell of charred wood blended with the stink of cattle and his own sweat. Spencer sat in the sun nearby. He clucked his tongue against the roof of his mouth as Tyler tried to talk with the Mexican boys.

Tyler pressed Paco to tell him more. Tyler learned that the boys had seen four riders come through the valley two days before. He thought he saw a gleam in Eloy's eyes when Paco spoke of the girl with them. Tyler's stomach jumped to think Eloy had seen Luak. But knowing she hadn't been with the men when they rode into the trap Spencer had set made him feel hollow inside.

Any time Tyler mentioned Fox's name, Paco looked at the ground and refused to say more. By waving his hands and pointing at the mountains, Tyler learned that Spencer had been right. Mesita was a long day's ride from the boy's cow camp.

A snort from the black mule let Tyler know that Bowie was close. Spencer pulled the knife from his boot top and trimmed the thorns from a mesquite branch, all the while watching the mountains to the west.

Tyler looked at Eloy and Paco. "I wish you spoke better English or I could talk better *Español*." Tyler let the words drift from his mouth without thinking.

261

Eloy sat straight up. He pointed to a single tower of blood-colored sandstone that stood alone against the slopes and angles of the desert mountains. The pinnacle stabbed at the sky like the chimney of a burned-out house.

"That rock's gotta be halfway to Mesita, Eloy." Tyler rubbed his forehead.

"Sí. *Curandera.*" Eloy buried his fingers in Paco's shirt. *"Curandera. Curandera."*

"What's Eloy jabbering about, Paco?"

The older boy looked to where Eloy pointed. He shook his head. Flies buzzed around his lips.

Eloy pulled harder on Paco's shirt.

"Paco, what's he tryin' to say?"

"Mujer —" Paco searched for the right words. "Old woman. *Muy* — " He touched two fingers on his head. "— Knows much. She live there. Speaks *Inglés.*"

"Think she could tell us somethin' 'bout Luak and Fox?"

Paco scratched at the dirt with his fingers. "Sí."

Spencer looked out to the red rock tower, then at the two boys and Tyler.

"Might be worth talkin' to this woman. Maybe she can tell us somethin'. What do you think, Spencer?"

"We can use any edge we can get. Tell

262

Paco and Eloy they're going to show us this here *Curandera.*"

The black mule brayed again. Bowie and the horses filed into the boys' camp. Spencer got to his feet and brushed the wood shavings from his pants.

Tyler stood and caught Spencer's arm as the gunman started to walk away. Tyler took a deep breath. "If I wouldn't have come after you, would you have killed those boys?"

Spencer pulled his arm away. "Tyler, you left the Krag on the mountain with Bowie. Bad mistake. You never know when you might need a gun to stop bad trouble from happening. This time you didn't need it." He ambled away to meet Bowie and then turned to Tyler. "*Curandera.* Know what that means in their language?"

"Just an old woman, I reckon."

"No, it's Mexican for a witch."

Chapter Twenty-Three

The horse Tyler rode seemed to be a sound animal but it didn't compare to the Thoroughbred Fox had stolen. Mister Hutt's rifle in the scabbard of the dead man's saddle reminded Tyler of all he'd lost. He'd memorized every muscle under the Thoroughbred's hide, the easy way the horse turned to the pull on a rein and the quick response at the first touch of his heels on its ribs.

It was Luak he fought to remember.

Five days before Fox had stolen the Thoroughbred and taken Luak. Like the spokes of a turning wagon wheel, Luak's dark eyes, the flash of her teeth, even the slightest touch of her fingers on his arm made a blur across the thoughts Tyler did not want to lose.

He expected the first cool of the evening to sizzle in the blistering afternoon like bacon grease in a campfire skillet. They'd sat in what little shade they could find until

Spencer gave the signal. Every canteen and each spare bottle were filled with water from the stream. Tyler soaked his kerchief and loose-knotted it around his neck for what little relief it might give.

The horses drank their fill. Like they knew what was ahead, the animals stood stock still, casting long shadows as Tyler strapped saddles and supplies to their backs. Even the black mule did not swing its head to nip Bowie's legs when he pulled the cinch tight.

"Like some kind of circus carnival headin'" for the next town." Spencer shook his head. "A greenhorn, two wolf-pup Mexican kids, and a still-wet-behind-the-ears ranch hand ridin' dead men's horses off to talk to a witch." He rammed his tongue into his cheek so far that Tyler thought it would tear the skin on the other side. He grabbed his saddle horn and lifted a boot to the stirrup.

"And you're leadin' the parade," Tyler said just above a whisper. "Why Spencer? I want to find Luak. Bowie's here for the adventure of it all. Since we left El Paso, I ain't figured out why you're here." His voice found strength. "Ain't about findin' your pa? Or is it?"

Spencer's hand slipped off the saddle horn. His face leaned forward until the brim of his hat touched the stirrup leather. When he looked back at Tyler, his eyes squeezed into tight slits. "Get 'em on their horses. We'll ride most of the night to stay out of the heat." He climbed onto his horse and rode off, not waiting for the others to follow.

With Spencer in the lead, the ragged line of riders followed the setting sun across the land as pitted and ruddy as a rusted ax blade. Bowie brought up the end of the file of riders, leading the black mule. Dark clouds boiled up and blotted out the heavens. The air turned thick and smelled of rain.

"Spencer, storm comin' in," Tyler shouted but the wind stole the words as they left his mouth.

A saber point of lightning ripped across the sky. In the pulse of brightness, the witch's tower seemed an arm's length away and in the next instant, farther than when they had started. Like cannons from the devil's army, the boom of thunder rolled over them. Tyler's horse's ears stood up; it tossed his head and jerked on the reins.

Tyler turned in the saddle. Eloy rode Luak's pony. In the next flash of lightning, the little boy's eyes grew to the size of tin plates. Eloy's hand touched his forehead, the center of his chest, and then each shoulder.

Paco's horse tossed its head when the thunder shook the air.

"Spencer we gotta get off this ridgeline." Tyler smacked his reins across his horse's rump.

Blue-white fiery lines spider-webbed the night. One tendril split a tree on the next hillside and the gunshot of thunder stabbed into Tyler's ears. Wind-blasted sand stung his face like a thousand cactus spines.

Horses cried out and the next boom of thunder drowned their screams.

Tyler wheeled his horse around. He kicked the frightened animal back to Eloy and Paco. "Follow me," he screamed with his face so close to Eloy's he could see the sand cling to the boy's tears. He caught the pony's bridle with his free hand and tugged the wide-eyed animal off the hilltop.

He jerked to a stop at the foot of the hill. "Get off the horse," Tyler shouted. "Lay on the ground." He pushed Eloy from his saddle.

A ragged slash of lightning backlit Spencer and his buckskin horse. Paco perched on the saddle in front of the gunman and the Mexican boy's horse yanked at the reins in Spencer's hand.

"Help. Bowie." Tyler read the words on Spencer's lips more than he heard them.

Tyler galloped his horse up to the crest of the hill. Sagebrush bent flat in the wind. Waves of dust filled the air. Bowie fought the pack animal's lead rope. The black mule reared. Canvas tore away. Cooking pots flew from the packsaddle. Bowie wrapped the lead rope around his hand and fought the thrashing mule. The animal was too strong. It jerked on its lead rope. Bowie lost his balance and tumbled from the saddle.

Hairs along Tyler's horse's mane stood straight and danced in the strange power all around them. A ghostly blue haze haloed the horse with Bowie's empty saddle. Tyler threw himself from the saddle to the ground.

A white blaze lit the sky. As fast as the fire above, the sound sucked away everything else. The skies opened and spilled icy waves until the earth ran slick.

The last of the raindrops battered his hat. The storm had passed as suddenly as it began. The moon, not quite full, made the soaked sagebrush sparkle like the flecks of mica in a noonday streambed. Bowie sat cross-legged in a rain puddle. His eyeglasses dangled from one ear and the lead rope to the mule still wrapped around his left hand. The torn packsaddle hung under the animal's belly. The mule munched on a clump of cheatgrass. It raised its head, looked at Bowie, and brayed.

"That mule saved my life." Bowie pushed his glasses back in place. "It pulled me out of my saddle just before the last lightning bolt struck." He touched his face and then raised his free hand as if to check to be sure it was still there.

Tyler lifted himself from where he had sprawled facedown on the sandy soil. The ground under his body's outline was dry. All around, water puddled at the base of the sage and cactus. He looked down the hill.

Eloy sat on Spencer's shoulders. The gunman had Paco by the hand and the reins of their three horses in the other. They climbed the hill to Tyler and Bowic.

"You still in one piece?" Spencer swung Eloy to the ground.

Tyler nodded.

"What about you, Bowie?"

"Lightning killed my horse." Bowie pulled on the mule's rope. His lifeless horse sprawled in the sage at the top of the hill. Steam rose from its scorched fur.

"We got other horses." Spencer stepped

closer to where Bowie sat. "You wouldn't be talkin' if you was hurt. Now let's gather what we can and get ready to ride."

Tyler stood to his knees. "We need to find the other horses and get a fire goin'. We're soaked. We need to dry out."

"The horses didn't go far. Yours and the other pack animal are at the bottom of this arroyo. As for the fire —" He jerked a thumb over his shoulder. "— like she knew we was comin' and put up a signal."

The *Curandera*'s rocky tower built a black outline on the western horizon. At its base, a fire taller than one of Mister Hutt's barns blazed the night sky.

"Believe in witches, Tyler?" Spencer hooked a stirrup on his saddle horn and tightened the cinch around his horse's middle. "Might have been her that sent the storm. Now she lit a fire to show us the way. Let's go see what she has to say about Dalton Fox."

"And Luak." Tyler climbed to his feet.

Spencer turned his head from Tyler. "Bowie get your saddle off the dead horse. I'll catch another one for you."

Bowie wiped the mud from his hands. "I'll ride the mule."

Tyler clamped his teeth shut to fight the

trembles that coursed through his body. His rain-drenched shirt clung to his chest and each ripple of breeze found a way through to his bare skin underneath. Just hours before, he'd prayed for relief from the blistering afternoon sun. Now he'd trade his next full meal for sunlight, no matter how hot.

The two Mexican boys couldn't hide their shivers. They shared a saddle. Eloy's arms wrapped around Paco and even in the little light of the false dawn, Tyler could see his lips had turned as blue as a plum.

Any other time, Tyler would have laughed at the way that Bowie's legs nearly dragged the ground on each side of the black mule. The tall man jostled from one side to the other with each step the animal took. Bowie's back looked as stiff and clumsy as Tyler's fingers felt around the rope tied to the packhorse.

Only Spencer sat stone solid in his saddle. Tyler never saw a tremor of cold shake the gunman's shoulders. Why should it? Tyler was sure the gunman felt nothing.

Over his shoulder and far behind the storm that had killed Bowie's horse, a lightning bolt knifed the sky with a ragged slice of electricity. He started to count and reached forty-two before the grumble of the thunder found them.

Riding the sound, a bat swooped through the gray light just a hand-width from Tyler's horse's nose. It dodged near Spencer, no doubt filling its stomach with bugs stirred by the storm, and disappeared into the tops of the sage.

Spencer raised his hand. "Cougar tracks," he pointed at marks in the trail just where Tyler had his last glimpse of the bat. "Came through after the rain. Hold your horses up tight. This wet brush will hold the cat's smell. Bowie, watch that mule." He rode on toward the witch's tower.

The line of riders stopped on the top of a hill. A hovel, built of stones the color of the desert, nestled at the base of the chimney rock. The little hut seemed to have grown on the spot where no hands could have built it. The glow from *Curandera*'s fire danced off the base of the pinnacle. Yellow flames died away over the glowing red coals. Waves of heat Tyler could feel a quarter mile away enticed the chilled riders with a promise of warmth.

Nothing moved in the shadowy scene. A sweet aroma of cooking food floated on the still air.

Spencer studied each shadow and rock. "Ain't a tree big enough to shade a jackrabbit anywhere around, but she built a fire we could see from five miles." He looked at Tyler. "Careful from here on out." He touched his rifle in its scabbard. "Be ready."

Paco's nose quivered at the smell of food. He kicked his horse and the two boys galloped toward the witch's home. The black mule snorted and pulled to follow, but Bowie pulled up.

Spencer held his horse back. "Maybe that witch is countin' on us hurryin' in without thinkin'. We'll walk 'em in. Bowie, hold tight to that mule."

A shadow that Tyler was sure was a rock came to life. Hands reached out and offered a bowl to Eloy and Paco. The boys climbed from the horse and sat near the fire dipping their hands into the pot. Tyler rested his hand on the Krag's buttstock. The shadow became a woman. Bent and old. The gray of her hair blended with the dawn light.

They stopped their horses where the circle of firelight touched the last dark of night.

"Ma'am," Spencer called out. "The boys there say you speak English. That so?"

The *Curandera* slipped a shawl from her shoulders up over her head and wrapped the ends over her shriveled chest. "You have traveled a great distance and have far to go.

Come eat."

Spencer pulled up on his reins until his horse stepped back from the light. His hand wrapped around his rifle. "Gracias, but we are here to ask your help. Tell us what we need, we'll water our horses and move on."

"You want me to tell you about the man called Dalton Fox."

Tyler clamped his hand on his saddle horn to stay on the horse. His legs were weak from the long night. At Fox's name, the shivers that had left him shook his body again.

"What can you tell us 'bout Fox?" Spencer stayed at the dark edge.

"We will talk of Fox —" The woman limped toward them. "— after you eat the food I have made for you."

Cold stabbed Tyler's back. The woman turned toward him. Fine lines wrinkled her face. Yellowed teeth touched pale lips. Eyes that could see through skin and bone and find the thoughts in a man's mind before they began to form searched his face. "I knew you would come, Tyler."

His shivers stopped. His face burned as hot as the red coals of her fire. "You know my name?"

She smiled and brushed the twigs and dirt from her frayed dress. "Eat. You are tired

274

from the storm. Rest. Tell the others to come with you." She walked to the fire and touched Eloy's head as a grandmother might touch her grandson.

CHAPTER TWENTY-FOUR

Three half-grown, half-wild dogs lounged at
the edge of the firelight. Like hungry wolves,
they watched the newcomers fill clay bowls
from the steaming iron pot that hung over
the red coals. The hot stew stung Tyler's
fingers as he scooped it into his mouth.

The old woman's stooped shoulders and
crooked legs cast a long shadow as the sun
rose. She leaned on a twisted piece of piñon
she used as her walking stick. She stroked
Eloy's hair and watched the men eat. Tyler's skin prickled each time her stare fell
on him.

"Mighty good eating, ma'am." Bowie
dipped his bowl in the pot for the third
time. "Sweet tasting. This venison?" He
raised his eyebrows. "Deer meat?"

She pulled her shawl tight around her
shoulders. *"Perro."*

Tyler thought of the Spanish words Pilar
had taught him. He looked at the dogs.

Bowie sniffed at the steam rising from the kettle. "*Perro,* you say. Smells almost as good as it tastes."

"Dig deep." She pointed at the pot. "Puppy in the bottom."

Bowie shrugged his shoulder and then filled his bowl. He took his place by the fire next to Tyler. He filled his mouth with a piece of meat from the thick soup.

Tyler nudged Bowie. "*Perro* means dog." He lifted his plate towards the half-wolf pups that watched them. One's mouth stretched open in a yawn.

Bowie lowered the bowl to his lap. His Adam's apple moved up and down behind the skin in his throat. "I have a spaniel back in Michigan."

Tyler licked the edge of his bowl. "Don't reckon this is him."

Spencer moved from where he sat. "I'll have more." He lowered his plate into the stewpot. "Bowie, you better eat your fill. No tellin' when we'll get hot food again."

The steaming liquid dribbled from the bowl's rim onto Bowie's pants. The muscles along his jaws quivered. "I've had plenty."

When Spencer finished, he set his plate in the dirt beside the firepit. "Tyler, best check on the horses." Spencer picked up his rifle and rested its butt on the ground between his knees. He drew a slow circle on the inside of his cheek with the tip of his tongue the way he did when he was thinking, then looked at the old woman.

Tyler shook his head. "Let Bowie or one of the boys do it. I want to hear what she has to say. She might be able to tell me if Luak's —" If the old woman truly had some sort of powers, Tyler wasn't sure he wanted to hear what she might tell him.

Spencer tapped his thumb on his rifle. "All we need her to tell us is what she knows for sure 'bout Fox. No magic. Not what she thinks. Just what she knows for damn certain."

"Still, I'm stayin'." Tyler set his jaw. He plucked a pebble from the ground and tossed it at the boys. "Eloy, check the horses."

One of the old woman's calloused feet stepped near the bright orange glow at the edge of the fire. "You will not talk of me like I am not here." Though there was anger in the words, her voice was calm.

For the first time since she had said his name, Tyler found the courage to look at the *Curandera*. Blotchy skin, as thin as the pages in his Bible, draped her bones like warm candle wax. She gathered the loose strands of her filthy hair in gnarled fingers and tucked them under her shawl. The dog stew stained the front of her dress along with soot, dirt, and marks that had to be blood.

Though her lips smiled, her eyes showed no feeling. They were as yellow as the sunrise and the pupils were not round. Sharp-ended ovals, like a cat's, stared at him without blinking.

She turned so that she faced the morning sun and tilted her head back. The shawl fell from the top of her head. Her arms reached out. She held the palms of her hands up to the morning and let the new sun wash over her. Her lips moved and she spoke in a language Tyler had never heard.

When she finished her prayer, she knelt and took a pinch of ash from the fire, and tossed it into the air. She smoothed her wild hair. "I knew Tyler would come with the man they call Big Shoulders. The birds whispered it to me." She raised a bony hand and pointed at Bowie. "Him, One Who Follows."

Bowie's body jerked and the dog stew spilled into the firepit. He grabbed for the dish. His fingers grazed the still-hot coals and he pulled them back. He shook his hand and touched his fingers to his mouth.

The old woman's unfeeling smile tightened the wrinkles on her face. "You have done well to come so far. Before two more suns, you will see the things that brought you."

Tyler swallowed hard. He glanced at Spencer.

The gunman shook his head. "Ma'am, no disrespect, but we just came to ask about a man called Dalton Fox. Is he in Mesita?"

The woman raised her hand. "What do you do when the ghosts call your name in the night?"

The color leaked out of Spencer's face.

The *Curandera* steadied her steps with her stick and moved until she stood near the fire where Spencer sat. "I see your father in your face. Some nights he calls to me. I could not help him." She tapped the stick on Spencer's boot. "The flood will show you what you need."

Spencer pulled his feet away from the woman. He wet his lips with his tongue. "I just want to know about Fox."

The woman's eyes flashed in the sunlight. "Satan planted a seed dipped in blood and Dalton Fox grew up from it. He has taken the church in the village as his own. He spits on all that is holy. All the village is in fear of him. He takes their daughters. The lucky ones he sells as slaves." She drew in a ragged

280

breath. "The man called Villa is away now, with many riders. You will find the tracks of their horses along the trail to Mesita. Before you go to find Fox, send the little boys away."

Spencer nodded. "Tyler, give one of the horses to the boys. Send 'em back to their cattle. Tend to ours. I want to ride on."

Tyler climbed to his feet. He touched the woman's shawl. "Ma'am, there was a girl with us. Indian girl. Named Luak. Fox and his men." The words stuck in his throat. "They took her."

Spencer sided close to Tyler. "The horses."

"She might know something."

"She'll fill your head with fool talk. If we find tracks on the trail like she said, she told us what we need to know. Ain't no way she could know anything about the girl." He pushed his next words through his teeth, "Get the horses." Spencer buried his fingers in Tyler's shirtsleeve. "Now."

Tyler looked at the old woman.

Spencer pulled him by the shirt. "Tyler," he barked.

A scorpion dashed across the sand at their feet. The witch pinned it to the ground with the splintered end of her walking stick. Slowly she bent over and pinched the struggling bug between her twisted fingers. Its tiny feet clawed at the air. The woman flicked her wrist and tossed the insect onto the coals of the dying fire.

"Tyler. The horses." Spencer pushed him down the trail to where the animals were tied. He reached down and grabbed Bowie's hand and pulled him to his feet. Spencer backed away from the woman with his finger close to his Winchester's trigger.

Tyler helped Eloy onto the horse behind Paco. Spencer caught Paco by the front of his shirt and pulled the boy's face close to his. "You ride back to your cattle and never, never come back here. You hear me?"

Paco moved his head up and down. Spencer shoved him back into the saddle and slapped the horse across the rump. The horse with the little vaqueros trotted away into the rolling desert.

Spencer caught his buckskin's reins from Tyler's fist and climbed into the saddle. Bowie fell in behind him on the black mule. Tyler followed on his horse, leading Luak's pony.

The *Curandera* waited beside the trail near the hovel that was her house. Spencer walked his horse by her. Bowie turned his head as the mule passed.

She raised her gnarled hand to Tyler. *"Un*

momento." He pulled his horse to a stop.

The crone's twisted fingers plucked a cactus flower from the ground where Tyler had seen none before. Her cupped hands reached up and placed the blossom in Tyler's. The *Curandera*'s amber eyes stared into his. "She love you."

A cactus needle pierced his glove and bit into the soft flesh at the base of his thumb. A drop of his blood seeped into the leather next to the cactus blossom in his palm. The flower was as blue as the sky. As blue as a cornflower.

The words the old woman said stung Tyler's heart. He'd seen the words in books but never thought he'd claim them for his own. "Luak loves me?" he whispered so softly he didn't know if the witch would hear.

The old woman pushed strands of greasy hair out of her face. Her voice changed. Not the garbled words he heard from her before. "She loved you, *muchacho.*"

He crushed the flower in his fist. The thorn bit deeper into his hand. He put his heels into his horse's sides and galloped away from the old woman.

Each slap of his horse's hooves on the hard-packed trail batted the *Curandera*'s words across his brain. When he turned to look back, the witch was gone and a mountain lion slipped into the sagebrush where she had stood.

Tyler caught Spencer and Bowie at the top of the next hill and jerked his horse to a stop in front of Spencer. "Tell me about Luak," he shouted into the gunman's face.

"I don't know what you're talking about." Spencer reined his horse to pass.

Tyler moved to block him. "Ever since we killed those men in the canyon and found her pony, you've been keepin' somethin' from me. What do you know, Spencer?"

Spencer looked back to where the rock tower stabbed the sky. He touched the back of his hand to his mouth. "Followed their tracks up that canyon, 'bout a mile or more from where we cut 'em down. Found where —" Spencer raised his head and looked Tyler in the eye. "Wrapped her in that dead man's bedroll and buried her with my own two hands."

Every thought but one emptied from Tyler's mind. Like the desert wind searching for a place to end, currents of dread funneled between muscles and skin until they seeped from his mouth. "Did they —" Tyler fought to find the next words. "Was she —"

"Long as you live, never ask me more. Long as you live."

Tyler felt the horse beneath his saddle draw air into its lungs. The smell of mesquite filled his nose. Bitter dirt clung to his tongue. When he closed his eyes, a blue ribbon danced in Luak's shiny black hair. When they opened, Spencer stared back at him.

Tyler threw himself from his horse's back. His hands clamped around Spencer's throat. His fury pushed Spencer from his saddle and the two tumbled onto the ground. Horses screamed. Tyler's fist cracked Spencer's face. He cocked his arm and slammed his hand down again. Dust from frightened hooves swirled.

"Why, Spencer?" Tyler brought his fist down again. "Why didn't you tell me?" Tears as hot as the red coals on the witch's fire seared his eyes. Through that mist, Tyler saw no pain in Spencer's face. No fists fought back. Tyler pushed up and stood.

He stumbled to Luak's pony and tore the canvas away from the packsaddle and dug into the pouch. His hands found the gun belt Spencer had taken from one of the men they had killed in the valley. Tyler buckled it around his narrow hips and turned to face Spencer.

The wind held its breath. There were no sounds but the ones the horses made. The scrape of hooves as they shifted on the sandy soil, the creak of leather, and the clink of bits and buckles.

Spencer lifted himself onto one elbow. His tongue wiped away drops of blood from his split lip. He raised to his knees and the tips of his fingers found the hilt of the knife in his boot top.

Tyler mopped at his eyes. His voice quivered like the breeze across the sage. "Tell me what we have to do to kill Fox. I'll follow you into hell to do it."

CHAPTER TWENTY-FIVE

Spencer let the knife slip back into its sheath. His tongue touched the inside of one cheek and then the other. He watched for Tyler's next move, but the boy's hand never reached for the six-gun. Instead, Tyler's shoulders shook like aspen leaves, and rivulets of dirty tears streaked his face. There was no dishonor, no signs of fear, only hate. Hate that Spencer could mold.

"You'll do as I say." Spencer stood. "No questions. Do what I say, when I say. And if hell is where Fox lives, then hell is where we're bound."

Tyler bobbed his head up and down.

Spencer turned to where Bowie still sat the mule. Sunlight flashed off the gunmetal in the tall man's hand. "Which one of us were you goin' to use that on?"

Bowie looked down at the pistol he held. "All you had was that knife in your boot and Tyler had a gun. I think if it came to that, I'd have shot you."

Spencer nodded. "Right choice."

Bowie swung his long leg over the mule's back and stepped to the ground. He tucked his pistol into the front pocket of his trousers and wiped his hands down the front of his pants.

Spencer dabbed his bloody lips with his shirtsleeve. "Saddle up. I want to see if there're tracks along the wash like the old woman said."

Tyler tipped the canteen to his lips. He held the warm water in his mouth and let it trickle down his throat a drop at a time. He lifted the canteen to his ear and sloshed the water back and forth to hear how much was left. Less than half-full and no telling when they'd find the next water. If it came down to it, the horses would get the water before the men. And how far would the water in their canteens go between three horses and a mule?

Bowie's face was flush-white. Blotchy red lines streaked his cheekbones and blood from his cracked lips mixed with the dirt on his chin.

Tyler held out the canteen.

Bowie shook his head. "We need to save all we can."

Like gray ash on brimstone, the dust raised in puffs under the horses' hooves. Each breath Tyler sucked in was like lifting the anvil Mister Hutt used for horseshoeing off his chest.

But they followed Spencer.

A game trail led off the mesa top to the dry wash the *Curandera* had pointed out. The shade from the high rim blocked the midday sun but none of its heat. Tongues of hot air licked away the sweat before it could seep out on Tyler's skin.

Spencer raised his hand. Bowie pulled up on the black mule. Tyler stopped his horse. Spencer climbed down. "Tyler, tell me what you make of this." He pointed to the marks in the dirt.

Tyler swung off his horse and dropped onto one knee to study the tracks. "Like the old woman said. Riders through here yesterday, maybe the day before. Headed away from Mesita."

"How many?"

Tyler stood and walked up the wash a few steps. "Guessing ten, maybe more."

"Means ten less with Fox."

Tyler slipped his fingers under the gun belt and lifted up on the weight of the Colt on his hip. "Fox's all I care about."

He went to his horse. "We best hurry."

"No." Spencer tucked the toe of his boot in his stirrup. "No hurryin'. Fox knows we're comin'. He wants us to. That's why he tried to hang you. So he'd be sure I'd come after him."

Tyler touched the rough scab on his throat. He counted the tracks in the dirt again. The shadow of Bowie on the mule darkened the ground. Bowie lifted an arm. His hand pointed up the trail towards Mesita.

"Spencer," Bowie's voice croaked. "Rider on the trail."

Waves of heat rising from the desert blurred all but the dark shape of a man on a horse. Tyler guessed he was a quarter mile away. Maybe more. The rider pulled his horse to a stop and then whirled it around. Sunlight flashed off his spurs as he kicked the horse to a full gallop.

Spencer had the big Winchester in his hands before Tyler realized it. The gunman flopped onto his belly in the dry creek bed. He jacked open the rifle and checked to be sure there was a cartridge in the chamber. He tossed his hat aside and clamped his cheek along the rifle stock.

Rider and horse reached the top of the hill, skylined in the second of time before they would disappear over the ridge. Spencer's rifle boomed. Gunsmoke lifted in the still air. The man's arms stretched away from his sides like the figure on a crucifix. A second later Tyler heard the slap of a bullet hitting flesh. The rider toppled from his saddle.

"Got 'em. Better'n four hundred yards," Bowie whispered.

Spencer shook his head. "I was aimin' for the horse."

"Huh?"

"Dead man can't tell us more 'bout Fox."

Bowie covered his mouth with the back of his hand. He swayed like his long legs might forget to hold him up. "You killed a man. And by *accident*. 'Cause you missed the horse? You don't even know if he's one of Fox's."

Spencer stood up. "Only someone up to no good would be travelin' these parts in the heat of the day."

"We're here." Bowie wiped at his eyes.

"And we're on the way to kill a man." Spencer tucked his rifle into its scabbard. "C'mon, he might not be dead yet."

Bowie's lips trembled. "What will you do then? Beat him until he tells you what you want to hear?"

Tyler handed Bowie the reins to his mule. "If we have to."

Bowie's mouth dropped open and he stared at Tyler. "Do you hear what you're saying?"

"Bowie, this don't concern you." Tyler gathered the reins to his horse. "Spencer told you, we'll give you what supplies we can spare. Take the mule and get on outta here. Your choice."

Bowie drew in a deep breath. "I'll stay."

Spencer moved closer. He never took his eyes off of Tyler but spoke to Bowie, "You throw in with us, what I say goes."

"I heard you."

It was every bit of six hundred yards to where the rider fell. Spencer's bullet had torn through the center of his back. Inch-long, black ants swarmed over the bloody gore on the man's chest. The insects scurried away carrying bits of splintered bone and pieces of pink lung. Others had found their way to his eyes and lips.

Tyler recognized the bent nose and its shiny scar. "I know him."

"What?" Spencer dug into the dead man's pockets.

"He was there when they took Luak."

"You sure?"

"Fox called him Natalia, I think. Said he was an Apache. He could talk with Luak."

He touched the man's leg with the toe of his boot. "He tied the rope to the tree when they left me to hang." Tyler wanted to feel the hate. But he was numb inside. He held his hands out and looked at them. Not a tremble. As steady as a stone.

CHAPTER TWENTY-SIX

Spencer slung the wet-sided canteens over the dead branches of the paloverde tree that sheltered the place he'd chosen to camp. Thirsty dirt caught any drip and the dry air turned wet spots to clods of clay.

"Found fresh lion tracks between here and the horses." He held out one canteen to Bowie. "I want Tyler to stay with the stock 'til dawn. Boy's got a way with animals. He can keep 'em calm. Last thing we need is for them to put up a ruckus and let Fox and his know we're close." He looked out into the gray light settling over the desert. "Where's the boy?"

"Said he was gonna sneak out on that ridge and watch the village."

"I told you both to stay put."

"I tried to stop —"

"Damn him." Spencer squinted to where Tyler had left his saddle and gear. "He took that Krag rifle." Spencer snatched the

294

canteen back from Bowie, filled his mouth, and spat it on the ground.

Bowie got up from the ground and faced Spencer. "He's becoming just like you."

"What?"

"Since you told him about Luak, the only thing he sees is Fox in his rifle sights. You're going to turn that boy into a killer." Bowie tightened his face as if he was waiting for a snake to strike. "Like you."

Spencer bent over and stripped off his spurs. "C'mon." When he stood he turned up the collar on his jacket.

"What about that lion and the horses?"

"Not gettin' Tyler killed is more important than horses."

Like a giant had stretched his hand over the wrinkles in dirty bedclothes, the ridges and gullies spread out before him. Tyler found Luak's village at the web where the monster's thumb and first finger met. Woodsmoke drifted up the hill to the clump of spiny cactus he hid behind.

In the flat light before sunrise, three dozen adobe huts clustered around a larger stone building with a bell tower and cross. Candles flickered in the church and the rest of the village sat dark. A single figure crossed from the church to a well at the center square. The man leaned his rifle on the low stone wall and drew up a bucket to drink from. Tyler dipped his head down even though he knew the man could never spot him on the hill.

Goats and sheep crowded together in their corrals for the night. A horse nickered. The man at the well turned and waved. A shadow on the roof of the church became a man with a rifle in the crook of his elbow. Tyler's pulse throbbed in his temples and his breath came in short sups of air. The wooden doors of the church swung open. A blur of white stumbled into the dirt street and fell. Short snaps of a man's voice carried on the still air. Tyler squinted and willed that his eyes would pull together what little light the dawn allowed. The white-draped figure lifted itself and a cascade of hair, so black that it made the darkness gray, haloed a girl's head.

The man's voice barked again.

Tyler lifted the Krag rifle to his cheek and watched Dalton Fox step into a slash of candlelight. Tyler squinted through the V-shaped notch of the rifle's back sight until the bead on the front post blotted out Fox's tiny figure so far away. It would be a long shot. Farther than when Spencer killed the man on his horse.

Fox stepped to the girl and buried his fist in her hair. She squealed with pain. Fox and the man at the well laughed.

"Luak?" Tyler's lips made the word. Spencer had lied to him. Or he was wrong? It was another girl he had buried in the canyon. All Indian girls looked alike to Spencer. He'd said it himself.

Fox pulled the girl back into the church building.

A rooster crowed.

A gloved hand clamped over Tyler's mouth. The rifle wrenched from his hands.

"Damn it, Tyler," hissed in his ears.

"I saw her, Spencer. Luak's still alive. It musta been another girl you found."

"Hush." Spencer raised onto his knees and peeked over the tips of the cactus. Tyler struggled to sit up, but Spencer pushed him back to the ground.

"I saw her. She's in the church with Fox."

"Keep your mouth shut." Spencer's teeth flashed in the low light.

"It was Luak, I tell ya."

Spencer caught Tyler's throat with one hand and squeezed. He leaned in until the tip of his nose touched Tyler's. "Not one more sound." He shoved Tyler back. "Take your rifle," he whispered, "belly crawl down

297

that hill 'til you find Bowie. Don't look back. I'll be right behind you."

"Bowie, I saw Luak." Tyler dragged himself into a clump of twisted sage at the bottom of the hill. Cool night air settled all around him and shadows from the ridge held the night's darkness. Above them, the first rays of the dawn sun threw bright, spidery cracks in the fading night.

Tyler clutched Bowie by the shirt and pulled him up onto his knees. "She's in the church with Fox."

Spencer grabbed Tyler's shoulders and sat him back on the ground. "What you saw was some Indian girl Fox took up with. That old woman told us as much."

Tyler refused to let go of Bowie's shirt. "No, it was her. Just Fox and two others. We can sneak in there now and get her back."

"Keep your mouth shut and listen." Spencer pushed Tyler down again. "You saw Fox and two? How many didn't you see? How many uncorked a jug of mescal and are half-drunk somewhere? How many in the church you couldn't see?"

Tyler shook his head.

"Boy, you want it to be Luak. It's not. I swear it to you." Spencer let go of Tyler's shoulders and looked back up the hill. "I'm guessin' that Villa and the bunch the woman told us about is out looking for the men we killed. By now they will have followed them to the canyon and found the bodies. They'll cast about for our tracks. They're a day behind now. If they light out for here, they could show anytime."

Spencer caught Tyler by the chin and lifted his face to his. "I want you to think hard. Everything you saw from up there, remember it. Every part. Sun's going to be up in no more than half an hour. We're going to sneak back to our camp. When we get there, you're going to draw me a map of all that you saw."

With the tip of his jackknife in the dirt, Tyler sketched the village square, the huts and corrals, the well where the man drew the bucket of water, and the church. When he finished drawing the streets and paths of the village, he stabbed the blade into the spot where he saw Fox grab the girl by the hair.

He jammed his eyes shut and tried to remember every detail of the girl he'd seen.

Luak.

It had to be Luak.

Spencer picked up a stick and in long motions drew the hills and draws around the town. He scratched an "x" where they were camped. "If we're going to do this, it has to be tonight. Wait any longer and we risk Villa ridin' back." He tapped the stick on Tyler's chest. "No more goin' off on your own. We got one chance. You have to follow what I say or you're apt to get Bowie and me killed. You, too. And Fox'll be free to do what he pleases. Got it?"

Tyler nodded.

"Say it."

Tyler rocked his face up and down. "I'll do what you say 'til Fox is dead. Then I need to be sure. Sure about Luak."

CHAPTER TWENTY-SEVEN

Beneath the cartridge boxes, at the bottom of the dead man's saddlebags, Tyler found his Bible. He straightened the wrinkled pages and picked grains of sand from the bindings. Bowie offered the last scraps of their jerky but Tyler refused to eat.

Spencer got up from his spot of shade and hunkered down on his heels over the map Tyler had drawn in the dirt. The muscles in the gunman's jaws knotted and relaxed as he schooled himself on the lines and scratches. He raised his head and shut his eyes as if he were forcing every part of the map into his mind.

Tyler looked down at the book in his hands. The Lord of the Old Testament had sent the Israelite armies to smite the Philistines. Fox was a black sinner for sure, but Spencer was no prophet leading an army of God to cleanse the wicked.

Tyler closed his eyes. "Luak," he breathed

her name out, but his new hatred blocked his prayers before they reached Heaven.

Morning sun inched to noon. The afternoon blazed hellfire hot. They drank from their canteens and waited.

Gray clouds boiled up as the sun reached the western horizon.

"Storm comin'," Spencer said and he laid his kerchief out on the dirt in front of him. He took an oily rag from his saddlebags and wiped down his big Winchester. He dumped out a box of the .405 cartridges and, one by one, ran the cloth over each. When he had finished he loaded his rifle and filled his vest pockets with the remaining rounds. "Get your rifle, Tyler. It's time."

Tyler stood and strapped the gun belt around his waist and picked up the Krag.

Spencer rested the Winchester on his shoulder. "Let's go over this one more time." His tongue jabbed the inside of his cheek and Spencer knelt by the map in the dirt. "Bowie, you're gonna sit tight. Check that pocket watch of yours; when midnight comes, get the horses saddled and cross these two ridges." He pointed to the marks he'd drawn. "Picket the horses in the bottom and slip out on this finger of high ground." Spencer scooped up a handful of sand and let it sift through his fingers onto the place he wanted Bowie to wait. "Find a place to hide yourself where you can see the village and the trail in."

Spencer rubbed the dirt onto his pants. "When Tyler and me have done what we intend to, we'll find you and the horses and hightail it out of here. If you so much as see Villa and the others —"

Bowie raised a hand. "I know, use my rifle. Start shooting to warn you. Get the horses and meet you on the south side, at the last row of houses." He touched the map.

Spencer nodded. "You know your part."

Bowie reached out his hand and took Spencer's in his. "I'm not sure what to say, so I'll say good luck."

Tyler held out his hand.

Bowie took it in both of his. "Be careful, as foolish as that sounds."

Tyler and Spencer slipped away into the desert twilight.

Angry clouds blotted out the stars. Spencer raised his hand, dropped onto his knees, and crawled to the rim of the last hill. He motioned for Tyler to kneel beside him.

The village sat dark except for the sputter of candlelight that seeped from the windows of the church. The sounds of animals and the voices of men carried up on the wind.

"Tyler." Spencer's hand snaked out through inky darkness and tapped on the Krag's stock. "You sure about this? I can go in alone. You can find Bowie and wait 'til it's over."

"No. I need to find Luak."

Spencer wrapped his fingers over Tyler's grip on the rifle. "Tyler, sometimes a man can want somethin' too much. It blinds him to everything else. It was her I buried. Nothin' will change that."

Tyler shook his hand free. "I said I'm goin'."

The tips of yucca blades rustled in the wind and the whiff of sheep and goats drifted up from the village corrals. Moonlight leaked through a crack in the clouds.

Spencer took his hand away from the rifle. "I wanted to use your hate for my doings. Most likely, Fox caused my father . . ." His hands trembled. "I thought killin' Fox would bring me closer to the man I never knew." He looked out into the night. "Now I'm not so sure."

"Are you afraid, Spencer? You never back down from nothin'."

Spencer pushed his face close to Tyler's. The boy's eyes peeled wide. "I am afraid. And you better be, too." He pushed the

304

words through his teeth. "Men will die tonight. We might be among 'em. Listen to me. All my life I never answered to no one. Never stepped aside for no man. Never been tied down." He drew in a deep breath. "And never had nothin', 'cept the clothes I have on and this Winchester to call my own." The rifle felt heavy in his hand. "If I tell you I decided not to do this?"

Lightning ripped the sky and the boom of its thunder rolled in from far away.

Tyler hiked the gun belt up his skinny hips. "I'll do it myself."

Spencer's chin dropped onto his chest. He took his father's Colt from his jacket pocket. His thumb rubbed the Bootheel brand burned into its grip and he wished he had never come to Virgil Hutt's ranch. He tucked the revolver into his belt. "Get over the ridge as quick as you can so they don't see our silhouettes. Keep low and do what I tell you."

The first icy raindrop splattered on Tyler's cheek. Two more thunked his hat. Then, as if an ocean in the heavens opened, great sheets of water tumbled to earth and splashed up from the ground. Tyler's boots slid on the slippery clay. He flattened his back against the wall of an adobe hut next to where Spencer stood.

Across from the shadows where they hid, a woman's face, wrinkled and dark, showed in a window. Tyler sucked in a breath and held it.

The woman wrapped a frayed blanket over her shoulders. Lightning snapped. She found a cross on a loop of silver chain around her neck, touched it to her lips, and disappeared into the darkness of her little home.

Beads of water spilled off the brim of Spencer's hat. He dodged to the corner of the next hut. Tyler tensed and then threw himself after Spencer.

It was Spencer's plan for Tyler to hide in the corral at the edge of the village square. From there, Tyler could see the front doors to the church building and the rifleman on the roof. Spencer would creep to the other side of the square. On his signal, Tyler would throw open the gates to the corral, fire his pistol, and stampede the horses into the plaza. Spencer said the men would come out of the church and flatten their backs against the wall so they'd be hard to pick out in the dark. Fox would come out last.

Tyler was to find cover and stay still. When the men moved to gather the horses, Spencer would pick out Fox and cut him down.

Tyler was to keep an eye out for the guard on the roof. With Fox dead, Spencer would open up on the others. Tyler was to join the cross fire.

Tyler hugged the Krag rifle to his chest. Spencer's plan would work. The men they killed in the canyon had done just what he had said. Spencer knew how men that killed as a part of their living would act. He was one of them. Before the night was over, Tyler would be one too.

The boy flopped under the bottom rail of the corral. He grabbed mashed handfuls of hay, horse droppings, and mud mixed with animal piss to inch through the feet of the horses. At the gate post, he mopped his face with the sleeve of his jacket. He perched his rifle against the pole and trained it on the church.

Tyler saw only the smallest glimpse in the next flash of linghtning. Spencer darted from the well to the buildings on the other side of the plaza. Before the thunder stole it away, Tyler heard the notes of a girl's voice from the church.

He lifted himself on his elbows, straining to hear more. Every part of the night dripped with shiny rain. Tyler's fingers reached up and fumbled for the thongs that tied the gate.

The church doors swung open and the outline of a man stepped out onto the portico. A match flared. The man's hands cupped the flame to a cigarette in his lips.

Dalton Fox sucked the flame into his tobacco.

Rainwater sloshed from Spencer's hat.

Fox turned. A column on the portico blocked Spencer's rifle sights from all but Fox's legs. Spencer lifted his face from the rifle's stock and looked across the plaza.

Take the shot, Tyler. End it now.

Tyler let his arm drop from the leather straps that held the gate closed. He raised the Krag rifle a fraction at a time.

Fox leaned against the building. An orange dot glowed at his lips. He stuck one hand out into the stream of water that spilled from the roof and let the liquid dance through his fingers.

Tyler's thumb flipped the safety catch on his rifle. He gritted his teeth and took up the slack on the trigger. Wind-driven rainwater flowed down his forehead into his eyes. Tyler blinked it away.

Spencer rose from his knees to his feet, hugging his face to the corner of the rough adobe building, straining to find a clean shot at Fox. A spear point of electricity arced the sky.

Caught in the space between the brightness and the thunder's crash, Spencer saw a man in the bell tower aim his rifle at Tyler in the corral. Spencer threw the Winchester to his shoulder and fired at the man.

White flame flared from the muzzle. Gunshot blended with thunder. Lead slapped the church bell. A ghostly gong vibrated through the air.

Fox dove through the church doors. Spencer's next shot splintered wood.

The rifleman on the roof leaned out of the bell tower, rifle pointing at the flash from Spencer's gun. Tyler found the man's back in his sights and jerked the trigger.

Black blood splattered from the man's shoulders. The rifle pitched from his hands. A lifeless body slumped onto the wet roof tiles.

Tyler threw open the gate. Terrified horses scrambled over each other fighting to escape through the opening. Globs of mud, tossed from hooves, filled the air. Tyler grabbed the halter of one of the fleeing horses. The animal jerked him from his feet and dragged him through the rain-drenched streets into the plaza. The Krag slipped from his hand. Tyler let go of the horse and slid behind the low stone wall at the well.

He jerked the Colt from the holster on his hip and pointed it at the doors to the church.

"Stay down," Spencer yelled at Tyler.

Wanting to draw the attention of the men in the church, he jumped the broken fence that surrounded the little graveyard next to the church. He dove into the mud behind a weathered wooden cross.

The church doors opened. A shotgun blasted. Inches from his face the top of the cross exploded into an angry swarm of splinters.

Two shots snapped from Tyler's pistol. The man with the shotgun fell limp on the portico.

Lightning and its thunder came as one. The crash shook the buildings and opened the clouds. Hailstones raked the village like pistol bullets.

Tyler leaped from behind the well and charged through the curtain of falling ice for the church. He kicked the shotgun out of the dead man's hand and threw himself through the doors.

Spencer clawed in the mud to get to his feet.

Above the din of the falling hail, a gunshot split the night. A burst of light pulsed at every window of the church.

Spencer slipped and fell to his knees. "No-o-o, Tyler."

Candle flames laid flat by the wind through the open door painted pale swirls on the church walls. Burnt gunpowder hung thick in the chapel's air. Tyler's pistol slipped from his fingers and fell to the floor.

An Indian girl cried.

Overturned pews, broken tables, and a bullet-scarred cross showed Fox's desecration of the holy place. Dalton Fox sprawled at the altar. Blood pooled beneath his lifeless shell.

Spencer leaned his Winchester on the basin where the village churchgoers would stop to dip their fingers in the Holy Water. He picked up Tyler's revolver and tucked it in the waist of his muddy pants.

"I killed him, Spencer." Tyler's arms hung limp at his sides.

Slowly, Spencer lifted his hand to touch the boy's shoulder. Tyler turned away.

The girl huddled in the corner of the church

on a pallet of filthy blankets. Broken bottles and torn clothes lay all around. She flinched when Tyler touched her hair and tried to pull away.

"It's over. He'll never hurt you again," Tyler whispered. His fingers touched her lightly as if he were trying to whisk a shadow away. She lifted her face and he caught her tears on his fingertips. Coal-black hair fell over her dark eyes.

"Como se llama?"

"Isabel."

"Familia?"

"Sí."

"Go to them."

He helped her stand.

She tilted her face up at him. "Gracias," like a song of a bird released from its cage. She walked to the door, paused to look back at Tyler, and then dashed out into the rain.

CHAPTER TWENTY-EIGHT

Dark wet streaks on the adobe huts turned golden in the morning light. One by one the horses Tyler had freed wandered back into the village square. They drank from rain puddles in the street with scrawny chickens and bony dogs. Feathers of vapor drifted up from the earth and the day draped Spencer's shoulders like a damp shirt.

He found Tyler's Krag rifle near the corral. He rubbed the mud from the stock and wiped the action clean with his kerchief.

Tyler stepped out of the church doors. His shirt hung open across the leathery muscles of his bare chest. He shaded his eyes and looked at the empty street of the little village. "Where is everybody? Why haven't they come out?"

"I'm guessin' they think we're no different than Fox. That we came to kill or take what's theirs."

Tyler's hand fell to the empty holster on

his hip. "We are different. Aren't we?"

Spencer leaned the Krag on the church wall next to his Winchester. "C'mon, there's men that need burying. Bowie and the animals will be here shortly."

They carried Fox's body from the church and laid it with the two others near the fence of the cemetery.

"Spencer —" Tyler pointed to the well at the center of the village square. "— it's that old woman we saw when we snuck into the village."

The woman kept her face down. Spencer could not see her eyes. At the well, she filled a wooden pail, covered her head with a shawl, and walked to the church. At the entryway, she made the sign of the cross, bowed her head, and walked in.

Spencer followed Tyler to the doorway.

At the little chapel's altar, the woman knelt and squeezed her hands together. After a long moment, she lifted the silver cross that hung from the chain around her neck and touched it to her lips. The woman took a rag from the folds of her worn dress, dipped it into the bucket, and began to scrub Dalton Fox's blood from the church floor.

There was not so much as a scuff from Tyler's boots as he walked to where the woman knelt. He stripped off his shirt and dropped onto his knees beside her. Tyler wet his shirt in the bucket and helped her wash away the terrible stain.

Spencer gathered broken furniture and empty bottles. An armload at a time he carried the refuse out to the village square. Tyler joined him and the two men righted the overturned pews. They sat the priest's table in its place near the still-wet floor.

For the first time, he could remember, Spencer knelt at an altar and watched the old woman light a candle.

A mule brayed.

Spencer ran for the church door.

Bowie, on the black mule, leading their string of horses, galloped into the village. He swung off the mule, bent over, and grabbed his knees with both hands. "Where's Tyler?"

Spencer moved to where Bowie stood. "In the church."

"Is he all right?"

"Yeah."

"Fox?"

"Tyler killed him."

Bowie hacked out a cough and spit on the ground. "Villa and more than a dozen riders. Be here anytime. We gotta get away."

Spencer peered over Bowie. Dust hung in the desert sky above the trail leading to the village. "Get your rifle and get into that church." He grabbed the mule's reins from Bowie.

Bowie tugged the Savage from the mule's saddle as it passed.

Spencer popped the mule on the rump and slammed the corral gate shut behind the horses. "Tyler," he yelled. He pulled the pistol Tyler had dropped on the church floor from his belt and tossed it to the boy as he came onto the portico. Dirt clung to the sweat on Tyler's bare chest.

Tyler plucked the Colt out of the air.

Horse hooves thumped hard-packed dirt and echoed back from the sides of the village huts. Chickens scattered. Dogs sulked away. Tyler slipped the sixth bullet into the Colt's cylinder. He jammed the pistol into its holster and pulled the belt tight on his hips.

Spencer peeled off his jacket and let it drop to the ground. He levered open the Winchester and fed a cartridge into its chamber.

"Bowie, climb up that bell tower. Don't you shoot 'til you know you have to." Spencer's tongue jabbed the inside of his cheek.

"Once you start, don't stop until everything in this street is dead."

Bowie's feet clattered up the rickety ladder.

Spencer rested the rifle in the crook of his elbow and turned to the plaza. "Tyler, there's no time to run. We're gonna stand in this street and face 'em. If this comes to what I think it might, there's no other man I'd want standin' next to me."

Tyler tried to swallow but his mouth was as dry as every mile of the desert they'd ridden. He stepped from the shade of the church and stood beside Spencer. He flexed his fingers open and shut and rested his hand on the pistol.

Pancho Villa rode Mister Hutt's Thoroughbred. Sunlight sparkled off the brass cartridges tucked in the bandoliers that crossed his chest. Tyler counted fifteen mounted men behind him. Each rested a new Winchester across his saddle.

Villa stopped the Thoroughbred near the village well and leaned down from the saddle to dip his hand into a bucket that rested on the stone wall. He filled his cupped hand with water and brought it to his mouth. Slurping sounds made Tyler think of how cool the water would taste. Droplets spilled down Villa's chin and caught in his mustache. He smacked his lips and shook the water from his fingers.

Tyler ground his bootheels in the dust. A tremble crossed the muscles in his arms and shoulders.

The Thoroughbred pulled on its reins and shook its muzzle at Tyler. The horse blew its breath through lips. A small noise escaped in recognition of its old friend.

Tyler curled his lip over his bottom teeth and bit down.

Villa tipped back the broad brim of his sombrero. He nudged the horse with his knees and the Thoroughbred stepped closer to Tyler and Spencer. His men spread out and formed a fan shape around the well. Tyler felt their eyes on his bare chest.

"Amigos." Villa was careful to hold the reins high and away from his body. "I see you have done my work for me." He nodded towards the place near the churchyard where Fox's body lay. "*Hombre muy malo. Sí?*"

The Thoroughbred stretched out its neck and licked the sweat from Tyler's skin. Villa jerked its head back.

"Which one of you killed Fox?"

Spencer seemed to fasten his eyes on Villa and ignore the men that formed the half-circle in front of him. "He's dead. That's all that matters."

The door of the church squeaked on its hinges. Tyler turned his head enough to see the old woman step into the shadows of the doorway.

"Only one of you could be top dog, is that it, Villa?" Spencer's voice never trembled. "If you wanted him dead, job's been done for you. You and your men can ride on."

"Maybe you ride on and leave this village for me." Villa's right hand dropped onto his leg, just inches from a shiny Colt on his belt.

Tyler drew in his breath and held it until his chest burned.

One of Villa's men raised his rifle from where it lay across his saddle and propped the buttstock on his leg. His finger curled around the trigger. Another did the same. Then another. Soon fifteen Winchesters stood at the ready.

The old woman walked from the church and stood between Spencer and Tyler. In her hands, she held a battered crucifix.

As silently as spirits, the villagers emerged from their doorways and alleys. Tyler saw Isabel. Behind her stood a man with an ax. Another gripped a weather-beaten shovel. Others held twisted branches and chunks of firewood. Brown-skinned women in threadbare dresses stood close to their men.

"It's your choice." Spencer turned so that the rifle that rested in his arm pointed at Villa's belly. "Appears these people don't want you."

"Many will die, Señor." Villa inched his fingers closer to his pistol.

"You'll be the first." Spencer jabbed his tongue into his cheek. He raised his voice. "Bowie."

Sounds rustled from the rooftop above. Shadows took shape on the dusty ground. Tyler glanced up. Bowie leaned from the belfry with his rifle trained on Villa.

The old woman's voice chanted a prayer.

Villa raised his hand to his mustache. "*Bueno,* there is nothing in this village that pleases me." He turned his head and barked a command to his men. One by one they lowered their rifles. Villa stood in the stirrups and then let himself drop onto the saddle's seat. "We ride on."

Before Villa could pull the Thoroughbred's reins, Tyler stepped forward and wrapped his fingers in the horse's bridle.

"This here's Mister Hutt's horse. I aim to take him back to The Bootheel with me."

Saddles creaked and rifles moved. Villagers gripped their tools tighter.

Villa laughed. "Amigo, what would you

have me ride? That old mule in the corral there?"

Tyler's free hand lifted the Colt from its holster. He swung the muzzle to the side of the horse's head. "You don't leave me this horse, nobody's gonna ride outta here on it." He cocked the hammer.

"You would shoot this fine horse?"

"If I had to keep a man like you from ridin' outta here on it, I would."

All went quiet except the song of the woman's prayer.

Villa swung his leg over the saddle and dropped to the ground. He moved in until the brim of his hat touched Tyler's forehead. The smell of mescal flooded Tyler's face. Evil as sharp as cactus spines flared in the bandit's eyes.

"Who is this Mister Hutt?"

Tyler never blinked. "My boss."

"This Mister Hutt, he knows good horses —" Villa turned his head to look at Spencer. "— and good men." He stepped back, pulled off his sombrero, and bowed his head to Tyler.

"Esteban," the outlaw shouted.

One of Villa's men rode in where they stood. He jumped from the back of the horse. Villa took the reins and climbed into the saddle.

321

"Adios, amigo. Next time." He wagged a finger at Tyler, "Next time."

Villa pulled hard on the horse's reins. The animal reared. When its feet touched the ground, Villa spurred it into a gallop. A rider trotted in and caught Esteban's hand. Esteban jumped up behind the saddle and the line of outlaws followed their leader out into the desert.

Only when the dust of their horses had settled did Tyler lower his gun. He tangled his finger in the Thoroughbred's mane. The muscles along his shoulders ached and his fingers trembled. Tyler thought of The Bootheel and knew Mister Hutt would not be waiting.

The old woman caught his hand and pulled until he bent at the waist. She held out her cross and silver chain and slipped it over his head.

"For the next hundred years, this village will tell stories about what happened today." Spencer took the pistol from Tyler's hand. "Might even make up a song about the man who killed Dalton Fox and stood eye to eye with a bandit leader. Just to get back his boss's horse." He rested his hand on Tyler's shoulder.

"I was scared, Spencer." Only his grip on the Thoroughbred's mane held him up.

"You bargained with the devil and your God closed the deal."

Tyler squeezed the woman's cross until it bit into his palm. "I'd never kill this horse."

"I knew that. Villa didn't."

CHAPTER TWENTY-NINE

From the debris they carried from the church, the villagers built a fire in the plaza. Flames licked the sky. The inferno consumed all the evil the village had known. A whole goat roasting on a spit set at the edge of the fire. Bowls of *frijoles* and plates of *tortillas* were carried from the houses. Children laughed. Dogs barked. Women sang.

Bowie danced with the old woman. His long legs kicked in the air. She twirled on little-girl feet in front of him.

Spencer slipped away from the *fiesta*. He climbed to the church tower with his Winchester and watched to be sure Villa would not return. All through the hot noonday, he studied a cloud of dust until it disappeared into the Valley of Visions.

Below, Tyler sat with Isabel. He smiled for the first time since Luak.

When Spencer climbed down from his

watch, white ash covered the red embers in the firepit. Tyler tended to the horses. Bowie, wrapped in a borrowed blanket, dozed against the church wall. Spencer walked to the corral.

Tyler rubbed the Thoroughbred's back. "What's next, Spencer?"

"When we've rested, we head back to The Bootheel."

"What about your father?"

"What about him?"

"That's why we came. Mister Hutt sent us to find out what happened to your pa." Tyler stroked the Thoroughbred's face.

"We've done what we can. Whatever Fox knew died with him. It's time to head back."

"Mister Hutt woulda . . ."

"Hutt sent you on this trip to harden you. Teach you things he'd never get to." Spencer rested his hand on the top rail of the corral. "He's countin' on you runnin' that ranch when he's gone. That was what this was all about. He woulda brought you here or someplace else hisself but he was dyin' a bit more each day. Tellin' me to find my father was just his excuse."

"You sure about that?"

"I am now. And it worked."

"What?"

325

"You're a man." Spencer looked Tyler in the eye.

" 'Cause I stood down Villa and killed Fox."

"No, 'cause you wouldn't give up until you knew for yourself about Luak." Spencer brushed his hand across his mouth. " 'Cause ya knelt down beside that woman to wash the blood from the church floor. You're a good man. More good than I'll ever be."

Tyler turned his back to Spencer. "Then we should go back."

"Yeah. In the mornin'. Now help me. We need to bury the men we killed. These folks shouldn't oughta do it."

Not even the heat of the day could lift the death chill from the bodies. Tyler feared the food from the feast would spill out his mouth. He grasped Fox's ankles, clamped his eyes shut, and hoisted the stiff carcass. Flies, which seconds earlier had swarmed the body's face, flew to his.

Spencer had the corpse by the shoulders. The two half-dragged, half-carried the dead body to the single grave they had dug just outside the little fence that circled the churchyard. With a heave, they swung the bulk over the pit and let it drop. As what was left of Fox smashed onto it, foul air whooshed from the bloated bodies at the bottom of the pit. One grave for three men.

Tyler turned away. He doubled over and swallowed hard. Dirt fell from Spencer's shovel into the hole.

Drips of rainwater from the night's storm still clung to the edge of the church roof. The same wind that carried the smell of the dead men coaxed lose a droplet and it splatted into the muddy clay. A wooden cross, almost hidden near the church, seemed ready to topple with the next gust. Tyler swatted at a stubborn fly. He stepped over the little fence and went to straighten the grave marker.

Water spilling from the roof had left deep gouges in the ground that covered the grave. Tyler righted the fallen cross and pressed it down into the dirt. A piece of yellow bone only a handspan deep in the rough soil caught the sunlight. Tyler kicked dirt over it. In a different water-torn gash, another fragment of bone and decaying denim jutted from the grave dirt. Tyler knelt and tried to smooth the soil over the remains. His fingertips brushed a piece of rough, corroded steel.

He pulled a rusty knife from the dirt. It had been a working man's tool. Ranch hands at The Bootheel carried similar blades and used them for all sorts of chores. The tip of this one was broken. No doubt from trying to pry something open. Rust covered the blade. The brass bolsters that held the wooden handle to the steel had turned green. Tyler rubbed his thumb over the grips to clean the dirt away. Beneath that layer of grime, a familiar set of lines took shape.

Tyler stood up. He wiped the knife's grips across his pants. First one side, then the other. The markings showed clear now. He lifted his face and gripped the lost knife all the tighter.

Tyler looked at the knife again and called out, "Spencer, you gotta take a look at this."

Spencer stabbed the shovel into the mound of grave dirt. He climbed the fence and walked to where Tyler waited. "What is it?"

"Just look." Tyler held out the knife.

Spencer took it. "What am I supposed to see?"

"Look close at the grips."

Spencer shifted the knife in his hands. The color drained from his face. "You just pick this up?"

"Last night's rain washed open this grave here." Tyler pointed to where he'd found the knife. "It's the Bootheel brand burnt into those handles, ain't it?"

"Yeah, don't mean nothing."

"Your pa's grave, Spencer?"

"Nameless man in an unmarked grave *don't mean nothin',*" he nearly shouted.

"Mister Hutt said your pa would mark things with the point of a hot knife. Just like he did with the grips of that Colt pistol. Look close Spencer, they're the same marks."

"Don't mean it's him. A thousand ways to explain how this got here. Traded for, stolen, lost, and found again. This don't mean a thing." Spencer threw the knife down.

"You don't want it to be him, do you?"

Spencer jammed the point of his tongue into the side of his cheek so hard Tyler thought it might stab through. "I never knew the man. Leave it be."

Bowie came around the corner of the church. "Look there." He pointed out to a hill near the trail that led away from the village. "I thought I heard a mountain lion scream. When I looked to see what it was, I saw her. It's her. It's that witch."

Sunlight shined on her wispy hair. The bent, old woman's dress whipped in the wind around her frail body. But the *Curandera* made no move to come closer.

Tyler grabbed Spencer's arm. "Remember what she told you? 'The flood will show you what you need.' That's what she said. We thought she was just crazy. Maybe she was sayin' the storm would show us this grave. What she said about Luak —" Tyler let go. "— was all true." He bent over to pick up the knife.

Spencer climbed the fence and started for the *Curandera.* Each stride became longer and soon he was running. Before he came close, the witch turned and faded into the brush and cactus.

At the top of the hill where she had stood, Spencer stooped. The pads of a mountain lion's paws left their marks in the dust. There was not a sign of a woman's footprints. And in the dirt among the animal's tracks lay a holster for a pistol. Burnt into the leather was the Bootheel brand.

"He's been out there near two hours." Tyler turned to Bowie. "It'll be dark soon."

"I think it's best we leave him alone. Spencer's a hard man to figure. He'll come back when he's ready."

"Do you think it's his pa's grave?"

"No way of knowing for sure. Maybe Spencer thinks so and this is his way to

330

grieve. Maybe with all, that's happened he just needs to be by himself."

Tyler woke to the sounds of a shovel slicing dirt and the smell of fresh earth. In the gray moonlight, Spencer dug a new hole next to the shallow one where Tyler had found the knife. When all Tyler could only see was the top of his head above the rim of the hole, Spencer climbed out.

As carefully as a mother with a new child, Spencer sifted through sandy clay beneath the grave marker Tyler had straightened. He gathered bits and pieces from the soil.

Though Tyler could not see clearly in the dark, he knew what Spencer was doing. Three times Spencer climbed into the new grave to deposit the things he had found.

Then a shovelful at a time Spencer filled the grave. With his bare hands, he smoothed the dirt on the new mound. He sat back on his heels and bowed his head. The stars above him grew brighter. The gunman climbed to his feet and pressed the wooden cross into the earth.

Then Spencer brushed the dirt from his clothes, walked to the village well for a drink, and never said a word to Tyler.

CHAPTER THIRTY

"I've decided to stay here in Mesita."

"Bowie, you're bein' a fool. Get on that mule and come with me and Tyler."

Bowie shook his head. "I've thought this over and I'm staying. I came to Mexico to explore the Valley of Visions and I'm here."

Spencer leaned forward and rested his elbow on his saddle horn. "Get on the mule."

"Hear me out. I wrote a letter I want you to mail when you get back to the States. It will let my family know where I am and that I'm safe." He handed an envelope up to Tyler on the back of the Thoroughbred. "I intend on hiring some of the village men to go with me and retrieve my equipment. I'll make Mesita my home base and prospect in the mountains all around."

"What about Villa and others like him?"

"I've learned well from you, Spencer. I can take care of myself."

332

"What's ya think, Tyler?"

Tyler nudged the Thoroughbred closer to Spencer's horse. "I think a man should make his own choices." He reached down and took Bowie's hand.

"So be it." Spencer tilted back his hat. "Bowie, you keep your nose in the wind, an eye on the skyline, and that rifle handy. We don't have hardly any supplies to leave with you."

"If it's all right I'd like to keep the black mule. I've grown rather fond of the animal. It has a personality quite like an uncle of mine. I think I'll name him Bartholomew."

Spencer shook his head. "Bowie, take a better look at that jackass. You might want to call *her* Betty."

Bowie smiled and reached up to shake Spencer's hand. "It's been a grand adventure."

CHAPTER THIRTY-ONE

Tyler and the Thoroughbred led the way.

On the fifth day, they crossed the Rio Grande and camped that night in the *bosque.* Spencer shot a deer. On a strip on a sandy riverbank, Tyler made a fire.

Spencer skewered chunks of the backstraps on green willow sticks. Globs of fat popped as they dripped onto the red coals. Night built walls around them and the noise of the river stood guard.

"Day after tomorrow we'll make The Bootheel." Tyler pushed a handful of cottonwood branches on the fire. Heat moved from the glowing embers to the dry wood. Flames flared up and touched the river with yellow and orange. "I got a hankerin' to see that ranch like nothin' I ever felt before."

"It'll be different this time."

"You mean Mister Hutt'll be gone?" Tyler tossed a piece of a branch into the fire. "He's dead, ain't he?" Sap bubbled up from the wood. Bark peeled away in the heat. And in an instant, the branch was gone. "I remember the first day I saw The Bootheel. Mister Hutt rode back to the wagon and had me jump up behind him on his horse. We rode up to the rimrock above the ranch house and buildings. He just pointed at the cattle and horses down below. Never said a word. I thought I was seein' heaven."

Tyler listened to the sounds the river made. The glow of the fire painted shadows on Spencer's face. "What will you do Spencer? Stay and work the ranch?"

Spencer shifted his weight on the sand. He took a spear of roasted meat from the campfire. A trail of steam disappeared into the darkness over their heads. "You should be thankful."

"Thankful?"

"A man's got to be thankful when he finishes a job he never should have started in the first place. Thankful he got something he's good at doin'. Hutt said you're goin' to be one helluva cowman. You need to be thankful you got a place to go to."

" 'Til I left The Bootheel with you, I thought the whole world came to an end at the top of the rimrocks out the front gate. Now I know there's more out there."

"Tyler, right now our world is this ring of

335

light the fire casts. Tomorrow, in the day-time, it'll be the next horizon. This here world changes with how you see it."

They were in their saddles before first light. Tyler chewed cold venison and hunched his shoulders against the morning chill. He pointed the Thoroughbred north. Spencer fell in behind.

By midmorning, the country rolled out before them like a wrinkled blanket on a working man's bunk. In the farthest fold, a tinge of green promised trees and water. The air was cool. A flock of cranes rode high on the thermals until the tips of their wings flicked the clouds. Each squawk the birds made seemed to tell all of nature they were on their way home.

Spencer pulled his horse to a stop next to Tyler's. He filled his lungs with air. "What say we run these horses?"

"Why?"

"For the pure simple joy of sittin' a runnin' horse." And he snapped the reins across his horse's rump.

The Thoroughbred caught Spencer's horse within a hundred yards. Riders and animals raced across the broken desert. Hoofbeats and dust filled the air. Grit coated Tyler's teeth. His eyes burned, but he pushed the horse on.

He eased to a stop on the crest of the hillock.

Spencer's horse, lathered and panting, galloped in. A smile showed on Spencer's face. "There'll be a day when this land will be crossed by train tracks and roads and fences. Gallopin' a horse for a mile like that won't be an easy thing to do." Spencer took the canteen that Tyler offered. "Maybe that day's sooner than we know —" He spit a mouthful of water on the ground. "— if the lawyers, bankers, and politicians have their way."

"Law's lookin' for you. Maybe you should turn around right now and head back to Mexico."

Spencer handed back the canteen. "I gave my word to Hutt that I'd bring you back to The Bootheel. That's what I intend on doin'."

"Then what?"

Spencer touched his spurs to his horse's sides. "Best walk these animals a piece to let 'em cool."

"He's dead."

Spencer sat next to him, but Tyler spoke to no one but himself.

Tyler wanted to dab his eyes with the back

of his glove but didn't. The Thoroughbred straddled the naked ruts on the wagon trail that led to the buildings and corrals in the basin below. "See that gate behind the barns? The stock's out on the pasture ground, but the gate's swingin' free. Wind can catch a gate and slam it against the fence. Mister Hutt'd tan me good if I didn't tie a gate back." His voice caught in his throat. "Weeds growin' along the side of the barn there. Mister Hutt would trim them back hisself. Didn't want burrs where boots pick 'em up and bring 'em in the house."

The Thoroughbred pulled at the reins and tossed its head side to side. Horses in the side corrals bunched up at the fence and whinnied. The Thoroughbred answered. Tyler stroked its mane, but the horse fought him.

A man came from the barn. He shaded his eyes with a straw hat and looked up the hill.

Tyler tugged back on the reins. He turned the horse in a tight circle around Spencer.

"They know we're here, we can go on in now."

Spencer followed Tyler and the Thoroughbred through the gate. Chickens scattered in front of their horses. Tyler dropped from the saddle before his horse stopped. The reins slipped from his fingers and the animal walked loose.

Spencer pulled his horse up and waited in his saddle.

An old Mexican woman hurried onto the front porch of the ranch house wiping her hands on a stained apron. When she saw Tyler she covered her face with her hands and began to weep. "I cook best steaks. Everyone eat inside tonight." She wrapped her thick arms around Tyler and tugged his face down to meet hers. "Jesus," she called to the man near the barn. "Go tell Miller and others. Tyler is home."

Tyler's arms hung stiff at his sides while the woman wrapped hers around him. "Pilar —" He raised his head. "— Mister Hutt?"

"Muerto, muchacho." Tears covered her cheeks. "Not long, maybe three days after you left. We bury him by the big rock on the hill."

Tyler pushed away. He caught the Thoroughbred and pressed his face into its mane.

A shadow moved in the ranch house door. A new calico dress rustled in the wind. Curly brown hair caught a stray sunbeam.

Pilar glanced back and then looked up to Spencer on his horse. "She comes with your letter." Pilar moved into the shadows, took the woman by the arm, and led her into the sun.

Eyes, more green than brown, found Spencer's. Smooth skin shimmered with a sheen of sweat. She lifted her face. A thick red scar smudged a throat the color of warm whiskey.

"You saved me." The words seeped from her mouth beneath a ragged breath.

Spencer kicked free of his stirrups and swung off the horse. He could only say her name.

"Christmas."

Every person gathered around the table in the ranch house sat silent as Tyler finished his story. His words hung in the air as thick as the scent of Pilar's cooking. "Fox took Luak. Left me to hang. Spencer found her body the next day. He buried her."

"Madre de Dios." A tin plate fell from Pilar's hand. It clattered on the floor.

Christmas snatched up the dish and took the others from Pilar. She went to the kitchen.

"Miller." Pilar took a thick envelope from the mantel. "Tell Tyler and Spencer what Mister Hutt wants for them." She laid the envelope near Tyler.

340

Mister Hutt's foreman nodded. "Don't know the fancy lawyer words. It's simple. Both of you own The Bootheel."

Tyler bit down on his lip. He turned to Spencer.

Miller went on. "His will was set up that way. He did leave me two sections of ground on the river and fifty head of cattle on the condition that I stay on as foreman for the next five years. If you'll have me." He tipped his head at the Mexican woman. "Pilar is to stay in this house as long as she wants. He left money in the town bank for her. But every horse, head of cattle, acre of ground, and blade of grass is yours. You two are partners now. It's all in them papers there, good and proper."

"You're son he never had." Pilar touched Tyler's shoulders. "Spencer his best friend's son. The way he wanted."

Tyler leaned back in his chair. His mind gathered in each pasture, water hole, ridge, and gully he'd ridden with Mister Hutt. He knew which cow threw the best calves, which horse was due to foal, and where the spring's grass would grow first. If it was a lean year, he knew where Mister Hutt would buy winter feed. He knew which buyer paid top dollar for the cattle. He could pull a breech calf. Mister Hutt had taught him to cipher the accounts.

Mister Hutt trusted Miller, that was for certain. He could boss Jesus and the other hands. If trouble came no one was better than Spencer. But what were Spencer's thoughts about partnering up? Tyler tipped his chair back and looked across the table.

Spencer watched the mulatto girl in the kitchen.

Tyler remembered seeing Christmas in the shacks behind Jimmy Six's place that night in El Paso. He knew where the ugly scar on her throat came from but had no idea how she had ended up at The Bootheel.

Partners shouldn't have secrets.

"Best food I've had in a long time, Pilar." Tyler stood up and took his hat from a peg on the wall. " 'Bout an hour from now can we talk over the herd and such, Miller? I'm going to walk around the place a bit. I got a lot to think over."

"I'll put your things in the little room off the kitchen," Pilar said.

Tyler looked at Spencer.

"Let Spencer have that room. I'll stay with the hands in the bunkhouse."

Spencer found Christmas on the back stoop. An apron hung from her rounded hips. She had gathered the front of the cloth up to make a sort of bag. Chickens clucked and jostled with one another, begging for the next morsels she tossed from the folds in the apron.

Christmas turned when she heard Spencer. Sun shone on her hair and flashed from her teeth. She smiled and traced her chipped front tooth with the tip of her tongue. "Deese chickens make me laugh."

"You know this ranch is half mine now?"

"I heard da men talkin'."

Spencer moved closer. He reached out and touched the red scar on her neck. "You're welcome to stay as long as you like."

Her eyes closed and she tilted her head back. The puckered, angry slash ran from the point of her jaw across her throat to her left ear. Red dots, where the doctor had stitched the wound, still showed on her skin.

She pushed his hand away. "Seem so long ago. Don't want to think 'bout it no more." She brushed the last of the seed from her apron to the chickens and twirled on her tiptoes among the birds. "I feel all brand new. I stay here a long time."

Spencer's tongue found the inside of his cheek. He let the afternoon sunshine warm his face. "Then I'll stay with you."

Miller shook his head.

"I'll tell him in the morning." Tyler reached out over the corral fence and stroked the Thoroughbred's neck. Near the ranch house, Spencer and Christmas sat on the low fence around Pilar's garden. Her head rested on Spencer's shoulder. A striped barn cat rubbed against Spencer's legs.

"Miller, 'member that chisel and hammer Mister Hutt used when we cut stone for the well house? They still in the barn?"

"They'd be with his tools. Your tools now." Miller turned down his shirtsleeves. "What we just talked about? You sure?" He looked at Spencer.

"I'm sure. Go on now."

Miller jammed his hands in his pockets and shuffled to the bunkhouse.

Tyler wrapped his fingers in the horse's mane. A dozen sturdy cow ponies milled in the corral with the Thoroughbred. As many more, and just as sound, grazed with the cattle out on the ranch ground. Tyler could call every horse by name.

Like the bayonet leaves on a yucca plant, spears of golden light spread across the sky. The orange-rimmed sun fought the turning of the earth and then surrendered to day's end. Shadows lengthened and turned as black as an Indian girl's hair.

Tyler put a match to the lantern that hung

by a nail just inside the barn door. He found the hammer and chisel on Mister Hutt's workbench. With the tools in one hand and the kerosene lamp in the other, Tyler climbed the hill where Mister Hutt rested. He set the light on the grave mound, placed the point of the chisel on the stone, and swung the hammer.

Christmas's fingernails traced the scrapes and scratches on Spencer's arm. She rested her face in the hollow of his shoulder. Outside, far away, a hammer struck metal. Inside, the only sound was Spencer's calloused palms on her skin. Air slipped from her mouth and cooled the sweat on his face. As gently as he'd ever done anything in his life, Spencer touched the place on her throat that moved to the beat of her heart. His fingers grazed her scar.

Christmas twisted in the bedclothes and came to him.

Outside, a chisel struck stone.

As the sun rose, Tyler blew the last chips of stone away and looked at his work. Carved into the rough slab of granite, the Bootheel brand would forever mark Mister Hutt's grave. No words, just his brand.

Tyler hung the lantern back on its nail

and put the tools where he had found them. He took his gear from the tack room, caught the Thoroughbred, and saddled the horse.

Spencer crossed the ranch yard. The striped cat trotted at his heels. "Gonna check on the stock?"

"I'm leavin'."

"What?"

Tyler put the toe of his boot in the stirrup and swung up onto the horse. "All I ever wanted was to be was a cowhand. You showed me there's more and I want to see it."

"Tyler, half of this is yours."

Tyler pulled on his gloves. "I'm afraid if I stay any longer, I'll stay forever."

Spencer looked back at the ranch house. Christmas, wrapped in their blanket, stepped onto the porch. He turned back to Tyler. "Where you headed?"

"There's a lot of world to see." He tipped his head toward the hills. "I'll decide at the rimrock."

"You love The Bootheel."

"Mister Hutt said, 'It's all about country to call your own and horses and cattle that are yours, knowing a job gets done 'cause you do it.' " Tyler grinned. "It's not about those things at all. It's choosin' who you say sir to."

346

Christmas slipped up beside Spencer. He wrapped his arm around her waist.

"If I do no greater thing in my life —" Tyler sat up in the saddle. "— I can tell folks I rode to Mexico with Case Spencer."

"Half of this is yours when you're ready to come back."

Tyler looked over the horses in the corral and out to the cattle in the pastures. "I trust you, *sir.*" Tyler bit down on his lip and then winked at Spencer. "Weeds need cut along the side of the barn. Don't want to track no burrs into the house."

"I'll get to it."

Spencer and Christmas followed him to the gate. Tyler stayed away from the trail road and let the Thoroughbred weave its way through the sage and mesquite. Horse and rider climbed up through the broken slabs of granite where God's own finger had shattered the rimrock. At the top, he paused.

Then Tyler pointed the Thoroughbred south towards the Rio Grande and rode to Mexico.

To say a prayer at Luak's grave.

ABOUT THE AUTHOR

Kevin Wolf's novel, *The Homeplace,* was the winner of the 2015 Tony Hillerman Award. The novel was a finalist for the 2016 Strand Critics Award for Debut Mystery. His short story, "Belthanger," was selected by the Western Writers of America as the 2021 Spur Award Winner for Best Short fiction. The great-grandson of Colorado homesteaders, he enjoys fly fishing, old Winchesters, and 1950's Western movies. He lives in Estes Park, Colorado, with his wife. Rocky Mountain National Park is his backyard. Visit his website at www.kevinwolfstory teller.com.

The employees of Thorndike Press hope you have enjoyed this Large Print book. All our Thorndike, Wheeler, and Kennebec Large Print titles are designed for easy reading, and all our books are made to last. Other Thorndike Press Large Print books are available at your library, through selected bookstores, or directly from us.

For information about titles, please call:
(800) 223-1244

or visit our website at:
gale.com/thorndike

To share your comments, please write:

Publisher
Thorndike Press
10 Water St., Suite 310
Waterville, ME 04901